U0127362

所寶惟賢

冀伯文物鑑賞

卷二　玉器

目錄

卷二

Contents

Volume 2

雅俗共賞—清代觀賞性玉器

前國立歷史博物館編輯　林淑心

一、前言

中國玉雕藝術源遠流長，可溯及新石器時代早期，最初乃始於原始的石器宗教性崇拜所產生。經歷代工藝的不斷發展，至唐宋時期，因社會變化的影響，玉器已由玄秘崇高具宗教禮儀性質的象徵物，逐漸轉化成為實用性，趨於生活化而以觀賞與裝飾性功能為主，元明時期則成為高層貴族及豪家文士等玩賞的重要物品。明代隨著商業的發展，雕刻工藝有著飛躍性的進步，尤以玉器工藝的發展最令人注目！「玉作」工藝，由政府設立「御用監」專事監督，力求品質提升，民間則因玉器普及化、生活化而需求的數量大增，推動民間玉雕的繁盛，所謂「良玉雖集京師，工巧首推蘇郡」，除宮廷之玉作，蘇州已成南方玉器雕刻的中心。

清代玉雕工藝益加精進，玉料來源因回部的平定，新疆的和闐玉料，源源不斷輸入而不虞匱乏，且因王室貴族的喜愛與倡導，更促進玉雕技藝的進一步提昇。宮廷設立玉作部門，由造辦處督工監造，極力追求工巧、質美，不惜工本以產生令人驚嘆絕美的作品為目標。約在乾隆年間，因大小金川的平定，翡翠玉材隨即大量輸入，激發玉雕技法的巧思用心與追求。民間更在明代以來良好的基礎及好玉風潮推波助瀾之下，玉器使用更為廣泛，普遍融入於生活之中。於是清一代玉雕工藝再度掀起高潮，成就漢代之後再次呈現玉雕工藝的巔峰時代，後世因此以「乾隆工」，代表精湛絕美的玉雕工藝，即為最佳的佐證，清代觀賞性的玉器，更是典型的代表作品。

二、品類

清代觀賞性的玉器，雖然以宮廷玉為多，但民間作品亦成果卓著。玉作的審美觀點，基本上以「裝飾美」的角度取向，因緊密地與社會生活各階層相結合，藝術的表現形式與人們生活密不可分，是以寫實形式主義的手法，表現精巧、華麗、多變的藝術風格。因為表現技法過分拘泥於細節的呈現，不免有流於纖巧繁縟之感，但流露出的俗世風情，卻贏得雅俗共賞。依其用途約可分為下列類別：

（一）陳設器：玉山子、屏風、插屏、花插、花薰、玉罐、盆景等。

（二）肖生器：玉人物（神道釋佛像、仕女、童子、漁翁等）、玉動物（鳥獸蟲鱗）、植物（花果）祥瑞物等。

（三）文玩器：玉如意、筆筒、筆架、筆洗、臂擱、文鎮、水盂、爐、瓶、盒、奩、花薰。

（四）日用器：玉碗、盤、杯、盞、燈、鼻煙壺等。

（五）其他：傳統禮儀器如磬、璧、圭等。

三、材質

清代因政治統一，交通運輸通暢，新疆所產玉料作為貢玉，每年少則數千斤，多達萬斤，以供宮中玉作使用。主要來自兩大產區：

一為山產玉料，主要產地在葉爾羌密勒塔山區，以青玉為多，因是山中礦產，玉料特別巨大。根據清宮檔案記錄，最大的一塊為費時十年雕刻完成，後來安置在樂壽堂宮的「大禹治水玉山子」，其他如「秋山行旅玉山子」，「會昌九老玉山子」等均為代表性的山產玉料。

一為水產玉料，主要產地在和闐地區的白、綠玉河，即俗稱「籽玉」，多產於河牀中，每年在枯水期由回民從水中撈起，另一種由山中沖到河川中上游的玉籽，稱「山流水」，雖然其質地不如水產的籽玉溫潤，但因其體積較大，亦為普遍使用的玉材。

清代觀賞性的玉器，採用的玉材，除製作巨大的作品，如玉山子，大玉甕等使用山產玉外，仍以和闐所產的水產玉居十之八九，尤其以羊脂白玉，佔最大宗。主要原因是因為山產玉，玉料體積雖然碩大，但玉料比較乾燥，不如水產玉潤澤透亮，且山產玉常出現玉綹或雜質，無法與羊脂白玉的純淨潔白相比。其次則以和闐所產各類玉料如青白玉、黃玉、青玉、碧玉、灰玉、墨玉等雕製。另外亦使用翡翠、瑪瑙、水晶、青晶石、綠松石等多種質材，表現多元的審美觀點與藝術呈現。基本上玉質純正優良的玉材，經玉匠嚴加精選之後，多能「就材選樣」，將玉料作最適當的使用，並能達成最佳最完善的藝術效果。

四、工藝

清代觀賞性玉器，除部份純粹為藝術性的目的而製作外，事實上仍以兼具實用價值的作品為主流。但因為玉器所涵蓋的材質之美，嚴謹技藝所呈現的工藝之美，量材造型所發揮的設計之美，使玉器成為清代最具觀賞價值的代表性工藝，且成為社會各階層的人，都能欣賞而喜愛的作品。

綜合觀之，清代觀賞性玉器的器形，不僅繼承古玉器所展現的典雅器式，且吸取歷代各種傳統工藝造型美之精粹，以出神入化的技藝，表現為令人讚嘆的玉製品，因其件件皆由手工製作，所以件件都不相同，是玉器藝術最引人之處。

下列從工藝的角度加以分析：

(一) 器式

1 取形於古代青銅彝器：以仿自商周青銅器，器形優美的尊、觥、壺、簋、匜、鼎等。

2 取形於古陶瓷器：以宋代陶瓷的貫耳瓶、定窯碗、盤造形，最為常見。

3 取形於金銀器：尤以唐代的金銀器造型最多。

4 取形於自然界之肖生物：包括人物、動物、植物等自然形像。

5 將平面繪畫式的圖像，以浮雕、半浮雕，多層次雕刻、高雕、圓雕的表現技法，化平面為立體。以玉山子、插屏、屏風最多。

6 以金銀鑲嵌的技法，在玉器器面上鑲玻璃、水晶、寶石等方式，創新新式樣，開展器式新風格。

(二) 技法

清代玉器雕刻技法，在清光緒十七年（一八九一年），李澄淵所繪製〈玉作圖說〉中，已有詳盡的描述，將當時玉工雕刻玉器的過程，以圖文並茂的敘述手法，作完整的記錄，是瞭解清代玉雕最好的資料。根據其圖文內容記述，雕製玉器的工序，約分為下列步驟；

1搗砂 2研漿 3開玉 4扎堝 5衝堝 6磨堝 7掏膛 8上花 9打鑽 10透花 11打眼 12木堝 13皮堝等，需經十三項工序始可完成作品雕製。

清代玉器工藝的高峰期約為清中期，即所謂乾隆中至嘉慶初期的四十年左右，這段時期，是所謂「乾隆工」的成熟階段，這時期的製玉成就幾達精緻完美的境界。選材嚴謹、器型規整、設計新穎、拋光精細、雕琢細膩精巧，玉工治玉已達一絲不苟的程度，乾隆曾在御題詩中讚嘆曰：

「細起花文若有神，撫無留手卻平勻，
知其是玉疑非玉，謂此非珍孰是珍？」

可見其工巧之一斑。尤其來自印度蒙兀兒帝國所產「痕都斯坦玉」傳入以後，受其製作工法及藝術風格的影響，玉雕技法趨於細薄的追求製作，尤其是薄胎碗的瑩透精絕，映著燈光其紋飾清晰可見，乾隆曾在一首御題詩中，讚美此類玉作，曰：

「看去有花葉，撫來無跡痕，
表裏都圓渾，色形若混成。」

同時在玉器的薄作技法努力之外，玉的胎地上鑲嵌金銀絲、珠寶、玻璃、玉石的異國裝飾風，亦隨帝王的喜好而風行，玉器技法因此得以拓展。

（三）紋飾

清代玉器上的紋飾，其種類內容的豐富，堪稱數千年傳統玉器文化之集大成者。不僅涵蓋歷代玉器所呈現紋飾的綜合，更加以創新，約可分為下列數大類：

1 仿古彝器類：以龍鳳紋、雲紋、夔紋、螭紋、饕餮紋、瑞獸紋、穀紋、十二章紋等。

2 祥瑞紋飾類：包括五福（福、祿、壽、喜、財）三多（多福、多壽、多男子），富貴吉慶的象徵物，趨吉避邪的吉祥物，寓意諧音吉祥的代表物等。

3 主題故事類：神話傳說（八仙慶壽）、歷史故事（蘇武牧羊）、文人佳話（羲之愛鵝）、演義小說（西廂記）、仁義善行（二十四孝）等以開光式呈現。

4 山水風景類：四季景色、山川岩崖、河岸風光等入畫景象。

5 肖生生物類：包括動物、植物等。

（四）銘款

清代玉器上的題銘刻款，初期未見，可能在宮廷玉作玉工制度真正完備以後，始有年款刻製。傳世作品中最早的年款為「雍正年製」，數量最多的是「乾隆年製」，雖然還有「嘉慶年製」、「嘉慶御賞」、「道光年製」等，至清代末期則不見。年款以四字篆款或隸書款為主，偶見楷書款。乾隆時尚有「大清乾隆年製」、「乾隆仿古」、「大清乾隆仿古」、「乾隆御製」、「乾隆御用」等數種不同的款式。其中「乾隆御製」款，是皇帝賞賜品所使用，而「乾隆御用」款，則是真正在宮中所使用的物品。乾隆喜愛玉器，所以見到工好質佳作品，題御詩或銘記命玉工雕刻，此類玉器上的銘文，都刻工精美，書體端莊工整，特別值得細細品賞。

五、結語

綜觀清代的觀賞性玉器，不論是大至數噸重的巨作，如「大禹治水玉山子」、「秋山行旅玉山子」等，或是小僅方寸的擺件如「玉兔」、「玉狗」等，都是玉工以其神乎其技的雙手，所創作出來的作品。大件巨作由多數人通力合作完成，小件作品大都獨力雕作，玉器作品最大的特色，是純手工製作，每件玉器各自獨立，絕不會有兩件完全相同的作品。清代玉器以號稱「乾隆工」的作品自豪，所以一般屬於觀賞性玉器，都是工精質美「乾隆工」所雕成。其主要特徵如下：

（一）精與細：玉器上呈現的線條，都一絲不苟，條條分明，其力道與刀法一脈貫穿到底，呈現方式肯定有力，沒有任何不連續或猶疑的刀工痕跡。

（二）多層次：玉器的淺浮雕，所有凸起的弧面均圓潤光滑，撫之不留手，每個細節或底部，都一一照顧到。而多層次雕刻的每一層次，均順著玉石的肌理，逐步向內雕刻，線條分明比例精準，使器物更加立體化。

（三）薄而巧：深受痕都斯坦玉作的影響，玉胎要求趨向薄作，處理瑩潤透明的技法，高超卓絕。玉材的運用，因材施工隨形作器，視色巧製的「俏色」功力，幾達於出神入化之境。

清代觀賞性玉器，代表當代最具審美觀念及藝術性的玉器，不論是宮廷玉或民間玉，其技法無不出自「乾隆工」精巧的雙手，以精雕細琢的技法所製成，論工藝的技巧堪稱集歷代玉器之大成，再創一個玉器的黃金時代。但是因為過度追求纖巧新奇，藝術的表現趨於形式化、表面化，作品因缺乏精神文化的深刻內涵，其藝術性的顯現比較浮淺，讓人可直接看穿而無法深化。可是亦因為製作數量大增，玉器可普遍的深入社會，融入人們生活之中，使其庶民化、普及化，觀賞性玉器，成為一種雅俗共賞的清代絕美工藝藝術品。

B. Types of Jade

Although Qing Dynasty ornamental jade mostly came from the imperial palace, civilian artisans also accomplished much in the art. The basic perspective of the aesthetics of jade-making is that of "beautiful decoration." Due to a dense population and the mingling of different social classes, the expression of art became closely related to people's lives. The artistic style was one that appreciated refined skills, splendor, and variety, using realist and formalist methods. Because the artistic techniques are strongly circumscribed by the need to present details, the artifacts can't help but be extremely delicate and ornate. It exudes a sense of folk art, while still winning the praise of those with elegant taste. The types of jade can basically be divided into these categories:

1. Displays: jade boulders, screens, table screens, vases, incense burners, jade containers, and scenery.

2. Representations: Auspicious figures, such as people (including Taoist and Buddhist deities, female figures, children, and fishermen), animals (birds, beasts, insects, and fish), and plants (flowers and fruits).

3. Stationery: lucky ornaments, brush holders, brush stands, brush cleaners, arm rests, paperweights, tea basins, burners, bottles, boxes, cosmetics cases, and incense burners.

4. Household items: bowls, plates, cups, small cups, lamps, and snuff bottles.

5. Miscellaneous: traditional ceremonial items such as chime stones, jade disks, and jade tablets.

Fitting Both Refined and Popular Tastes — Qing Dynasty Ornamental Jade

Lin Shu-Xin
Former Editor
National Museum of History

A. Foreword

The art of jade carving has a long history in China, which can be traced back to the early neolithic period, originally spurred by the religious worship of stoneware. There was constant development of craftsmanship throughout the eras, and, because of changes in society, by the time of the Tang and Song dynasties, jade had gradually transformed from a symbolic object of obscure and elevated religious rituals into an ornamental and decorative item that was practical and closer to everyday life. By the time of the Yuan Dynasty, jade was an important object to be appreciated by high society and wealthy literati. In the Ming Dynasty, with the development of commercialism, carving craftsmanship progressed by leaps and bounds, and the developments in jade carving were especially fascinating. The Directorate of Imperial Accoutrements was established to supervise the production of jade ornaments in an effort to enhance quality. There was an increased demand for jade because of the popularization of jade among the common people. The imperial court was not the only place where fine jade could be produced, as Suzhou had become the center of jade carving for southern China.

In the Qing Dynasty, the art of jade carving became even more refined. Jade sources increased with the pacification of Huibu, and Xinjiang's abundant Hetian jade provided a continuous inflow of material. The fondness for and promotion of jade by the imperial court and nobles advanced the further development of jade carving skills. The imperial palace established the Jade Production Bureau to place jade under the supervision of the Imperial Workshop in the pursuit of skilled workmanship and high quality, sparing nothing in pursuit of the goal to produce the finest jade ornaments. Approximately during the reign of Qianlong, the large influx of jadeite that followed the pacification of the Jinchuan region inspired the refinement of jade carving skills. Since the Ming Dynasty, with the increasingly strong foundation enjoyed by the craft of jade carving and the popularity of jade, the use of jade by the common people greatly increased and it became a part of everyday life. Then, jade carving entered a golden age during the Qing Dynasty, which saw the highest achievements in jade carving since the Han Dynasty. Later generations used the term "Qianlong artisanship" to represent the perfection achieved in jade carving during that era. Qing Dynasty ornamental jade is an emblematic genre of that era.

D. Craftsmanship

With the exception of a portion that was made purely for artistic reasons, Qing Dynasty ornamental jade was actually created mainly with practical value in mind. Because of the beauty inherent in jade, however, the beauty displayed in the exact workmanship makes jade-making the craft that best represents the aesthetics of Qing Dynasty ornaments. It also became an artwork that people from all levels of society could appreciate and cherish. Taking an overall look at the forms of Qing Dynasty ornamental jade, they not only carried on the classic forms that had developed in ancient times, but also extracted the essence of the most beautiful forms of each era, creating amazing artworks reflecting the highest pinnacle of technique. Because each piece was created by hand, each is different, and this is the most fascinating aspect of the art of jade. Some analyses that can be made from the viewpoint of craftsmanship are as follows:

1. Styles

a. Patterned after ancient bronze ritual vessels: modeling after Shang-Zhou bronzeware, with exquisite forms like wine vessels, pots, food vessels, washbasins, and tripod vessels.

b. Patterned after ancient porcelain: the most commonly seen forms are patterned after Song Dynasty vases, bowls, and plates.

c. Patterned after metal ware: Tang Dynasty metal ware is the most common.

d. Patterned after representations of the natural world: including human figures, animals, plants, and natural shapes.

e. Those with images like two-dimensional paintings: layers of carving in relief and demi-relief, transforming the two-dimensional into three-dimensional, usually in jade boulders, table screens, and screens.

f. Using the technique similar to setting decorations in metal, such as setting glass, crystal, or gems in the jade, which developed into a new style in jade ornaments.

C. Sources of Jade

Because of political uniformity in the Qing Dynasty, transportation was efficient, and thousands of catties sometimes as many as ten thousand (a unit of measure equivalent to about half a kilogram) of raw jade from Xinjiang were given in tribute to the imperial palace each year.. The main sources were two production regions. One was the Yarkand River region with its raw mostly green jade mined from mountains. Since it was mined from the mountains, the raw jade was in especially large pieces, according to records from the Qing Dynasty. The largest piece took ten years to carve in its entirety, and was later placed in the Hall of Joyful Longevity as the "Regulation of Flood by Da Yu Jade Boulder". Other representative works of mountain-mined jade are the "Traveling in Autumn Mountains Jade Boulder" and the "Nine Elders of Huichang Jade Boulder". Another type was raw jade gathered from rivers, popularly called "seed jade", the main production regions of which were the White Jade River and the Green Jade River of Hetian, where jade was mostly found in the riverbeds. Each year during the dry season, the Hui people would pick raw jade out of the riverbed. Another kind was called "mountain wash" which was seed jade found in the upper reaches of rivers, in the mountains. Though its quality was not as lustrous as seed jade, it was commonly used as raw jade since it could be found in greater quantities.

Except in the creation of large artworks, such as jade boulders and urns, Qing Dynasty ornamental jade used the Hetian raw jade gathered from rivers about 89% of the time, especially suet white jade, which made up the great majority. The main reason was that although mountain-mined jade came in very large pieces, the quality was rather dry, not like the shiny lustrous jade gathered from rivers. The mountain-mined jade often had cracks and flaws and could not compare with the purity of suet white jade. After suet white jade, the next most popular jade types were the other types produced in Hetian, such as green-white jade, yellow jade, green jade, blue jade, gray jade, and black jade. Other types of materials were used, such as jadeite, achate, crystal, green quartz, and turquoise, which displayed diverse aesthetic viewpoints and artistic expressions. Basically, the ideal was that raw jade with pure and excellent jade quality could be strictly selected by a jade artisan to create the perfect artistic effect, depending on its intended use.

3. Decorations

The decorations on Qing Dynasty jade include many different types, as they were the culmination of thousands of years of traditional jade culture. It was not only the amalgamation of the decorations culled from history, furthermore; the era produced its own innovations, and they can be divided into the following categories:

a. Ancient ritualistic symbols: such as dragons and phoenixes, clouds, one-footed dragons, hornless dragons, ravenous beasts, auspicious beasts, grain, and the twelve ornaments.

b. Auspicious decorations: these include the five fortunes (good luck, official position, long life, happiness, and wealth), the three plentitudes (plentiful luck, plentiful long life, and plentiful sons), symbols of nobility and celebration, auspicious items that bring in luck and cast away evil, and symbols that are homonyms for lucky words.

c. Theme stories: legends (Eight Immortals Celebrate God of Longevity's Birthday), historical stories (Su Wu Herding Sheep), fictional tales (Xi Zhi's Beloved Goose), novels (Romance of the West Chamber), and tales of good deeds (Twenty-Four Paragons of Filial Respect).

d. Landscapes: Scenes of the four seasons, mountain rivers and cliffs, and riverbank panoramas.

e. Natural figures: animals and plants.

4. Inscriptions

Inscriptions cannot be found on Qing Dynasty jade from the early period; it was only after the palace jade production system was truly completed that inscriptions of the year of manufacture began to be made. The earliest surviving inscribed work bears the inscription, "Made in The Year of Yongzheng," while most inscribed pieces bear that of, "Made in the Year of Qianlong." Although there are inscriptions for the reigns of emperors Jiaqing and Guangdao, this practice died out towards the end of the Qing Dynasty. The years are usually inscribed with four characters in seal character script or clerical script, though regular script is occasionally seen. There were many different phrases used to designate the year during the time of Qianlong. There were different inscriptions for jade given as a gift by the emperor and jade to be used in the palace. Emperor Qianlong loved jade, so if he saw artwork that was of especially high quality, he would take up his brush and write an imperial poem or compose an inscription to memorialize the artisan. These types of inscriptions are carved with the greatest refinement, with perfect and dignified script especially worthy of careful appreciation to this day.

2. Skills

A clear description of the carving techniques of Qing Dynasty ornamental jade is given to us by the Jade Production Explanatory Illustrations, created by Li Cheng-Yuan in 1891. This document used illustrations and descriptions to compile a complete record of the processes used by jade carving artisans at the time. It is the best resource for understanding Qing Dynasty jade carving. In accordance with its descriptions, the process of jade carving is broken down into the following steps:

1) "ramming the sand"; 2) "grinding the paste"; 3) "revealing the jade"; 4) "piercing the crucible"; 5) "containing the crucible"; 6) "milling the crucible"; 7) "scooping the chamber" 8) "applying the pattern"; 9) "drilling the bore"; 10) "penetrating the pattern"; 11) "punching the hole"; 12) "wooden crucible"; and 13) "leather crucible". These are the thirteen steps described as the requirements for completing the process of jade carving.

The peak of Qing Dynasty jade craftsmanship was its middle period, which was approximately a forty-year period from the middle of the reign of Qianlong to the beginning of the reign of Jiaqing. It was the mature period of so-called "Qianlong artisanship", during which the artisanship of jade making-reached perfection. The selection of material was strict, the styles followed standards, the designs were novel, the burnish was exquisite, and the carving and engraving were finely skilled. Jade production had reached a level of utter perfection, as Emperor Qianlong himself expressed in imperial poetry in which he praised the work of jade artisans as heavenly treasures.

Looking at just a small aspect of the fine craftsmanship, we see how the pursuit of the finest details was the trend in jade carving, especially after "Hindustan jade" had been imported from the Mughal Empire of India and its production techniques and artistic style had exerted an influence. This was especially true in the case of the fine detail of thin-walled bowls, revealed through the reflection of light. Qianlong once praised the work involved in producing this kind of jade in imperial poetry, expressing his delight at the perfect blend of patterns and colors that can be seen in the jade.

In addition to the effort that went into the fine techniques of carving, there was also the embedding of decorations, such as precious metals, gems, glass, and quartz into the jade, in accordance with the preferences of the emperors, allowing for even more development of technique.

E. Conclusion

Taking an overall view of Qing Dynasty ornamental jade, be it a work of monumental size (such as the "Regulation of Flood by Da Yu Jade Boulder" or the "Traveling in Autumn Mountains Jade Boulder") or a decoration only a few inches in size, such as "jade rabbit" or "jade dog", they are all masterful artworks crafted with consummate skill. The large artworks were completed by many artisans working in tandem, while the small works were completed by a single artist. What sets jade-making apart is that it is done entirely by hand, so each and every piece of jade art is special and no two pieces are ever the same. The best of Qing Dynasty jade was labeled as "Qianlong artisanship", so most surviving ornamental jade of fine craftsmanship belongs to this category. Its main characteristics are as follows:

1. Fine and detailed: The lines that appear on jade are intricate and clearly defined, with a consistent technique that shows that the artisan never hesitated for a moment and completed all the artwork in one single-minded motion.

2. Multi-layered: all of the contours of the bas-relief of jade are smooth and round, and every detail and surface is carefully carved. Every layer of multi-layer relief smoothly follows the texture of the jade so that all lines are clear and accurate, making full use of the jade's three-dimensionality.

3. Thin and skillful: profoundly influenced by Hindustan jade, with workmanship that requires the highest quality of thin and translucent walls. The highest level of skill was required to make use of the natural color of the raw jade to create the most suitable style of jade art.

Qing Dynasty ornamental jade represents the jade that was considered the most beautiful and the most artistic of its time. Whether it was made in the palace or by a civilian artist, the techniques were all influenced by the "Qianlong artisanship" style, created with the highest refinement of carving skill. The jade of this era can be justifiably called the greatest achievement in the history of jade-making in China, creating a new golden age of jade artistry. Since it was preoccupied with the pursuit of cleverness and novelty, however, the art form tended towards being too formalist and superficial, lacking an inner significance that could portray the spiritual side of the culture. It can therefore appear somewhat shallow, giving the impression that there is no deeper level to explore. On the other hand, the large quantity of jade artworks that was produced allowed them to become part of the everyday life of people of all levels of society. It allowed the common people as well as the noble classes to be able to appreciate the beauty of Qing Dynasty jade artistry.

璽印

清宮舊藏御用璽印四組件

清宮舊藏御用璽印四組件：

一、「肇祖原皇后之寶」（漢清文）。清（滿）文印文的「祖始」可辨識，楷書寫體。

二、「宣皇后寶」（漢清文）。滿文也是楷書寫體，意為宣皇「太」后。案《欽定大清會典則例》卷二十八：「鑄印，凡鑄造金寶金印，皇太后金寶盤龍紐。」

三、碧玉盤螭紐璽印組。「嘉慶御筆」、「所寶惟賢」、「所其無逸」三件，置一檀木匣。

四、「光緒尊親之寶」。

「璽」自從秦朝時「天子獨以印稱璽」，定位為皇室專用；「印」是信物，今天在華人或日本的社會還是在使用中。蒙古、滿清雖然不是漢族，也是使用璽印為信物，再根據自己的民族加入蒙文、清（滿）文（清代稱「國書」）。《大清會典則例》卷六十三，清廷設有「鑄印局」。「鑄造寶印、關防、鈐記，順治年間定，凡鑄造寶印，禮部鑄印局職掌。印文清文左，漢文右。字樣由內院撰發。」滿洲皇室用印的習慣，早在努爾哈赤時代，受賜於明朝使用「建洲左衛之印」，稱帝時，使用老滿文的璽印。滿人也一樣的相信天命說，當獲得元順帝的傳國玉璽「制誥之命」璽，也大事盛行典禮一番。大致而言，清朝的帝后用印習慣，承襲明朝的舊制。

從皇帝「朕及天下」的觀念，雖然都是皇室用印，然而也可細分為二：公領域與私領域。公領域的用印，也是官文書用印，皇帝的用印因各種場合不同而使用不同璽印。它的制度載於《欽定大清會典》卷二。據清乾隆十三年欽定「御寶為二十五顆」。乾隆皇帝作「交泰殿貯御寶二十有五」。首句：「國朝受天命，采古制為璽。掌以宮殿監正；襲以重盝，承以髹幾，設交泰殿中，以次左右列。當用則內閣請而用之。」因其用處不同，印文名稱各異。如：「皇帝之寶」、「制誥之寶」、「皇帝尊親之寶」、「敬天勤民之寶」、「廣運之寶」等，均註明用途，其中「皇帝尊親之寶」條下注：「以薦徽號」，「白玉，方二寸一分，厚七分。盤龍紐，高一寸三分。」上引雖是乾隆年間的刊本，目前尚可見到「雍正尊親之寶」、「乾隆尊親之這兩件璽印，應該是清廷太廟列帝列后的「謚寶」。滿文用楷體，璽印上清文（國書）的篆法是：「（乾隆）十三年諭，國家寶璽，朕依次排定，其數二十有五。向兼清漢文，漢文皆用篆體，清文則有專用篆體者，亦有即用本字者，今國書經朕指授，篆法宜用之於國寶。」北京故宮今日猶保有原藏太廟列帝列后的謚寶，其中就另有「肇祖原皇帝寶」（十三點六公分見方）。

另兩件是嘉慶皇帝與光緒皇帝璽印。清仁宗睿皇帝嘉慶，全名愛新覺羅顒琰（一七六〇——一八二〇年）嘉慶君為清代入關後第五帝，在位二十五年，終年六十一歲。顒琰是乾隆的第十五個兒子，乾隆六十年（一七七三年）乾隆帝因即位時許下心願，做皇帝在位不敢超過他的祖父康熙的「六十一年」，因此，把皇位禪讓給嘉親王，改元「嘉慶」，乾隆帝為太上皇而「歸政仍訓政」。清德宗光緒帝，全名愛新覺羅載湉（同治十年六月二十八日（一八七一年八月十四日）生於北京太平湖醇王府，光緒三十四年十月二十一日酉刻（一九〇八年十一月十四日傍晚）過世於北京。

清代每逢三大節，即元旦、萬壽、冬至，內外臣工須具表、箋以慶賀。光緒二十年十月正值慈禧太后六十歲壽辰，光緒皇帝特上賀表祝萬壽無疆，尊號「慈禧端佑康頤昭豫庄誠壽恭欽獻崇熙皇太后」就蓋有此「光緒尊親之寶」的大印。

碧玉盤螭紐印璽組「嘉慶御筆」、「所寶惟賢」、「所其無逸」三件，含金絲紫檀木匣。三印成一組在乾隆時代也多見，其中一方為主人或宮殿名，另兩方為自勉的警語。看來這三印也是同乾隆舊制。這三件應該是屬於私領域使用的「閒章」。「嘉慶御筆」，就如他的先祖康熙、雍正、乾隆，或者各個皇帝鈐在書寫的文字後，落款鈐印。這也可以用「閒章」來蓋括。「所寶惟賢」、「所其無逸」兩件多是皇帝的口氣。雍正、乾隆兩帝都有此四字印，只是篆法及朱白文的不同。即使是末代皇帝退居小朝廷的溥儀，也有「無逸齋精鑑璽」一方。

「所寶惟賢」，「寶」為珍寶、敬重之意。所以尊寶者就是「賢」人。語出《尚書．旅獒》：「不寶遠物，則遠人格；所寶惟賢，則邇人安。」

所其無逸」語出《尚書．無逸》篇，是周公訓誡成王所作，其言曰：「嗚呼！君子所其無逸。先知稼穡
乃逸，則知小人之依。」

嘉慶御筆」、「所寶惟賢」、兩方印皆可於今日台北故宮的書畫上見到，其例是台北故宮藏《清黃鉞畫
康冊》，惟未見連鈐「所其無逸」。

日清宮在書畫上鈐印，其例見於兩岸故宮，書畫收藏，題材佛道兩家為「祕殿珠林」；一般者為「石渠
，共有三編，第三編成於嘉慶二十一年，書畫鈐印例有其定制。這三印，尤其是「所其無逸」並未隨同
出現在這一冊之內。嘉慶的用印，顯然比其父親乾隆要少得多，在收藏書畫的題跋也一樣。

印的製作，雍正時期有御書處所屬的刻字作，是專門為皇帝刻印，後來乾隆朝玉璽的製作，也發交到蘇
承作。嘉慶朝應該還是循乾隆舊制。從專門負責皇室生活用品製作的造辦處，所留下的《內務府各作成
檔》，刻成一印，「篆樣」要先呈覽奉准，如清初的書法名家張照，就曾參予。惜未見嘉慶朝所記。

宮用印篆法，「本朝定例大內寶文皆玉筋篆」。皇室的喜好與表現，總以雍容華貴為宜，端莊凝重的玉
自是為所採用。如「所寶惟賢」就是。

themselves have different names. Examples of these names are "Imperial Seal of the Emperor", "Imperial Seal of the Emperor's Edict", "Imperial Seal of the Emperor's Heritage", "Imperial Seal of Respecting Heaven and Serving the People", and "Imperial Seal of Grand Destiny", and each has its own use. In Qianlong's time, the "Imperial Seal of the Emperor's Heritage" was recorded to be made of white jade and used for presenting titles of honor. We also have existing samples of Emperor Yongzheng's (reigned 1722 – 1735) "Imperial Seal of the Emperor's Heritage" seal as well as the one used by Qianlong. Presenting titles of honor, the official use for this imperial seal, referred to honoring the emperor's royal parents by conferring noble titles on them. It was recorded that the administrative officials of the Qing court oversaw the production of all types of imperial seals according to all their different uses.

As for the owners of the seals, before the time of the first Qing Dynasty emperor in China, there was their "Ancestral Emperor" Mengtemu, who ruled six generations before Nurhaci.

The records of empresses and concubines in the History of the Qing Dynasty start with the "Empress Who Honors the Ancestors", whose surname was Hitara, given name Emuci, and title Agunu. She was the birth mother of Qing Emperor Nurhaci, and her highest status before his birth was simply that of queen dowager. Since she was the mother of the emperor, her status was posthumously elevated to the "Empress Who Honors the Ancestors" in the year 1648 in honor of Nurhaci's father, Taksi. She gave birth to three sons and a daughter, and so was given the title because of the value of the contribution of bearing sons. As recorded in the History of the Qing Dynasty, she was pregnant with the emperor for 13 months. After Nurhaci was born, Hitara gave birth to two sons, Surhaci and Yarhaci, who were put to death by Nurhaci, and a daughter who was married off to another clan. The date of birth of the empress is not clear, but she gave birth to Nurhaci in 1559, and died nine years later, in 1568.

These two imperial seals are most likely "Posthumous Seals" of the Qing court made in honor of past emperors and empresses. The Manchurian is written in regular script, and the official method of writing the Manchurian on the imperial seal is explained as: "In the 13th Year (of Emperor Qianlong's reign), it is ordered that the emperor's imperial seals are to be arranged by rank, for a total of twenty-five. They are to be written in both Manchurian and Chinese, with the Chinese written in standard seal character script and the Manchurian with a specialized seal character script. They are to be used to signify that a document was personally written by the emperor, and this seal character script is only to be used for imperial seals." The Palace Museum in Beijing currently preserves the posthumous seals of past emperors and empresses, including the "Imperial Seal of the Ancestral Emperor".

Four Sets of Imperial Seals from the Collection of the Qing Court

Set of Four Imperial Seals from the Collection of the Qing Court:

1. *"Imperial Seal of the Ancestral Emperor" (in Chinese and Manchurian). The Manchurian words for "first ancestor" are still legible, written in regular script.*

2. *"Imperial Seal of the Empress" (in Chinese and Manchurian). The Manchurian is written in regular script, with a word that signifies it is for the empress dowager. Volume 28 of the Collected Regulations and Precedents of the Qing states that the seal of the empress dowager is to be a golden imperial seal with a coiling dragon body.*

3. *Green jade hornless dragon body imperial seal set. Three pieces set in a sandalwood case: the "Seal of the Jiaqing Emperor", the "Seal of Precious Virtue", and the "Seal Against Luxurious Ease".*

4. *"Imperial Seal of the Heritage of the Guangxu Emperor".*

Ever since the Qin Dynasty (221 – 207 BC), there have been imperial seals specifically for use by the imperial court. A seal is a pledge of the owner's word, and seals are still used in Chinese and Japanese societies to this day. Though the Mongolians and the Manchurians were not Han Chinese, they also used the imperial seal in this way, using their own languages instead of Chinese. In Volume 63 of the Collected Regulations and Precedents of the Qing, the Manchu government established the "Bureau of Seal Casting" as the official agency for casting authorized imperial seals and for the regulation of their use. The custom of using seals in the Manchurian court started as early as the time of Emperor Nurhaci (reigned 1616 – 1626), who received the "Seal of the Jianzhou Left Guard" from the Ming Dynasty. When he was named emperor, the imperial seal was used with Manchurian language. The Manchurians also believed in the concept of the Mandate of Heaven, and a magnificent ceremony was always held when the Yuan Dynasty Emperor Shundi's imperial seal was passed down to each subsequent emperor. Overall, the customs involved in using seals among emperors and empresses in the Qing Dynasty (1644 – 1912) closely followed the traditions of the Ming Dynasty (1368 – 1644).

Although imperial seals were only for use by the imperial court, they were divided into two types. One type was for public use, and the other was for private use. The seals for public use were for official documents, and different types of imperial seals were used for different types of occasions. The system was recorded in Volume 2 of the Collected Regulations of the Qing. According to a document written by the Qing Dynasty Emperor Qianlong (reigned 1735 – 1796), the dynasty receives the Mandate of Heaven and uses the imperial seals passed down from ancient times in many different ways to administer the imperial court. Because there are different uses for the seals, the seals

The meaning of the "Seal Against Luxurious Ease" is found in "Against Luxurious Ease" from the Shang Shu, in which the Duke of Zhou admonishes King Cheng: "Oh! The superior man rests in this, that he will indulge in no luxurious ease. He first understands how the painful toil of sowing and reaping makes for ease, and thus he understands how the lower people depend on this toil (for their support)."

The "Seal of the Jiaqing Emperor" and the "Seal of Precious Virtue" can both be found on Qing Dynasty calligraphy and paintings in the Palace Museum in Taipei, though the "Seal Against Luxurious Ease" is not represented there.

Examples of calligraphy and paintings imprinted with imperial seals from the Qing court can be found in the Palace Museums in Taipei and Beijing and in private collections. Paintings with subjects from Buddhism and Taoism are collected in the Mi Dian Zhu Lin. Paintings with general subjects are collected in the Shi Qu Bao Ji. There are three collections in all, and the third was compiled in 1816, with calligraphy and paintings collected by the order of Emperor Jiaqing. These three seals, especially "Seal Against Luxurious Ease" are not easily found in prints of these collections. Emperor Jiaqing apparently used his seal more infrequently than did his sire, Emperor Qianlong, so it is harder to find his calligraphy and paintings in collections today.

As for the making of imperial seals, there were special artisans that were part of the court who carved imperial seals during the reign of Emperor Yongzheng. By the time of Qianlong, the work was commissioned to artisans in Suzhou. The court of Jiaqing most likely followed the same system as Qianlong. In an official document of standards and regulations used by the administrative office that was in charge of making items of daily use for the imperial court, the carving of a seal required approval of a standard of excellent calligraphic script such as that of the famous calligraphist Zhang Zhao from the early Qing Dynasty. It is unfortunate, however, that similar records from the court of Emperor Jiaqing are incomplete.

The manufacture and use of imperial seals were both art forms, and the use of exquisite jade seals was meant to show the good taste and grandiosity of the imperial court. The "Seal of Precious Virtue" is an example of this.

Wang Yao-Ting

Former Chief Curator

Department of Painting and Calligraphy, National Palace Museum

The other two sets of imperial seals belonged to Emperor Jiaqing and Emperor Guangxu. The Qing Dynasty Emperor Jiaqing was named Aisin Giorro Yongyan (b. 1760 – d. 1820), the fifth Qing Dynasty emperor since the beginning of Manchu rule over China. He reigned for 25 years, and died at the age of 61. He was the 15th son of Qianlong, who had made a vow when he took the throne in 1773 not to stay on the throne past his 61st year, in honor of his grandfather Emperor Kangxi. Qianlong therefore, passed on the throne to Prince Jiaqin, who took the official name Emperor Jiaqing. Qianlong then became a valuable advisor to the new emperor. The Guangxu Emperor, who ruled for ten years, six months, and 28 days, was named Aisin Giorro Zaitian. He was born in Beijing on August 14, 1871, at Taiping Lake's Chunwang Palace, and died on the evening of November 14, 1908, in Beijing.

There were three main festivals in the Qing Dynasty, namely New Year's Day, the Emperor's Birthday, and Winter Solstice, and all nobles and officials were required to offer congratulations to the emperor in memorials and in writing. In October 1894, on the 60th birthday of Empress Dowager Cixi, Emperor Guangxu presented a memorial wishing her long life and honoring her with a grand and solemn imperial title. This memorial was sealed with the "Imperial Seal of the Heritage of the Guangxu Emperor".

The three jasper hornless dragon body imperial seals, "Seal of the Jiaqing Emperor", "Seal of Precious Virtue", and "Seal Against Luxurious Ease" are contained in a sandalwood case. Sets of three seals were common in the time of Emperor Qianlong. One of the three was inscribed in the name of the owner or the name of the palace. The other two were inscribed with phrases to accentuate the authority of the owner. These three seals use the same system as that of Qianlong. These three items were "poetry seals" used in the private realm. The "Seal of the Jiaqing Emperor" was used to mark personal writings by Emperor Jiaqing, in the tradition of his ancestors, Kangxi, Yongzheng, Qianlong, and other emperors. The two items of the "Seal of Precious Virtue" and the "Seal Against Luxurious Ease" expressed the emperor's personal philosophy. The two emperors Yongzheng and Qianlong also had imperial seals with similar words, only differing by the script style and embellishments. Even the last emperor, Puyi, in his court in exile had a similar imperial seal.

The "Seal of Precious Virtue" has four characters that express the idea that the emperor should be respected because he is a wise and virtuous man. This is a concept that can be seen in the "Hounds of Lu" from the Shang Shu: "When he does not look on foreign things as precious, foreigners will come to him; when it is real worth that is precious to him, (his own) people near at hand will be in a state of repose."

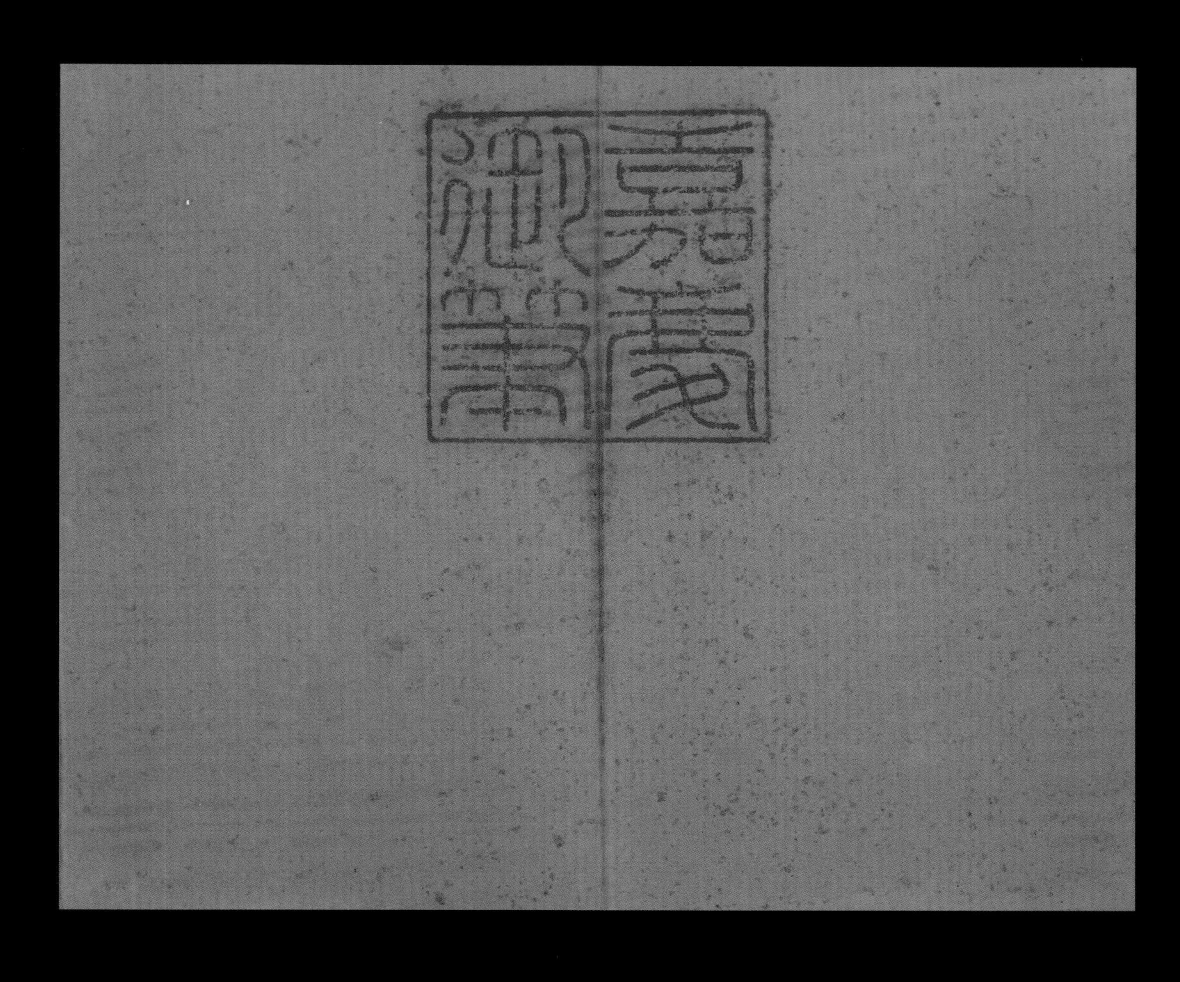

Qing Dynasty
Huang Yue "Album of the Suburb Concert for Annual Celebration" (detail)

It is currently collected in the National Palace Museum

清　白玉　肇祖原皇帝之寶璽印

長12.8公分　寬12.8公分　高8公分

此璽為清太祖努爾哈赤的六世祖孟特穆之謚寶，原應置放於列帝列后的太廟中。和闐白玉質，玉質溫潤而淨透，局部玉瑕綹紋處，深沁黃褐色沁斑。此件玉璽鈕飾非常特殊，做編結繩紋飾，兩兩相交結於印鈕的正中央，此鈕式有「結交四方」，或「駕御四方、大權在握」的深遠寓意。鈕式簡捷有力，呈鏤空高圓雕立體形制，就現在力學來說，亦完全符合手掌持握與用印施力時的人體工學設計，尤其此印鈕形制非常的罕見，因此匠師琢製設計之初，當是完全拋開傳統的制式璽印鈕飾設計，而別出心裁，巧妙完成此前無古人之作，實為難得。

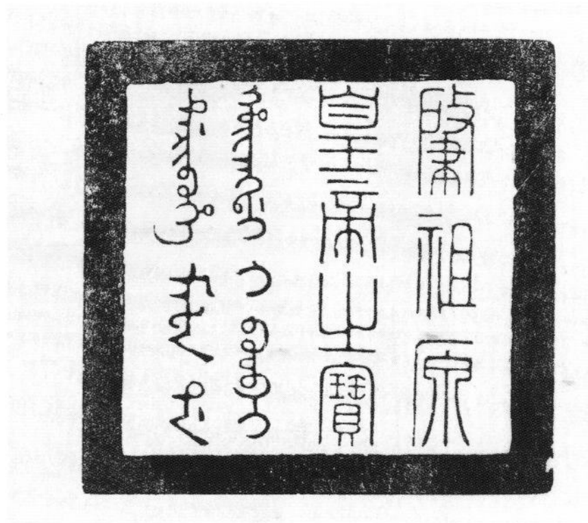

Qing Dynasty
White jade Zhao Zu Yuan Huang Di Zhi Bao Imperial seal

L/12.8cm, W/12.8cm, H/8cm

This seal is Taizu Emperor Nurhachi's sixth generation ancestor Mengtemu's "imperial seal" to be placed in the ancestral hall honoring previous emperors and empresses. Hetian white jade. The jade is smooth and pure, with a partial imperfection, and dark yellowish-brown spots. This imperial seal's body is special, with flat, knotted patterns intertwining to meet in the center. The seal body style signifies that the user has authority and power throughout the empire. The body style is simple and powerful, showing a pierced sculpture form. Today, we would say it conforms to the requirements of ergonomics, since it can be comfortably grasped. This type of seal body is very rare, showing how the artist moved away from traditional imperial seal designs to create this design of unprecedented dignity.

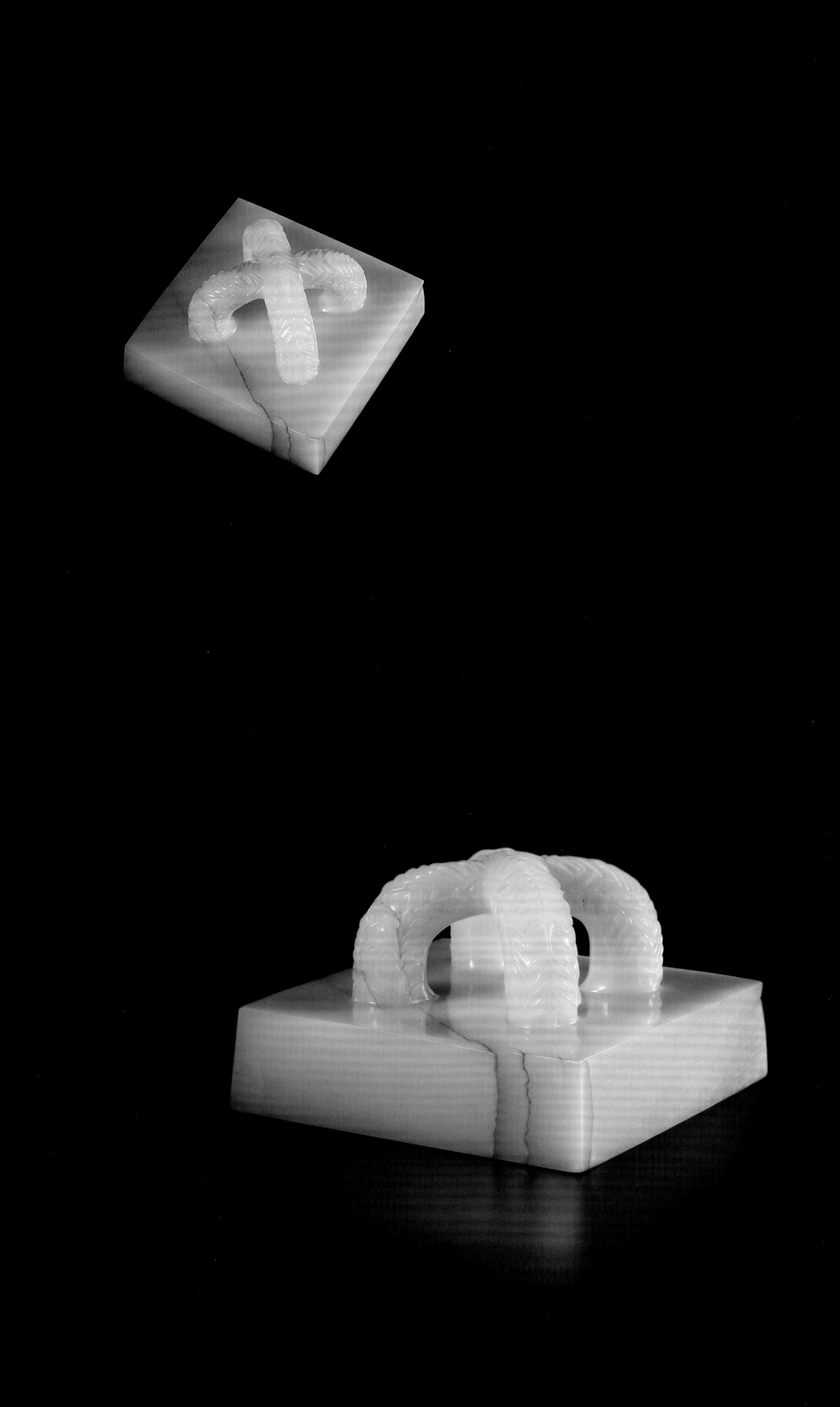

清 光緒 白玉 光緒尊親之寶璽印

長9.7公分 寬9.7公分 高9.85公分

和闐白玉質，玉質溫潤，用料厚實，略帶自然褐色斑紋。清代皇室御用璽印「皇帝尊親之寶」條下注：「以薦徽號」，清朝規定：國有慶典，必于皇太后尊號前疊加二字或四字，以示尊崇，是為上徽號。「白玉，方二寸一分，厚七分。盤龍紐，高一寸三分。」印鈕琢刻雙座龍，座龍以近圓雕形制的高浮雕手法製成，座龍壯碩，體態豐腴，龍尾夾藏於腹部四足之間。龍形鈕飾璽印，漢代以來即有，而歷代璽印用印尺寸，當屬清代皇室御用玉璽印為最大，無論器形、器式、選材、用料與琢刻工藝，也最為細緻與繁複。

Qing Dynasty Guangxu Era White jade Guang Xu Zun Qin Zhi Bao Imperial seal

L/9.7cm, W/9.7cm, H/9.85cm

Hetian white jade. The jade is smooth and the material is solid, with natural brown spots. Under the "Guang Xu Zun Qin Zhi Bao" inscription, it lists the specifications of the seal. The Qing Dynasty regulated that for state celebrations, the front of the empress dowager's symbol must have two or four characters carved to signify respect. It was an appellation of respect. The seal body is carved with two dragons in an almost sculpture-like style in high relief carving technique. The dragons are magnificent, with fully formed bodies and tails that hide their legs. Dragon shaped imperial seals were present in the Han Dynasty, but the Qing Dynasty emperors had the largest imperial seals. They were the essence of refinement and complexity in terms of shape, style, material, and carving technique.

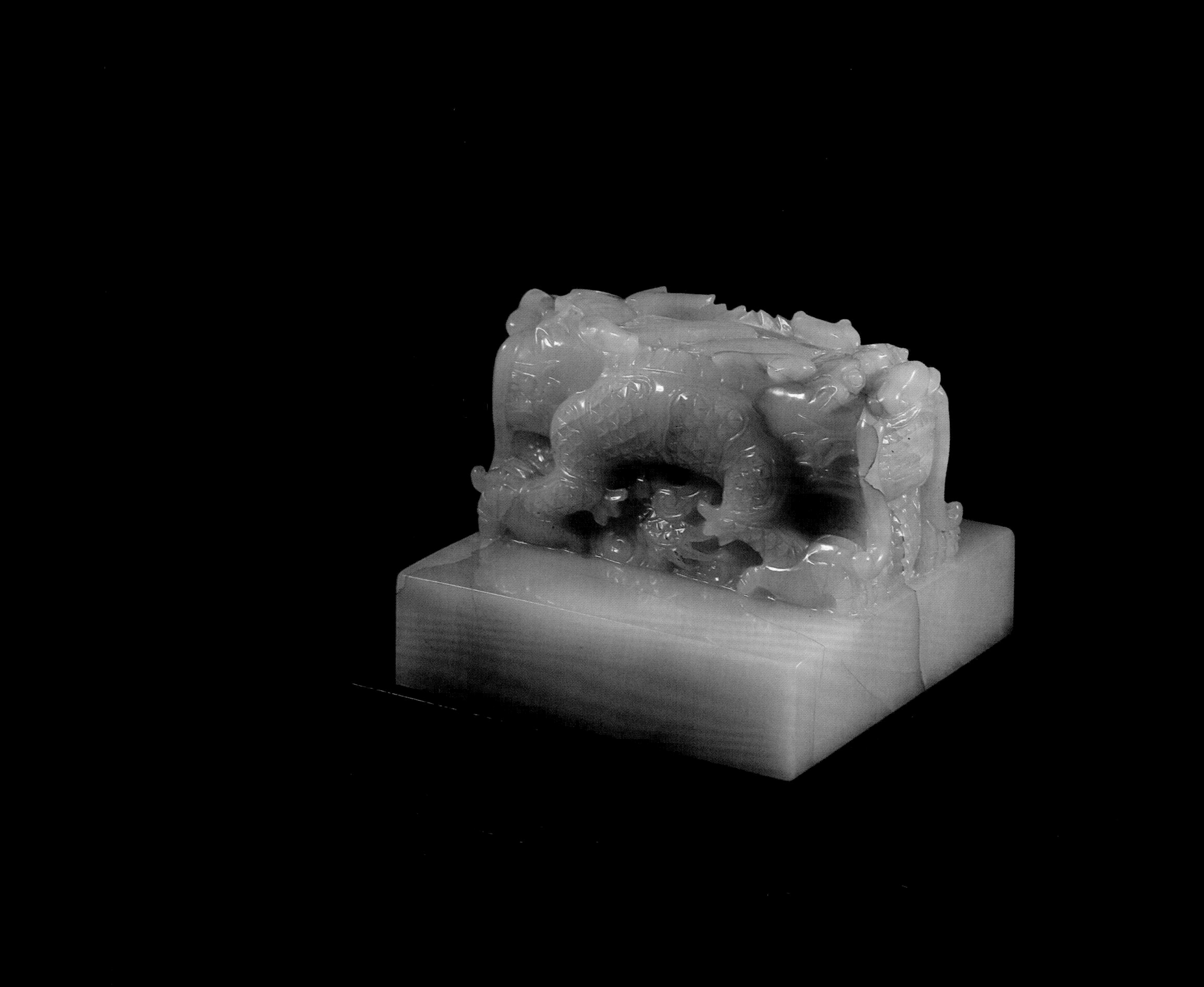

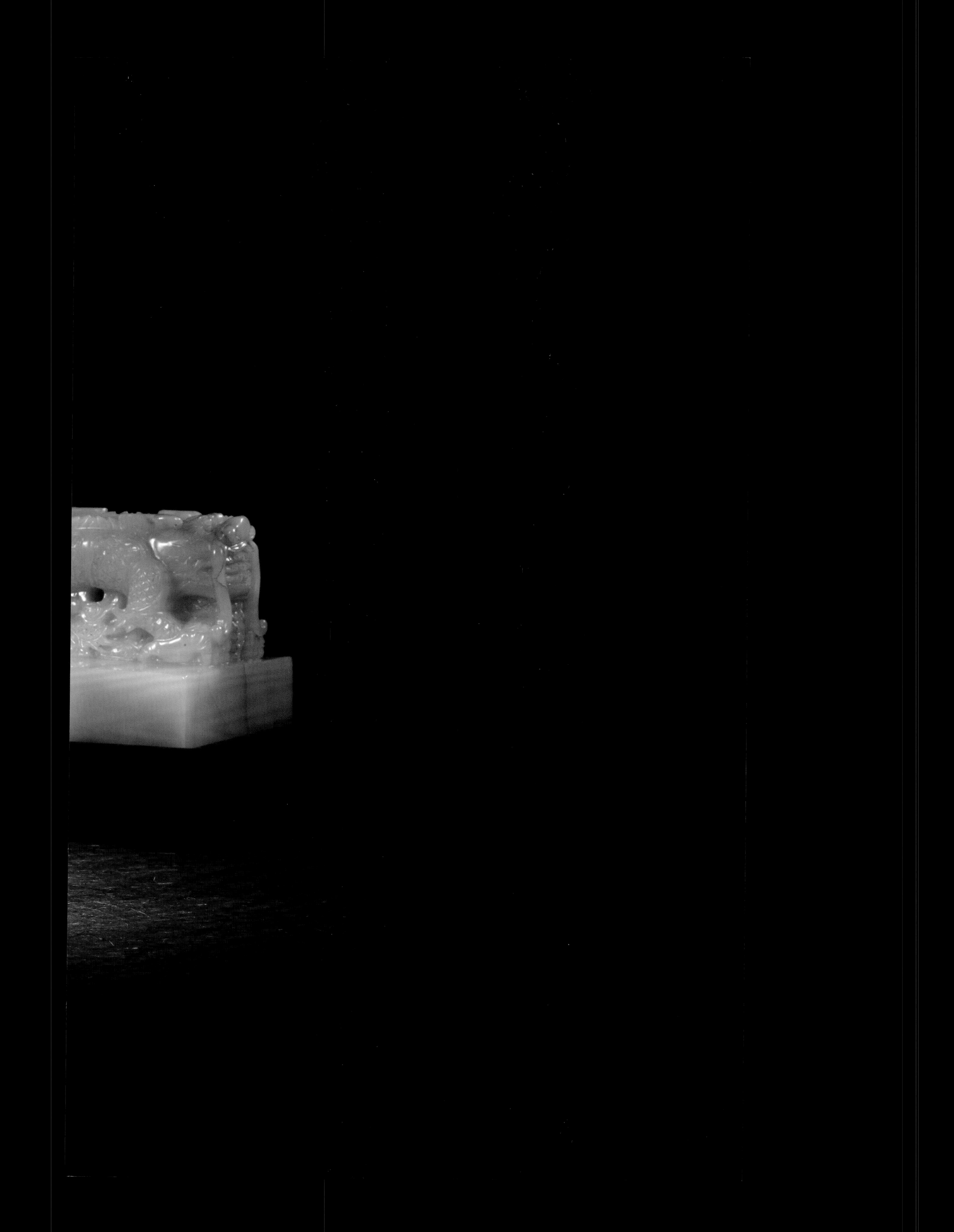

此璽為清太祖努爾哈赤生母喜塔臘氏之謚寶。喜塔臘氏名額穆齊，都督阿古女。於順治五年受追謚為「宣皇后」，此璽印應是清太廟列帝列后的「謚寶」。和闐青玉材質，「宣皇后寶」（漢滿文）璽印。意為宣皇「太」后。此方璽印，和闐青玉材質，正面端坐一昂首單座龍形制，案《欽定大清會典則例》卷二十八：「鑄印，凡鑄造金寶金印，皇太后金寶盤龍紐。」龍形設計雖不若皇帝玉璽的壯碩與大器，但卻依然使用皇室御用的五爪龍形制，爪與軀體略為平整而豐潤，青玉為清代玉雕常見用的大玉礦料，而此帝后之璽印用此琢刻而成，足見清代對和闐青玉的重視，可見一斑。

Qing Dynasty
Dark green jade Xuan Huang Hou Bao Imperial seal

L/13.8cm, W/13.8cm, H/14.8cm

This seal is Taizu Emperor Nurhachi's birth mother Lady Hitara's. In 1648, she was titled as "Empress Xuan" and this seal was an "imperial seal" in the Qing ancestral hall. Hetian dark green jade "Xuan Huang Hou Bao" imperial seal (in Chinese and Manchurian). The Manchurian refers to the empress dowager. This square imperial seal has a seated dragon with a raised head carved on the top. The historical records state that the seal of the empress dowager is a dragon seal. Although this dragon design cannot compare to the magnificence and tastefulness of the emperor's jade imperial seals, it uses the same imperial five-clawed dragon design. The claws and the body are regular and slightly plump. The dark green jade is the most commonly seen jade material in Qing Dynasty jade carvings, and the fine artisanship that went into this carving shows the importance that was placed on Hetian dark green jade.

清　碧玉　盤螭鈕璽印組（所寶惟賢、嘉慶御筆、所其無逸）

所寶惟賢　長6.9公分　寬6.9公分　高5.2公分
嘉慶御筆　長6.9公分　寬6.9公分　高4.7公分
所其無逸　長6.5公分　寬3.4公分　高3公分

「所寶惟賢」語出《尚書．旅獒》：「不寶遠物，則遠人格；所寶惟賢，則邇人安。」知古賢者對「所寶惟賢」亦極推崇，視為定國安民之根本。此璽，以明其求賢若渴，綏遠撫近之心跡。「所其無逸」語出《尚書．無逸》：「嗚呼！君子所其無逸。先知稼穡之難，乃逸；則知小人之依。…。」此璽以身居高位不可貪圖安逸享樂，以此自勵。和闐碧玉質，三件璽印配制於紫檀盒內，鈕式皆以盤螭龍紋為主要紋飾。清代玉螭，其最大特點是下唇有鬚，身較光素，頭部較大，身尾略短粗，此璽印正面上方高浮雕一隻呈盤俯姿勢的螭龍，龍身扭曲呈「弓」字形，曲線優美，身形靈巧。四周圍繞較小螭龍，螭龍下顎唇無鬚狀刻紋，十分精細。主龍首微仰，獨角，貓耳，圓睜眼大口，雙眉上翹。四肢伸出，上飾螺旋紋。有雙岔尾，短尾蜷曲，長尾盤于末端。此組玉璽構思巧妙，刀法流暢，所雕螭龍活靈活現，為鈐用、把玩皆佳的珍稀之品。

Qing Dynasty
Dark green jade coiled hornless dragon body Imperial seal set
(Suo Bao Wei Xian, Jia Qing Yu Bi, and Suo Qi Wu Yi)

Suo Bao Wei Xian　L/6.9cm, W/6.9cm, H/5.2cm
Jia Qing Yu Bi　L/6.9cm, W/6.9cm, H/4.7cm
Suo Qi Wu Yi　L/6.5cm, W/3.4cm, H/3cm

The phrase "Suo Bao Wei Xian" comes from the Shang Shu, which says that the man who appreciates these treasures is a sage. The ancients considered that the sage who can appreciate rare treasures will keep the kingdom and the people at peace. This seal shows that its owner understands this. The phrase "Suo Qi Wu Yi" also comes from the Shang Shu, which says that the superior man will not indulge in leisure because understands that the people depend on labor to survive. This seal is used to show that its owner does not waste time in luxurious ease Hetian dark green jade. Three piece imperial seal set in red sandalwood box. The seal body style is mainly that of a coiled hornless dragon pattern. The special characteristics of Qing Dynasty hornless dragons are beards on the lower lip, smoother bodies, larger heads, and shorter bodies. These imperial seals have one coiled hornless dragon carved in high relief on the top. The curves are beautiful, and the body is nimbly carved. There are four smaller hornless dragons around it, without beards on the lower lips that makes this piece special.The main dragon is slightly on its back, with one horn, catlike ears, large round eyes, and upraised eyebrows. Its four limbs are outstretched, decorated with a spiral pattern. It has a dual forked tail, with one short, curled tail and one long tail coiled toward the end. This set of imperial seals has amazing artistic imagination and smooth carving technique. The hornless dragons appear lively, making it a rare piece.

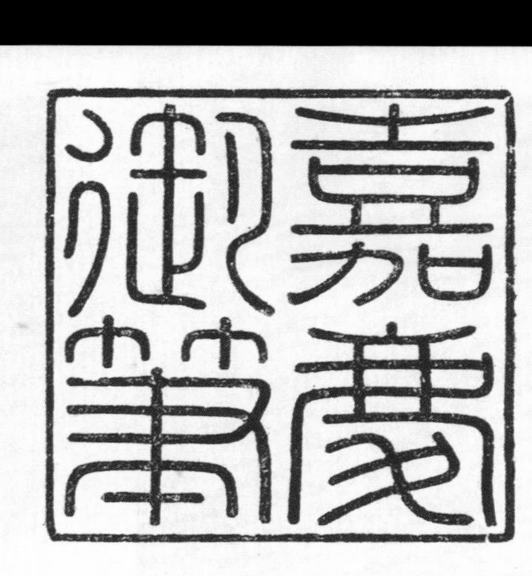
嘉慶御筆

嘉慶
所其無逸

所寶惟賢
御筆

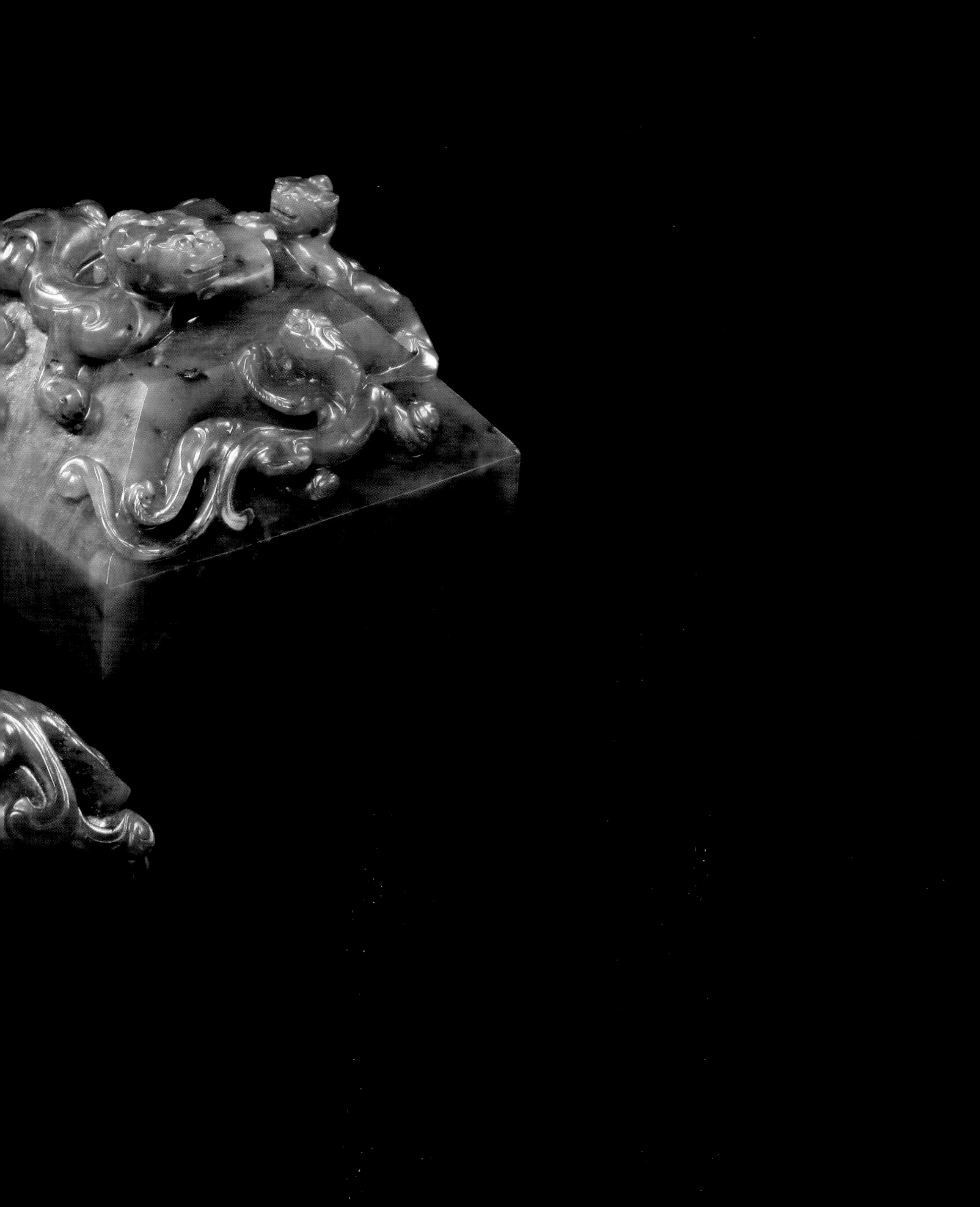

清　白玉　四方印

長3.2公分　寬3.2公分　高3.2公分

白玉質地，雕成方印，印面為朱文篆字「如日之恆」，屬吉語印，在印章印面邊緣，刻有「辰」字楷書款，或許曾屬於一系列套印中之一件。印章鈕部形如覆斗，上設環帶，以鏤刻技法表現，琢出螭龍蟠踞，雲氣繚繞。此件雕工溫雅精緻，羊脂白玉潔白凝膩，質地及雕工俱為精品。

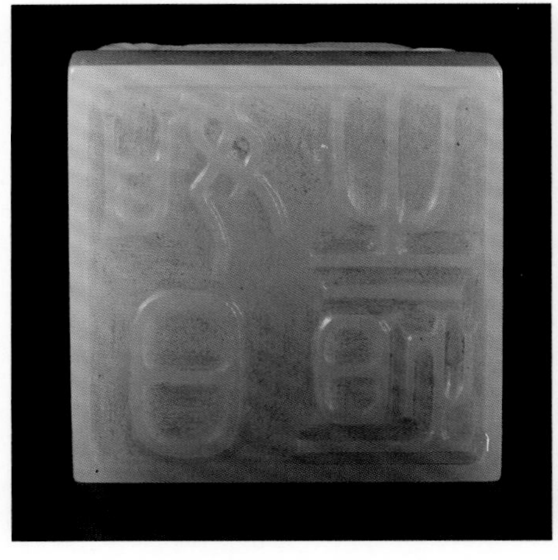

Qing Dynasty
White jade square seal

L/3.2cm, W/3.2cm, H/3.2cm

White jade carved into a square seal. On the seal face is carved in relief the words, "Ru Ri Zhi Heng," in seal script, making it an auspicious phrase seal. The side of the seal face is inscribed with the character for the number five, which means that this seal was probably one of a series. The seal body has an upside-down bowl shape and also circular ribbon shapes carved into a coiled hornless dragon with a hollowing out technique, giving it a suggestion of swirling clouds. The workmanship is elegant and exquisite and the suet jade is of the purest white, making this piece a refined artwork both in terms of technique and material.

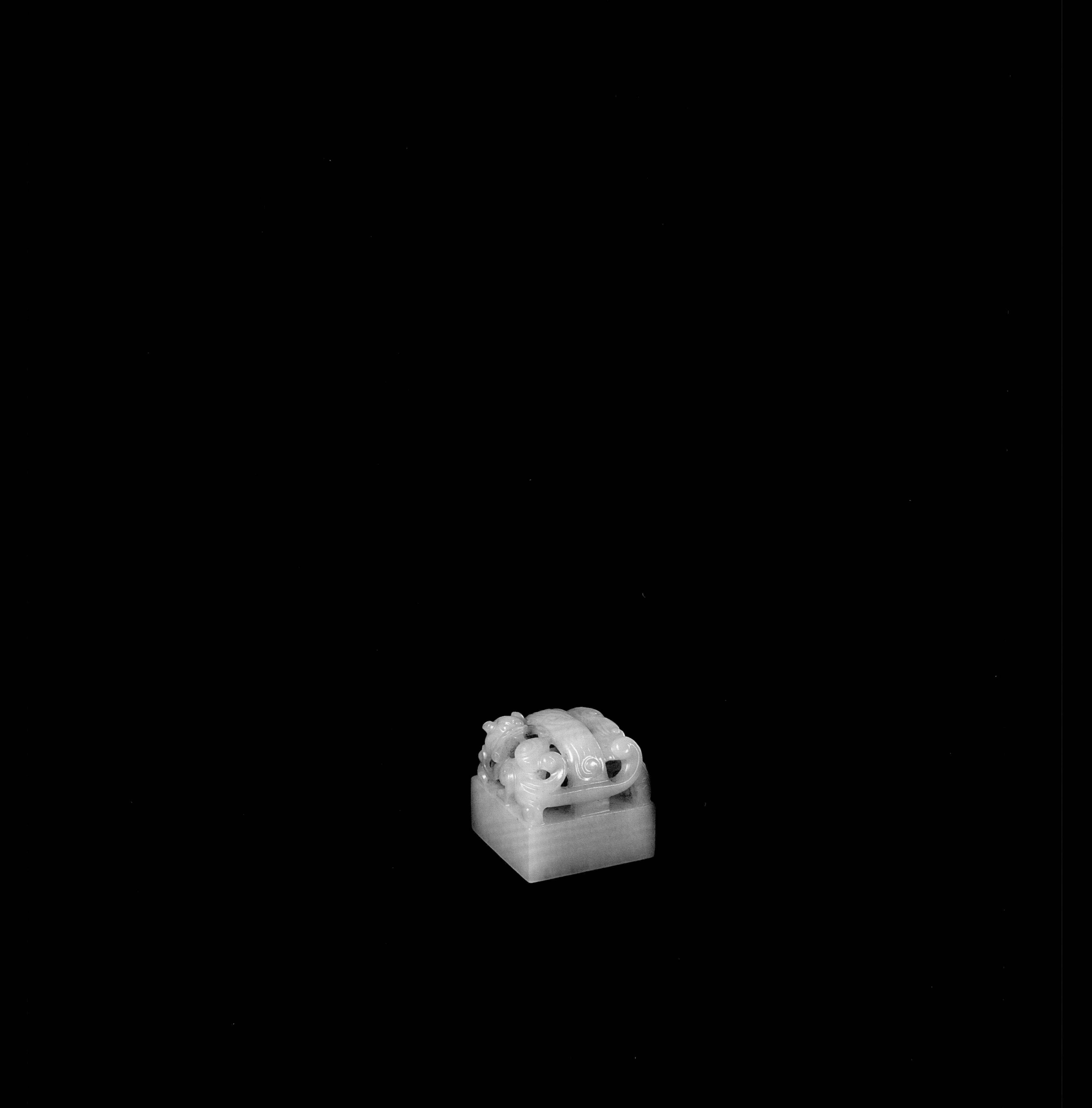

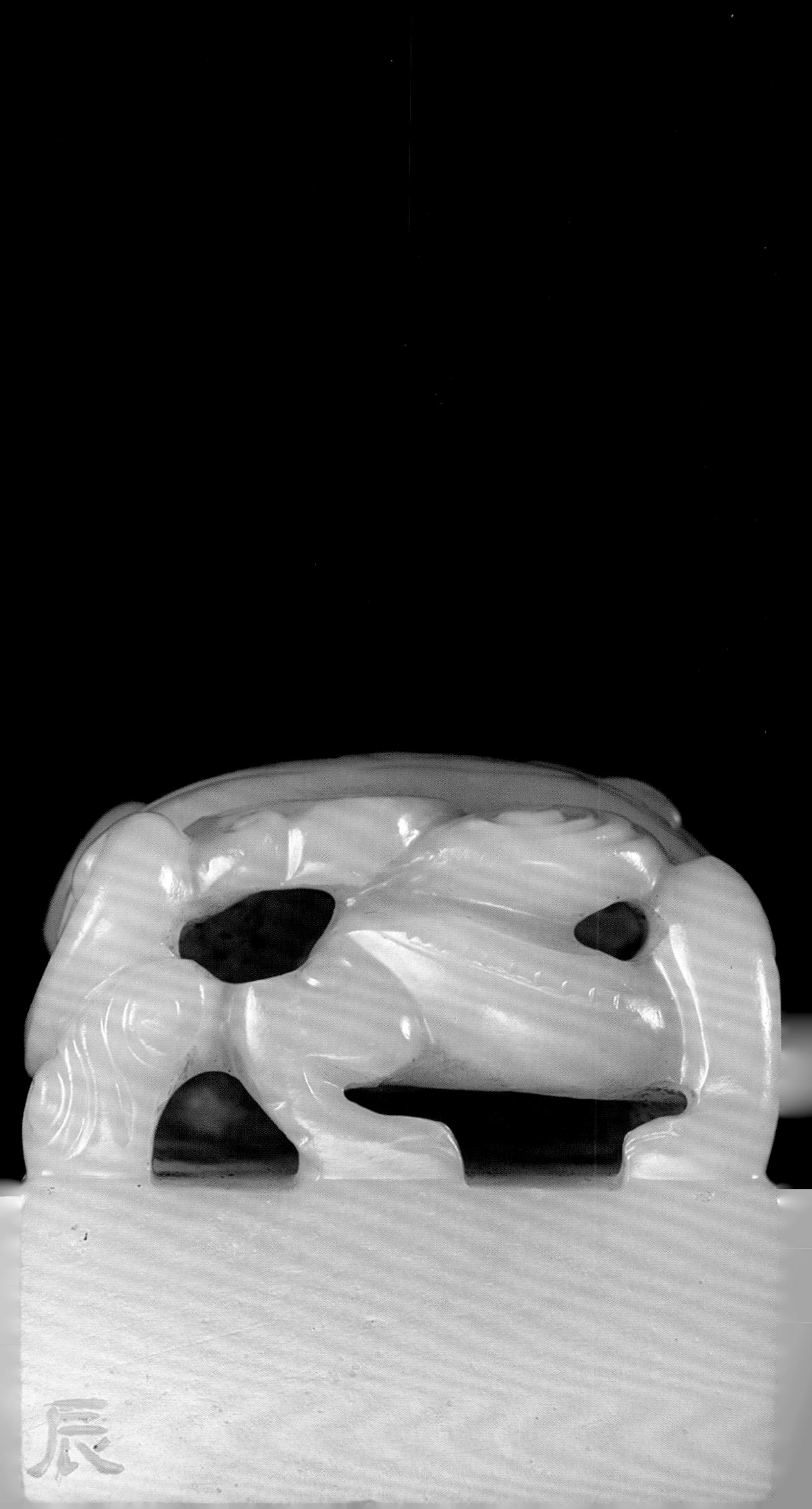
辰

清 白玉 圓印（品真、思華）

思華 印面 3.5公分 高3.1公分 品真 印面 3.5公分 高3.3公分

白玉質地，雕成圓形印章兩枚。一枚印面呈橢圓形，印面為白文篆字「品真」。另一枚印面呈花瓣形，刻白文篆字「思華」。兩枚印章均為小印，高不盈寸，玲瓏可愛，均約用於書畫中之名印。印身樸素無飾，印頂著意留存灑金沁色玉皮，溫潤中透古意。

QingDynasty
Two white jade seals,
inscribed with: Si Hua and Pin Zhen

H/3.1cm “Si Hua” seal face/3.5cm
H/3.3cm “Pin zhen” seal face/3.5cm

Two seals made of white jade carved into circular shapes. One seal has an elliptical shape and is inscribed with the words, “Pin Zhen,” in seal script. The other seal is in a flower petal shape and is inscribed with the words “Si Hua,” in seal script. Both are small seals of less than an inch in height. These bright and attractive name seals were used for calligraphy and painting. The seals are simple and unadorned, and on their tops they have golden spots and jade skin. They have a smooth texture and an ancient feel.

玉器

有清一朝，始自聖祖康熙皇帝，在內廷養心殿成立造辦處，負責宮廷器用的監造工作。造辦處下設各種作坊，如木作、玉作、……等，但瓷器及織品則另設於景德鎮及蘇杭、江寧等地。這些內廷器用，是為皇室所服務，因之各種活計的造型風格，也往往隨不同皇帝的喜好而有所差異化。這種由創意開發（或皇帝指定），到式樣定案的流程中，一定會出現畫樣呈覽、木（或竹）作模型、再經選料定樣、呈旨開工……等繁複嚴管的標準流程，這種生產於皇室內廷管理規範下的作品，風格明顯，工精料細，不但清楚的表現出皇家產品的標準，也體現出當朝皇帝的個人美學品味。

清朝自康熙至乾隆三朝，政治、經濟達到有史以來的巔峰，是難得的太平盛世，尤其乾隆在位時間長、武功強，是此段盛世的代表者。其個人因對藝術之雅好而重視收藏，在文化上成就非凡。康乾盛世的時代，正值歐西各國開拓亞洲航路的大探險年代，耶穌會傳教士隨著冒險家一路東來訪古探祕，部份教士也以一己的專才，服務於皇室內廷，直接引進了西方美學的表現形式。

乾隆（一七三六——一七九五年）一朝在位六十年，尤其乾隆二十年（一七五五年）平定準部、二十四年平定回部的大小和卓木，新疆納入大清的版圖，玉作的原料問題基本解決。在玉路斷絕的年代，玉料多靠私運內地，數量極少，質量亦難控制，而限制了玉作的發展。乾隆平西戰事結束後，玉路暢通，乾隆二十五年清廷部回部征克每年進貢玉料四千斤，和闐玉料通過春秋兩季的玉貢和私運內地，提供內廷玉作及京、津、蘇、杭等地玉作坊源源不斷的各色原料，讓乾隆一朝的玉器文化，在乾隆中期以後，達到史無前例的高峰。

乾隆曾自言：「朕自幼生長宮中，講誦二十年，未嘗少輟，實一書生也。」這位皇帝書生，自幼受教於碩學耆宿，如朱軾、蔡世遠等大儒，所學皆儒家經典。青年時期的寫作即匯輯成《御製樂善堂全集定本》三十卷。身為一國之尊，東征西討、勤於政務之餘，著詩四萬餘首，輯《御製詩集》。其中雖有代筆之作，但產量豐富，詩中大量論及對玉器之喜好與評價，留傳至今日，正好作為乾隆玉器鑑古存真的最佳比照。

明代高濂在其大作《遵生八箋》中，描述文人高士崇古的生活情趣：「時乎坐陳鐘鼎，几列琴書，拓帖松窗之下，展圖蘭室之中，窗櫳香藹，欄檻花妍，雖咽水餐雲，亦足以忘飢永日，沐玉吾齋，一洗人間氛垢矣。」「編考鐘鼎卣彝、書畫法帖、窯玉古玩、文房器具，纖細究心，更校古今鑒藻。」這《遵生八箋》中所描寫「居今之世與古人相見。」的生活情趣，不正是乾隆心繫之所在？當今兩岸的故宮清代藏畫中，有不少描繪乾隆漢裝生活的寫生作品，正是這種文人崇古生活的寫照。也因為乾隆養成教育中的崇古傾向，及其個人的尚古美學思維，對於乾隆一朝的崇古與摹古工藝風格，起了決定性的作用。

乾隆中期至嘉慶初年，是內廷玉作生產的高峰期，北京故宮藏玉共約二萬三千餘件，其中屬於乾隆收藏或製造、使用者即超過萬件。台北故宮藏玉中，乾隆時期的作品或收入重刻者，亦佔相當的比例，由此不難評鑑出乾隆的風格和品味。乾隆本身因崇古而摹古，尤其對玉器之崇愛；經常在製作過程中親自把關督造，在《活計檔》中，可以翻查出他對細節的要求嚴格，已達不盡情理的地步。大體而言，乾隆玉作用料講究、畫樣起稿高妙、造型大器、雕琢工藝精湛。對於當時清宮收藏的古董作品，無論材質，只要乾隆中意，直接命內廷太監傳旨交玉作坊仿作，連《西清古鑑》中的藏品也不例外。台北故宮即藏有《西清古鑑》卷三八唐飛熊表座的銅製原牛及乾隆摹古的玉製方牛，兩相對照展出，耐人尋味，由此也可以觀察出乾隆摹古錙銖必較的嚴謹精神。

這類摩古玉作，除上述仿古銅器造型外，摹寫書畫中之意境，亦是一大主流。此外對特別中意的作品，多刻有御題詩詞，褒獎器物、詠史述典之外，更透露乾隆當時的心境。御題詩大多以宮內習用的館閣體為之，字跡工整，鐫刻嚴謹，刻款有「乾隆年製」、「乾隆御用」、「大清乾隆年製」、「乾隆仿古」、「大清乾隆仿古」等。對於畫意題材的玉作，常刻有「比德」、「朗潤」兩款閒章；而摩古之作，則見「古香」、「太璞」兩款。由用印語詞的雅緻與作品內容的關連性，也可見乾隆內心深處的真性情。

乾隆由於個人美學的體認而崇古，相對於當時的新鮮事物，並不贊同而時有所貶。台北故宮所藏一件乾隆碧玉龍尾觥上的御題詩，即有「俗手好翻新樣奇，頓教瓊玖價增卑」的貶句。在《御製詩集》中有乾隆三十九年〈詠仿古夔紋斧珮〉：也有「不宜付俗匠，新樣殘瑤瑛」的詩句。詩中所提到的「俗手」、「俗匠」，指的就是蘇杭一帶玉作坊的巧匠，這些蘇杭等地的玉作坊，不時也接宮中代工玉作，但他們最大的謀生本領，是運用私採私運的玉料加工，以滿足市場的需求。乾隆四十三年派駐和闐的玉官高樸，因勾私盜採玉料而問斬，但利之所趨，並無法杜絕私採私運之風。乾隆詩中的「新樣」、「時樣」是相對於仿古而言，仿古是有所本的；宮中玉作的流程嚴謹，未通過御批呈覽的畫樣，是不得開工製作的。御製詩中曾出現「和闐採玉春秋貢，琢器頻翻博古圖」的詩句，充分的表現出乾隆對玉材使用的規範。

然而民間市場，卻因皇帝好玉而群起效尤，尤其蘇揚等地的官吏，呈進皇室討好皇帝的物件。民間使用玉料，自有其工本，玉材來源以重量計，因此施作時多遷就材料原形，捨不得過分汰琢，因此販售時亦以重量計費。清《高宗純皇帝實錄》曾記載乾隆五十九年頒佈的一則禁令，對蘇揚巧匠的時新之作，做徹底的禁止。「近來，蘇揚等處呈進物件，多有鏤空器皿……又有何用?此皆係該處奸猾匠人造作此等無用之物，以為新巧，希圖厚價獲利。而無識之徒，……呈進，朕於此等物件從不賞收。……著傳諭揚州、蘇州鹽政、織造等，以後務須嚴行飭禁，不准此等奸匠仍行刻鏤成作。並出示曉諭，令其一體知悉，以杜奇邪而歸純樸。」

乾隆因喜好博古而仿古，但他的摩古之作並非侷限於精準的仿古器形而已，時而出現不同時代的工藝造型、裝飾特徵與當時流行的吉祥用語與圖案，故意識上的結合再造，如北京故宮所藏純金鏤空葫蘆香薰，上刻」兩字；而南京博物院藏清乾隆官窯粉彩描金「大吉」葫蘆壁飾，北京藝術博物館藏乾隆緙絲群仙嬰戲」鏡心，也都有「大吉」二字。無獨有偶的，二〇〇五年香港佳士得"The Imperial Sale"專拍中，亦出清乾隆鎏金銅「大吉」葫蘆形音樂鐘。這種在葫蘆造型中，無論材質為何，均加刻（或繡畫）「大吉」其主要的意喻來自「福祿大吉」的吉祥圖案，而在乾隆時期將其意涵定型化、風格化，這是乾隆摩古風追尋儒家祥瑞吉兆思維的具體呈現。

隆品評玉器造型的標準，認為纖巧繁縟、瑣碎華囂的新巧風格，呈現出粗鄙而低俗的品味，視為浪費玉厄。對於追尋三代古銅器造型，則視為傳襲古雅、內涵豐盛的古禮象徵。而摹寫山水勝景，表現畫意情視為文人書生古雅情趣的表徵。也因此在乾隆玉作的另一特點，除開為玉器賦詩作文之外，常在他個人的摩古作品中，留下「古香」、「太璞」兩印；而在山水畫意的作品中，會留下「比德」、「朗潤」兩有甚者，會在作品的底部，直接刻上「甲」、「乙」、「丙」……的評鑑等第，處處表達出他對玉作的用心之深遠。

隆在位六十年，文治武功不可一世，他崇尚儒家祥瑞文化，獻瑞者投其所好，絡繹不絕。他認為玉器是行的理想材質，可以表達出藝術審美的最高格調。在乾隆二十五年以前，玉料罕少的年代，翻刻各種宮；平西之後，玉料源源不絕，則多琢宮中大小擺件，瓮、瓶、壺、碗、屏、大至萬斤以上的玉山子《大圖》，縱使耗時十餘年，費銀一萬五千餘兩都在所不惜。乾隆因好崇古而模仿，為後世留下龐大的藝術「御製」玉器也為中國玉器文化劃下了一個完美的句點。

Kingdom. Even though some of it was written by others on his behalf, there is still a large amount of poetry that dealt with his love for jade carvings, which have been bequeathed to later generations. This is the best example of how Qianlong used jade to learn the truths passed down from the ancients.

The writer Gao Lian (1573–1620), who lived during the Ming Dynasty, described the interests and tastes of scholars and gentlemen, and how pleasant it was to appreciate the fine curios in the literati study while contemplating the virtues of the ancients. This is a good way to explain the feelings of Emperor Qianlong. In the collection of the Palace Museums in Beijing and Taipei, there are many realistic paintings of Qianlong wearing Chinese clothing that show him to be the very picture of a scholar and a gentleman emulating the ancients. But it was also the tendency to honor the ancients in the education that Qianlong received, and the ancient orientation of his aesthetics that were decisive factors influencing the emphasis on ancient forms in the handicraft styles of his era.

The period from the middle of the Qianlong era to the beginning of the Jiaqing era was the peak period for jade carving production in the palace. There are over 23,000 pieces of jade art displayed in the Beijing Palace Museum, of which over 10,000 were collected, produced, or used under Qianlong. A large proportion of the jade collection in the National Palace Museum in Taipei were produced or re-carved during the Qianlong era. This allows us easily to understand the style and the taste of Qianlong. His veneration of ancient culture led the emperor to emulate ancient styles, especially in his esteem for jade artwork. He often personally supervised the jade production process, and he had such strict requirements for the tiniest details that it sometimes reached unreasonable levels. In general, Qianlong required the finest material, the most elegant subjects, the most tasteful forms, and the most exquisite carving skill. Whenever Qianlong took a liking to any item of treasure in the palace collection — even the most ancient bronzeware — he would have a palace eunuch send it to the jade workshop to use as a model for copying. In the National Palace Museum in Taipei the original bronze bear-shaped wine vessel stands next to the jade copy made by the order of Qianlong for comparison, and it is interesting to see the high standards that Qianlong demanded. Besides ancient bronze vessels, other items that were copied were ancient calligraphy and painting. Imperial poetry, commendations, and historical memorials were carved on artworks that caught Qianlong's eye, which reveal his state of mind at that time. The imperial poetry was mostly in the academic style used in the palace, and the characters had to be neat, while the carving standards were strict. There were a few different types of seal inscription, such as "Made in the year of Qianlong", "For use by Emperor Qianlong", or "Copy of ancient art by Qianlong". Seal inscriptions for jade that had painting-like scenes were the characters, "Bi De," or "Lang Run". Those for copies of ancient implements were the characters, "Gu Xiang" or "Tai Pu". Qianlong's true inner thoughts can be seen by the connection between the

The Emulation of Antiquity and the Pursuit of Novelty in a Golden Age

The imperial workshop was established at the time of Qing Dynasty Emperor Kangx reigned 1662–1722) inside the imperial palace, and was responsible for supervisin he production of implements for use in the palace. There were many workshop ubordinate to the imperial workshop, such as the wood carving workshop and the jad carving workshop, but the porcelain workshop and the textile workshop were each se ıp in other areas. These palace utensils were used to serve the emperor, so their style changed with the different preferences of different emperors. As a result of creativ nspiration or by the emperor's decree, new standards for the styles and specification would appear in terms of the subjects of paintings, the shapes of wood or bamboo carvings, and the types of material selected. Works that were produced under the stric standards of the palace showed a clearly recognizable style, with exquisite workmanshi and material. This not only clearly displayed the standards of the palace, but als demonstrated the personal aesthetics and taste of the emperor of the day.

The Qing Dynasty saw a peak of political and economic power from the reign o Kangxi to the reign of Qianlong, making this time a rare age of peace and prosperity Because of the length of his reign and great political talents, Emperor Qianlong is th embodiment of that golden age. He also made outstanding contributions to the worl of art, with his elegant taste and passion for collecting fine works. This was the era i which many European nations dared the high seas to explore the Asian continent, an esuit missionaries came along with the explorers to see the mysterious Orient. Some o he missionaries were talented persons, and they served in the imperial palace, directl ntroducing forms of expression from Western art.

n the 60-year reign of Qianlong (1736–1795), the problem of finding sources fo ade material was solved with the pacification of Zhunbu in 1755 and Huibu in 1759 making the Xinjiang region a part of the territory of the Qing Dynasty. In the age whe sources of jade were blocked, raw jade mostly came from private importers, makin t a rare commodity for which there was no way to ensure quality. This restricted th development of the art of jade carving. After Qianlong pacified the western regions ade flowed into China and there was an official decree about the amount of jade tha was to be sent as tribute from Huibu. Unending supplies of Hetian jade of all color were provided for jade production in Beijing, Tianjin, Suzhou, and Hangzhou throug he tribute occurring in spring and autumn of each year. It allowed the art of jad carving to see an unprecedented and subsequently unreplicated peak of glory after th middle of Qianlong's reign.

Qianlong once said that he was constantly studying during his first 20 years as he grev ıp in the palace. This studious emperor had famous scholars to tutor him from a youn ıge, and he studied all the Confucian classics. The writings of his youth were collecte n an imperial anthology made up of 30 volumes. As the absolute ruler, he still wrot voluminous amounts of poetry while he was conquering enemies and running th

"Da Ji," inscribed on it. There is a Qianlong era official kiln famille rose gourd-shaped wall decoration with, "Da Ji," painted in gold in the Nanjing Museum. There is a Qianlong era tapestry with, "Da Ji," in the Beijing Museum of Art. Also, in the Christie's, "The Imperial Sale," 2005 auction in Hong Kong, there was a Qianlong era gourd-shaped musical clock with the words, "Da Ji," written in gold. All of these gourd-shaped objects, regardless of the type of material, were carved or embroidered with the words, "Da Ji". This is an auspicious phrase which comes from the idiom "great auspiciousness of fortune and office". This phrase was given a stylistic format during the Qianlong era. This is a concrete manifestation of the pursuit of the Confucian concept of auspicious signs in Qianlong's emulation of ancient styles.

In the standards set down by Qianlong in the assessment of jade styles, he felt that the new styles that were delicately fancy and frivolously decorated displayed a taste that was low and vulgar, and it was seen as a disastrous waste of jade. The pursuit of the copying of ancient styles of bronzeware was seen as the symbol of a return to the elegant past and rich artistic intent. Copying the landscape masterpieces to display the artistic intent of the painting was seen as the symbol of scholars and students emulating the ancients. Another special characteristic of jade that came out of Qianlong's imperial workshop was that, in addition to carving poetry on the artworks, he had the characters, "Gu Xiang," or, "Tai Pu," carved on ancient replicas that he favored, and on works with the feel of landscape paintings, he carved the words, "Bi De," or, "Lang Run". In some cases, he even had numbers carved on the bottoms of the pieces to indicate his rating of their quality. He expressed his love and careful consideration of jade in every place possible. In Qianlong's 60-year reign, his pride in his accomplishments at home and abroad knew no bounds, and he venerated the Confucian culture of auspicious signs, so his advisors endlessly played to these tendencies. He thought that jade was the perfect material for cultivating virtuous action and that it could express the pinnacle of aesthetic achievement. Before 1760, jade was a scarce item, just used to make replicas of ancient jade artifacts in the palace. After the west was pacified, the flow of raw jade never stopped, and the art of jade carving mostly pursued the copying of small and large decorations in the palace, such as urns, vases, bottles, bowls, screens, and even jade boulders as heavy as 5,000 kilograms, which took over 10 years to complete and cost 15,000 taels to produce. Qianlong emulated the ancient styles because he venerated ancient culture. He left a vast artistic heritage for future generations, and his imperial inscriptions on jade marked the last great era of Chinese jade culture.

Wang Hsin-Kong

Former Editor
National Palace Museum

elegance of the seal inscription and the contents of the artwork.

Compared with Qianlong's veneration of ancient forms, which was a result of his understanding of his personal aesthetics, new styles did not always meet his approval, and often earned his denigration. There is a dark green jade dragon-tail wine vessel in the National Palace Museum in Taipei, with a deprecating imperial inscription that says it is a new style and that its vulgarity makes the jade less valuable. In the anthology of imperial poetry, there are many examples in which the commonness of new artworks is pointed out and devalued in comparison to ancient works. Imperial poetry mentions, "common artisans," or, "vulgar craftsmen," which refer to the civilian artisans of jade workshops in Suzhou and Yangzhou. These workshops occasionally did work commissioned by the palace, but they earned their living by working on jade acquired through private importers to meet the demand of the market. In 1778, the official in charge of Hetian jade was executed for privately smuggling in jade material, but this did not stop the flow of smuggled jade as intended. When Qianlong's poetry mentions "new styles" or "fashionable styles", it does so by way of comparison with copies of ancient styles. Jade production in the palace involved strict procedures, and nothing could be made without the emperor's approval of the style. There was a line in an imperial poem that said the Hetian jade given in tribute was to be carved into the style of every piece of ancient art in the catalog of the palace's ancient art, which shows the enormous scale of Qianlong's need for jade. The civilian market also copied these styles because of the emperor's preferences, especially for the use of officials from Suzhou and Yangzhou to present to the emperor as gifts. The jade used by civilian artisans was costly, and the raw jade was sold by its weight. The artisans used the natural shape of the jade as much as possible since they could not bear to cut away too much. This costliness led to even the finished artworks being sold by weight. The historical records of the Qing Dynasty recorded that a prohibition was announced in 1794, that was a complete ban on new styles of artwork made by the artisans of Suzhou and Yangzhou. The prohibition said that, "the objects made by Suzhou and Yangzhou artists were mostly hollow vessels that were useless. There have been cases of deceitful craftsmen from the workshop simply trying to create something new and fashionable in order to make a profit, but they are ignorant knaves. The emperor has never accepted any of these kinds of objects. It is ordered that the Yangzhou and Suzhou Salt Administrations and Textile Administrations strictly prohibit carving work by these deceitful artisans. It should be made known that the goal of workmanship is not to seek novelty but, to return to simplicity."

Qianlong promoted the copying of ancient styles because he loved studying the ancients, but his emulation of antiquity was not limited to precise replicas of ancient implements. There occasionally appeared artworks with combinations of styles and characteristics from different ages, and contemporary auspicious words and patterns. For example, there is a gold, hollow, gourd-shaped censer that has the two characters

和闐白玉質地，器作中孔圓形大璧形制，孔、器邊緣均留飾有一小圈弦帶紋，器面滿佈穀紋，排列工整，琢磨製作相當規矩，表現戰漢特色。穀紋璧始於東周時期，戰漢沿襲製作，此器原為入土後再重出與傳世的古玉大璧，白玉質器面，留有自然沁成的黑褐色沁斑，全器呈色自然斑爛，是古代禮瑞器。青白色玉璧，為古代禮天之大器，器邊緣上有琢刻「惟土物愛厥心臧：乾隆天子春御題」篆書款識，大璧應為故宮舊藏古璧，明記於清乾隆四十五年（一七八〇年）琢刻此文。

璧，古玉器名，有孔的圓形玉器，中間孔大的叫「瑗」，中間孔小的叫「璧」，介於兩者之間的叫「環」，多素璧，少數有弦文、穀紋、蒲紋、獸紋、乳丁紋、雲紋、龍紋、螭紋、鳥紋等。璧源自「天圓」之說，乃六器之一，璧分大璧、穀璧、蒲璧、繫璧等。大璧徑長一尺二寸，天子禮天之器。諸侯享天子者亦用之。禮天須用蒼色，蓋璧形圓，象天蒼，象天之色。穀璧子爵所執，飾穀紋，取「養人」之義。薄璧男爵所執，琢飾為蒲形，蒲為席，取「安人」之義。前三者統稱為「拱璧」，因皆須兩手拱執故。商周時代的璧，厚薄不勻，形制也不規整，內外大多不夠圓。春秋戰國時，璧則已相當規整，並有蠶紋、穀紋、蒲紋、獸面紋等雕飾。此璧應為西漢早期繼承戰國時期玉大璧的風格，雕工與紋飾比較精細與規矩工整，其圓潤與排列規矩的穀紋形制，是漢代的標準形制，穀紋代表著穀子發芽時的生生不息的生命力量，也是平安與富裕的象徵，此件大璧，尺寸大且用料厚實，紋飾琢刻工藝精緻，拋光細緻，是一件質、工、料、沁、形、紋皆完美的藝術品。

此件大璧曾為英國J.C.THOMSON爵士及DAVID SALMAN所收藏。

題舊玉穀璧

惟土物愛厥心臧璧刻以穀寓意長詎祇子執明朝章佳城誰氏出深藏肉倍於好規製良如雲籠月不礙光而光自葆非赫揚把吟
古仍慨慷

Warring States
Ancient jade grain pattern jade disk

Diam./21cm

Hetian white jade, shaped into a large disk with a hole in the center. The inner and outer edges have a small circular belt pattern, and the face of the piece is filled with grain patterns carved in orderly lines, making it very uniform, which is a characteristic of the early Han Dynasty. The grain pattern disk originated in the Eastern Zhou, and was followed throughout the Han Dynasty. This piece is a large ancient jade disk that was excavated after being buried. The surface of the white jade has natural black and brown stains that make this ancient ceremonial implement naturally multi-colored. Grayish white jade disks were important instruments in ancient ceremonies. The edge of the jade disk is carved with an inscription honoring Emperor Qianlong in 1780, which means it was in the collection of the imperial palace during the Qing Dynasty.

The jade disk ("bi") is an ancient ceremonial object made of jade with a round hole in the center. Those with a large hole are called, "yuan," and those with a smaller hole are called, "bi". Those in between were called, "huan". Most jade disks are plain, and very few have decorations carved on them. The jade disk symbolizes the concept of the, "round heaven", and is one of the six ancient implements. There are various kinds of jade disks. Large ones were about 40 centimeters in diameter, used for the emperor's worship of heaven. Nobles also offered them to the emperor. The color and shape of the jade disk symbolized heaven. The grain pattern on the jade disk symbolizes the cultivation of mankind. The grain pattern is in the shape of cat-tails, which symbolize peace for mankind. Another term for the jade disk is "gong bi" because it needed to be held with both hands. The jade disks of the Shang and Zhou Dynasties were of uneven thickness, and the shapes were also uneven, meaning they were not completely round. During the Spring and Autumn Period and the Warring States Period, jade disks were very even and they included various types of decorative patterns. The style of large jade disks was passed on to the Eastern Han Dynasty from the Warring States Period. The carving work and the decorations became more and more refined and ordered. Smooth and orderly grain patterns were the trademark of the Han Dynasty jade disks. The grain pattern represents the endless vitality of sprouting grain, and it was also a symbol of peace and prosperity. This jade disk is large and thick, the carving technique is exquisite, and the polishing work is finely detailed. It is an artwork that is perfect in terms of quality, workmanship, material, color, and shape.

This large jade disk was once in the collections of the Englishmen J.C. Thompson and David Salman.

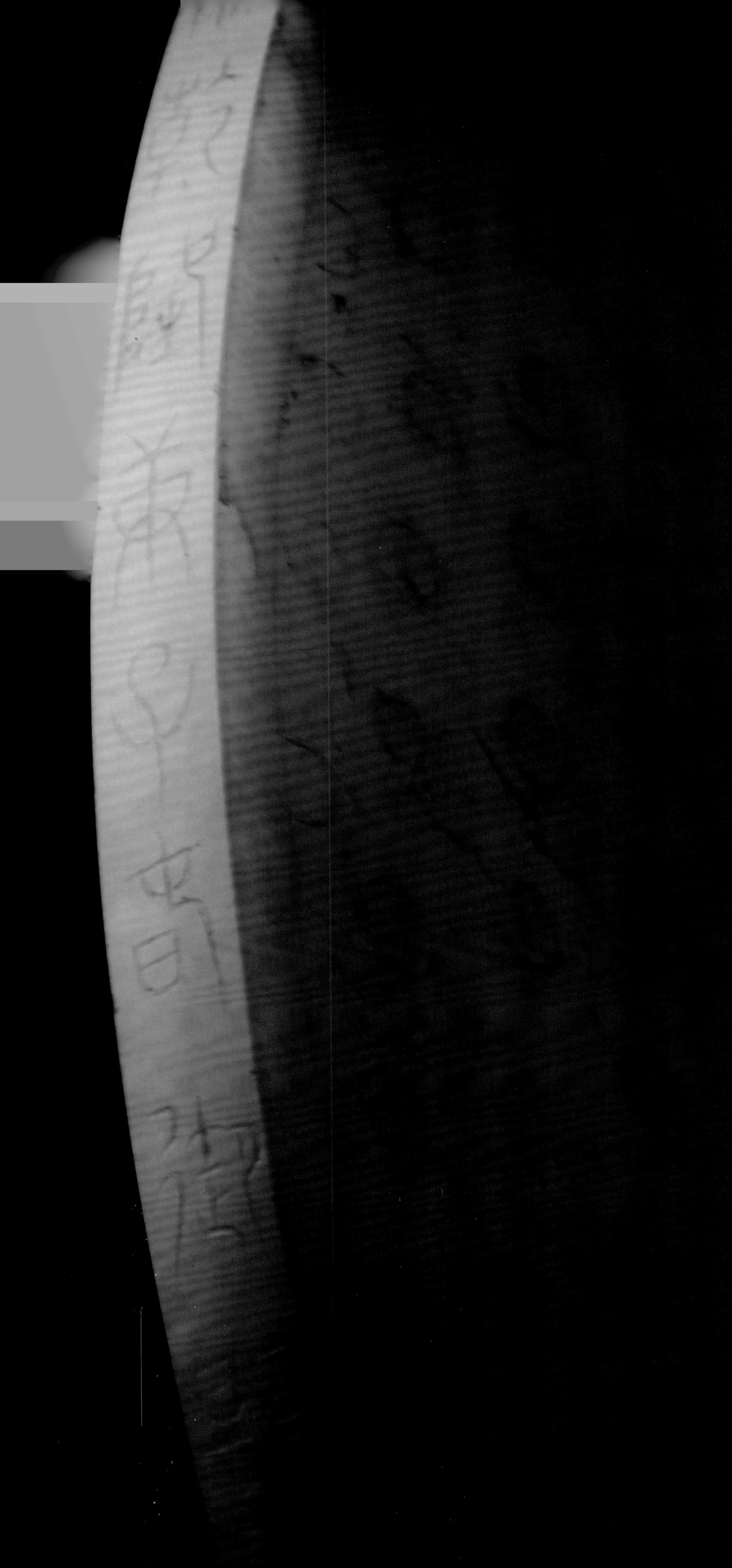

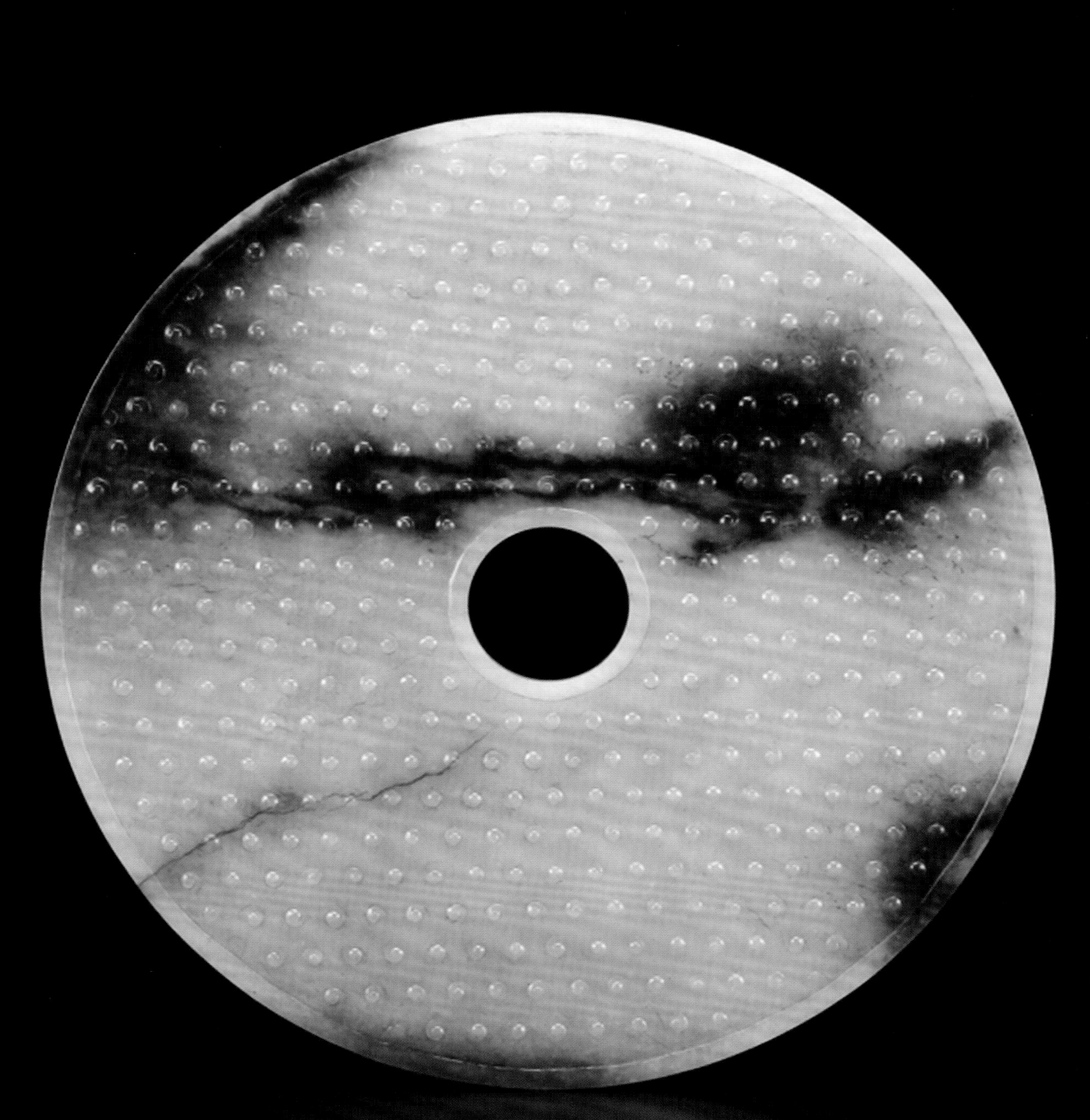

青白玉蘭花硯屏，由大塊和闐青白玉料製成，玉質溫潤光潔，呈圓斜頂，長方形插屏形制，屏器配有一和闐碧玉屏座，器座上緣正中偏後處刻有「甲」字款。屏上方正中央鈐刻圓形「古稀天子」四字朱文篆書描金款，左下方鈐刻長方形「几席有餘香」五字朱文篆書描金款，背後刻圓形「信天主人」四字朱文篆書描金款，右方刻「八徵耄念之寶」金款，下刻張照黃庭經長篇詩文。主題蘭草山石畫面上方空白處有乾隆皇帝倣趙孟頫書法寫蘇東坡詩長篇「道人胸中水鏡清，萬象起滅無逃形…」，背面刻有御題詩句「和闐良玉製為屏，並寫幽蘭滿意馨…」，末題「甲戌所倣趙孟頫書」。此屏傳約在一九〇〇年義和團事件八國聯軍自紫禁城中移走，後為美國Edward R. Carr所收藏。

硯屏是一種常裝飾於明清時期文房書齋的隔屏或几案上的擺設，器面以浮雕技法琢刻而成，蘭草山石琢刻線條自然轉折，山石表面以長條棱邊，似長披麻皴法，山石邊緣蘭草輪廓都雕琢得棱角鋒銳，技法高超卓越，拋光細緻，兼具寫生與畫境，猶如一幅生動的繪畫。此件蘭石玉硯屏，取材自和闐大塊山料礦石琢刻而成，淺浮雕蘭草琢刻雅致而幽靜，完整表現出芝蘭九畹的靚勁，玉屏的巧妙與精彩設計之處，除了有乾隆的御題詩文（趙孟頫書體，蘇東坡詩文）外，全屏在背光與透光的光影下，可照見蘭石背後天然的玉礦石紋路，都被收納成為隱約的山壁或石坡，恰與主題的幽蘭、雅石前後相呼應照。又其青白玉質地的選材，有冷冷霜雪的氛圍隱喻，更使幽蘭散發出冷香的質感。此屏不但是乾隆皇帝的珍愛之藏，更能由此硯屏所呈現出來的詩、書、畫、印、意等面面俱全的思維與佈置來說明，見證乾隆個人對玉石藝術的見解與熱情，是一件難能可貴的玉器珍稀之品。

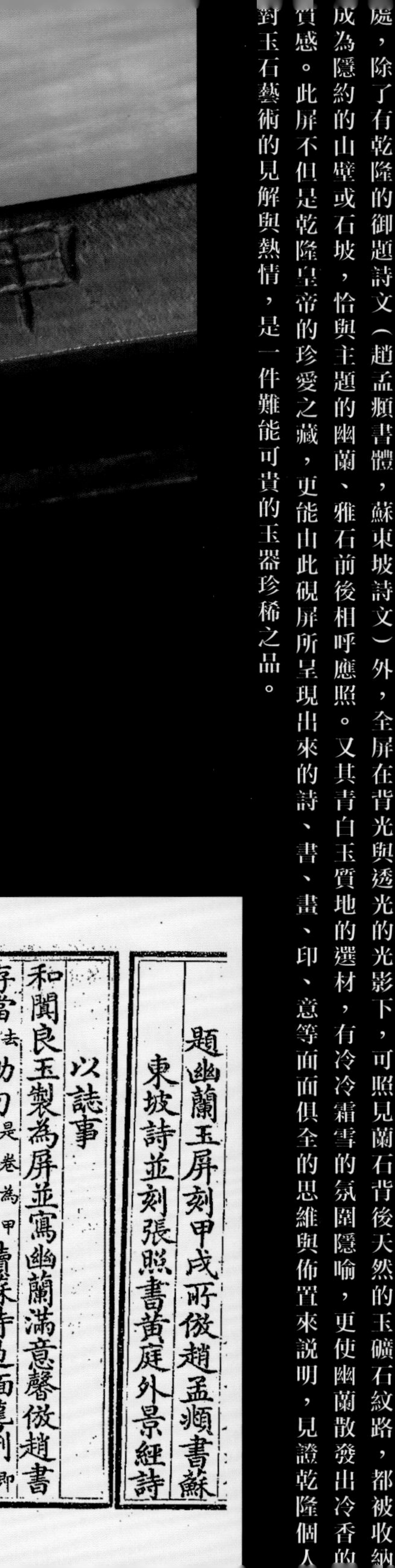

題幽蘭玉屏刻甲戌所倣趙孟頫書蘇東坡詩並刻張照書黃庭外景經詩以誌事

和闐良玉製為屏並寫幽蘭滿意馨倣趙書存當（去聲）泐句（是卷為甲戌所臨）讀蘇詩過緬襲硎（即用東坡句意）古稀不作蠅頭字（向每喜作蠅頭細書近以年逾古稀不復作昨秋題夷齊廟四景卷曾試為之目力仍前不資眼鏡並有詩紀事）昔憶與鐫外景經（內府舊存張照細書臨黃庭經扇面並命鉤摹刻於玉屏）三十年惟消一瞬（甲戌至今甲辰三十年矣）翰緣那復計相形（照書以楷體堪稱端莊雜流麗予書雖不及照而此則倣趙行書體於董其昌跋趙卷所云全類李北海者亦頗寓神會云）

和闐良玉製為屏
呂宮幽蘭滿意馨

道人胸中水鏡清萬象起滅無逃形
獨依古寺種秋菊要伴騷人餐落英
人間底處有南北紛紛鴻雁何曾寧閉
門坐穴一禪榻頭上歲月空崢嶸今
年偶出為米法欲與慧劍加礱砥雲
衲新磨山水生霜鬚不翦兒童驚公
家兒識不可得故知僧市無傾城秋
風吹夢過淮水想見橘柚垂空庭故
人久在天一角相望落落如晨星彭
城老守何足說棗林棠壁相邀迎手
山不憚荒店遠兩腳欲趁飛猱輕多
生綺語磨不盡尚有宛轉詩人情猿
吟鶴唳本無意不知下有行人行空
階夜雨自滴絕誰使挫抑啼孤惸
欲仙山拔瑤草傾筐坐歎何時盈簿
書鞅於畫填委煮茗燒栗宜宵征乞
取摩尼照濁水共看落月金盆傾
香光詩吳興此卷全類李北海故是
鷗波得意書甲戌夏子愚臨

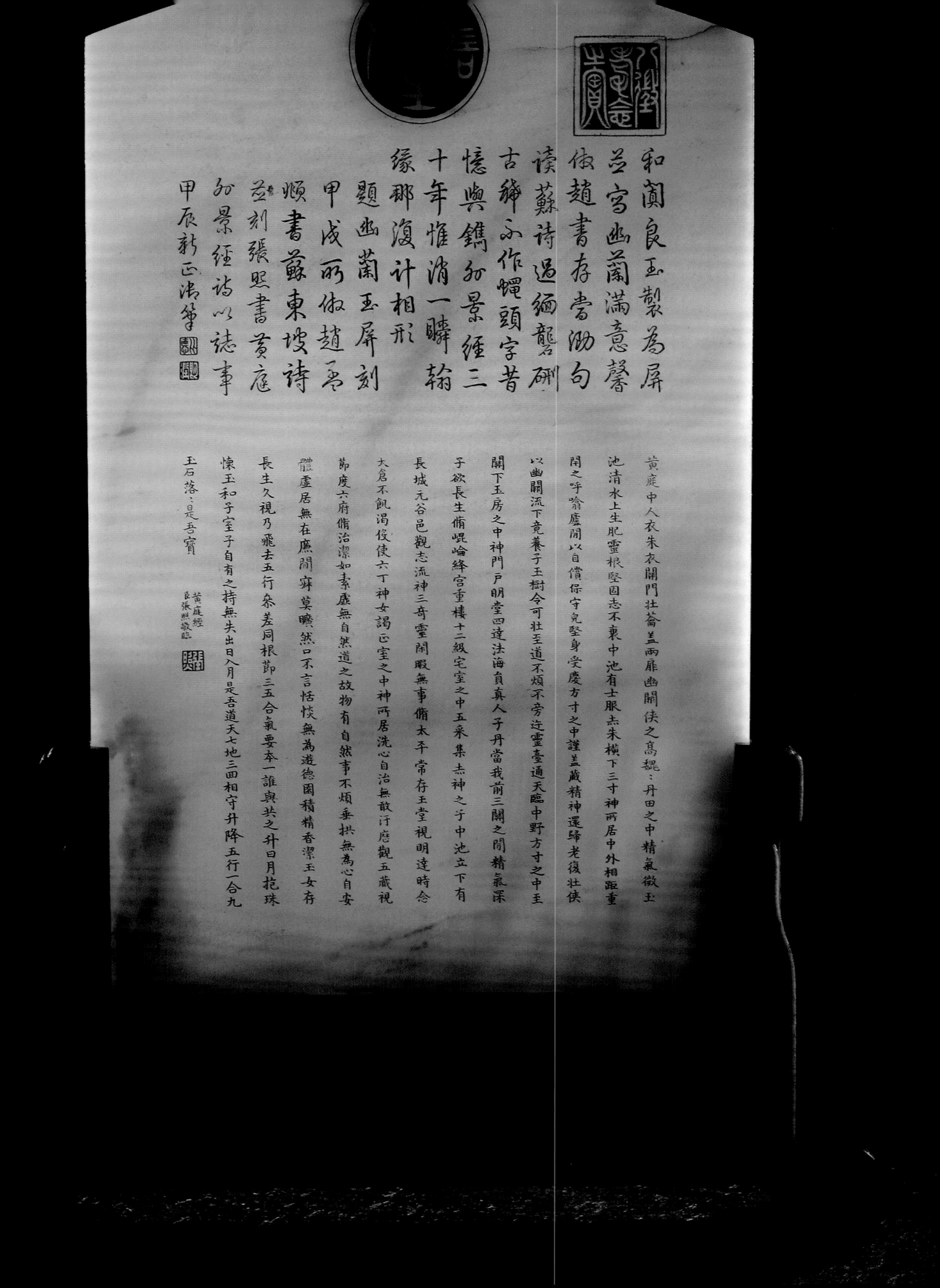

八徵耄念之寶

和闐良玉製為屏
並寫幽蘭滿意馨
依趙書存當泐句
讀蘇詩過緬礱硎
古稀亦作蠅頭字昔
憶與鐫外景經三
十年惟消一瞬翰
緣那復計相形
題幽蘭玉屏刻
甲戌所做趙孟
頫書蘇東坡詩
並刻張照書黃庭
外景經詩以誌事
甲辰新正御筆

黃庭中人衣朱衣關門壯籥盖兩扉幽闕俠之高魏：丹田之中精氣微玉
池清水上生肥靈根堅固志不衰中池有士服赤朱橫下三寸神所居中外相距重
開之呼喻廬間以自償保守兒堅身受慶方寸之中謹盖藏精神還歸老復壯俠
以幽闕流下竟養子玉樹令可壯至道不煩不旁迕靈臺通天臨中野方寸之中至
關下玉房之中神門戶明堂四達法海員真人子丹當我前三關之間精氣深
子欲長生脩崑崙絳宮重樓十二級宅室之中五采集赤神之子中池立下有
長城元谷邑觀志流神三奇靈閑暇無事脩太平常存玉堂視明達時念
大倉不飢渴役使六丁神女謁正室之中神所居洗心自治無敢汙歷觀五藏視
節度六府脩治潔如素虛無自然道之故物有自然事不煩垂拱無為心自安
體虛居無在廬間寂莫曠然口不言恬惔無為遊德園積精香潔玉女存
長生久視乃飛去五行參差同根節三五合氣要本一誰與共之升日月抱珠
懷玉和子室子自有之持無失出日入月是吾道天七地三回相守升降五行一合九
玉石落：是吾寶

黃庭經 臣張照敬臨

清　乾隆《和闐玉鏤東坡後赤壁賦圖》

寬36.5公分　高21.5公分

　　青白玉後赤壁賦山子，為和闐籽料琢治而成，青白玉質局部帶有黃褐玉皮色。山子由整塊自然形狀籽料雕琢成，制，巧雕巧作以赤壁景色，山壁險峻陡峭，夾岸林木扶疏，中、下段為江面，波濤洶湧，波光粼粼，近處舟船簑笠翁分明，各具形態詩意。這類山林景觀的雕刻，從取景、佈局，到層次排列都表現和滲透著繪畫的章法，山石表面以長法，山石邊緣、人物衣褶以及樹木輪廓都雕琢得稜角鋒銳，通景有如今天的微縮盆景一般，極富懷古之情趣與詩意。乾隆十九年時刻「後赤壁賦」詩文乙篇，末題「甲戌嘉平上　御臨於三希堂　御筆」，下鈐刻「乾」、「隆」珠文方章再題刻御題詩：「和闐貢玉歲來…」下鈐刻「比德」、「朗潤」方章，由此可知乾隆皇帝對此山子的重視程度。

　　清代的山子形式尤盛行於清高宗乾隆時期，從整體工藝美術史的角度觀察，刻意強調器物中「畫意」的成份，實開始，與繪畫之運筆、構景等相關的因素，在工藝美術的領域中逐步加重其份量。此類作品多是以山水人物及歷史故場景，其他知名作品如「秋山行旅」、「南山積翠」、「會昌九老」等。由於清代玉山雕琢，深受元人畫境與清初「石佈局講究均勢、穩重，層林疊嶂，意境清遠，因而在琢雕時皆力求古樸莊重，用刀起落、轉折圓潤而平穩，不同於翁的裁花鏤葉等裝飾作風。小型的玉山子也較常見，亦是以山水人物、亭臺樓閣、飛禽走獸等為題材，琢刻出一幅幅緻。有的運用巧作手法，利用玉石本身的顏色、紋理與厚薄差別，分別雕出雲霧、流水、蒼松、古道、隱士等景物，對比的特殊效果，此類作品尤其在強光透射下觀賞，極具特殊韻味。

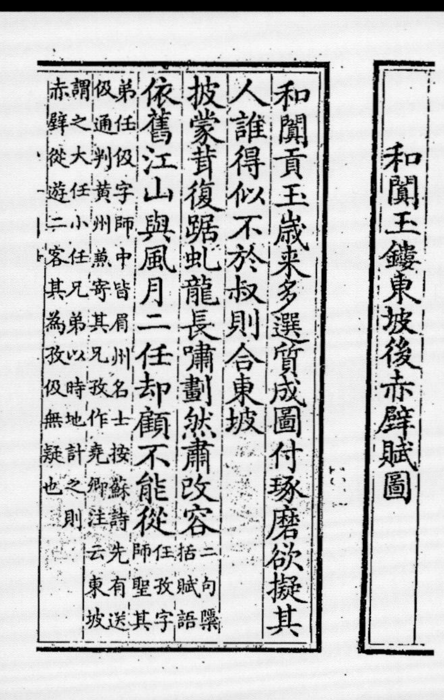

和闐玉鏤東坡後赤辟賦圖

和闐貢玉歲来多選質成圖付琢磨欲擬其人誰得似不於叔則合東坡二句檃括賦語披蒙茸復踞虬龍長嘯劃然肅改容任孜字師聖其依舊江山與風月二任却顧不能從弟任伋字師中皆眉州名士按蘇詩先有送伋通判黃州兼寄其兄孜作堯卿注云東坡謂之大任小任兄弟以時地計之則赤壁從遊二客其為孜伋無疑也

Qing Dynasty, Qianlong Era "Hetian Jade Inlay Dongpo's Latter Ode on the Red Cliffs"

W/36.5cm, H/21.5cm

This grayish white jade boulder with the, "Latter Ode on the Red Cliffs," is carved from Hetian jade seed. It has yellowish-brown jade skin color in places. The jade boulder is carved from a whole piece of naturally shaped jade seed material. The scene of the Red Cliffs was cleverly carved out using the natural shape of the mineral. The two cliff walls are steep and precarious, with luxuriant and well-spaced trees on both sides. There is a rushing river in the middle and the bottom. There is an indistinct image of fishermen in a boat on the river. The scene is divided into clear levels, and the scenes are full of poetic imagination. The carving of this mountain and forest scene is permeated with the orderliness of a painting, in its subject, its arrangement, and its levels. The stones display edges with long lines, which look like the long textural strokes of landscape paintings. The edges of the stones, the clothes of the human figures, and the outlines of the trees are carved sharply. The scene almost seems like a bonsai landscape, full of the feeling of a return to ancient times. In 1754, Emperor Qianlong had the "Latter Ode on the Red Cliffs" carved on this jade boulder. In 1772, another imperial verse was carved on this jade boulder, showing how much importance Emperor Qianlong placed on this piece.

The jade boulder style flourished in the Qianlong era of the Qing Dynasty. It can be observed, from the general perspective of the history of finely crafted art, that carving emphasized the painting-like quality of the art, which was undeniably the general trend. Starting in the Yuan Dynasty, the elements of painting, such as brush strokes and composition, gradually became an important part of the carving arts. These types of artworks were usually large scenes in jade, such as landscapes, human figures, and historical stories. Qing Dynasty jade carving was heavily influenced by Yuan Dynasty painting and the painting styles of the "Four Kings" of the early Qing. The arrangement of stone elements was careful, balanced, and solemn, and the layering of tree elements was serene and thoughtful. A certain kind of ancient seriousness was pursued in the carving technique. The movements of the carving knife were smooth and steady, unlike the unsophisticated decorative styles of folk jade carving. Smaller jade boulders are also commonly seen, in which elegant and peaceful scenes of landscapes, pavilions, and birds and animals are delicately carved. Some used skillful techniques, utilizing the differences in color, texture, and thickness of the jade itself to carve out elements like clouds, water, trees, paths, and hermits, while forming effects using contrasts, such as shallowness and depth. This type of artwork has an extremely special feel, especially when viewed with light shining through it.

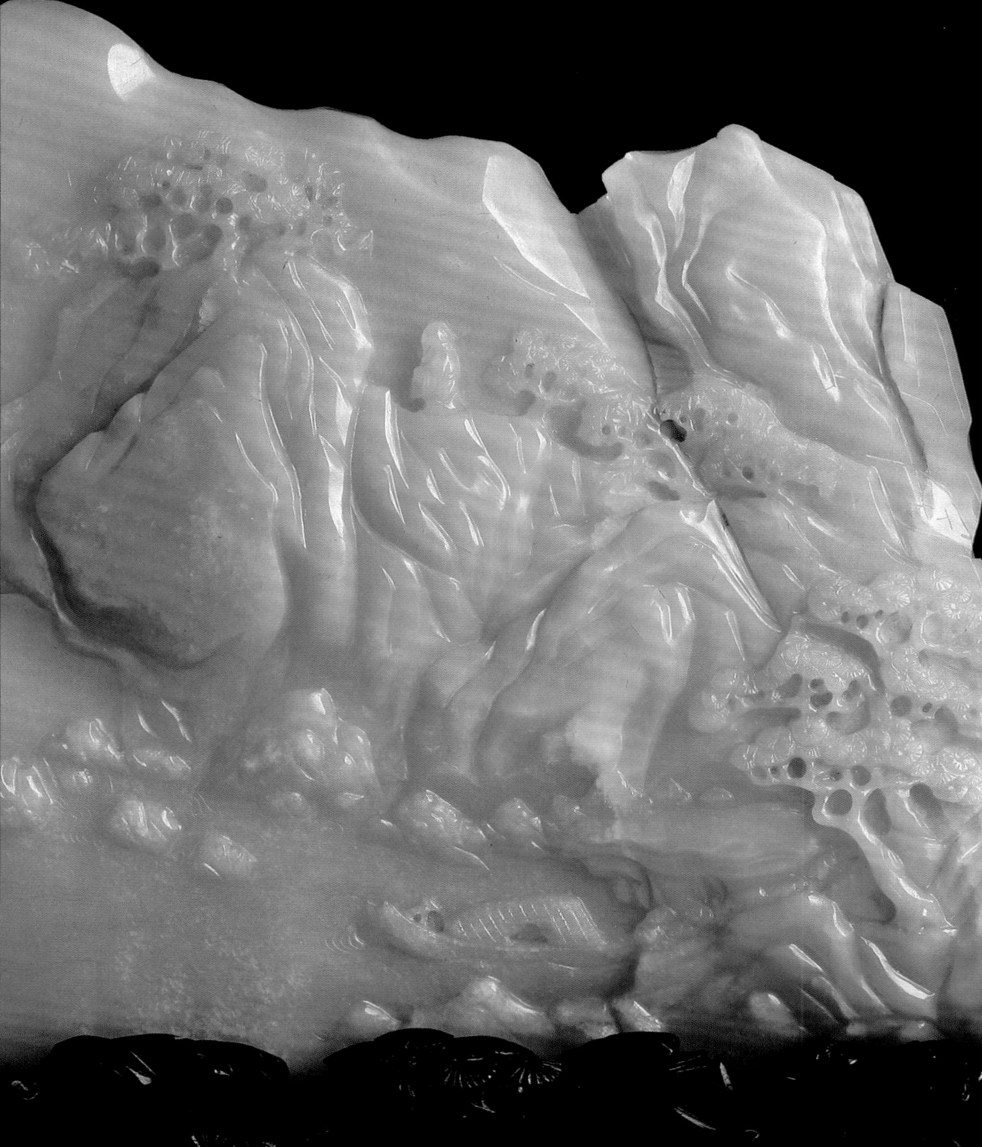

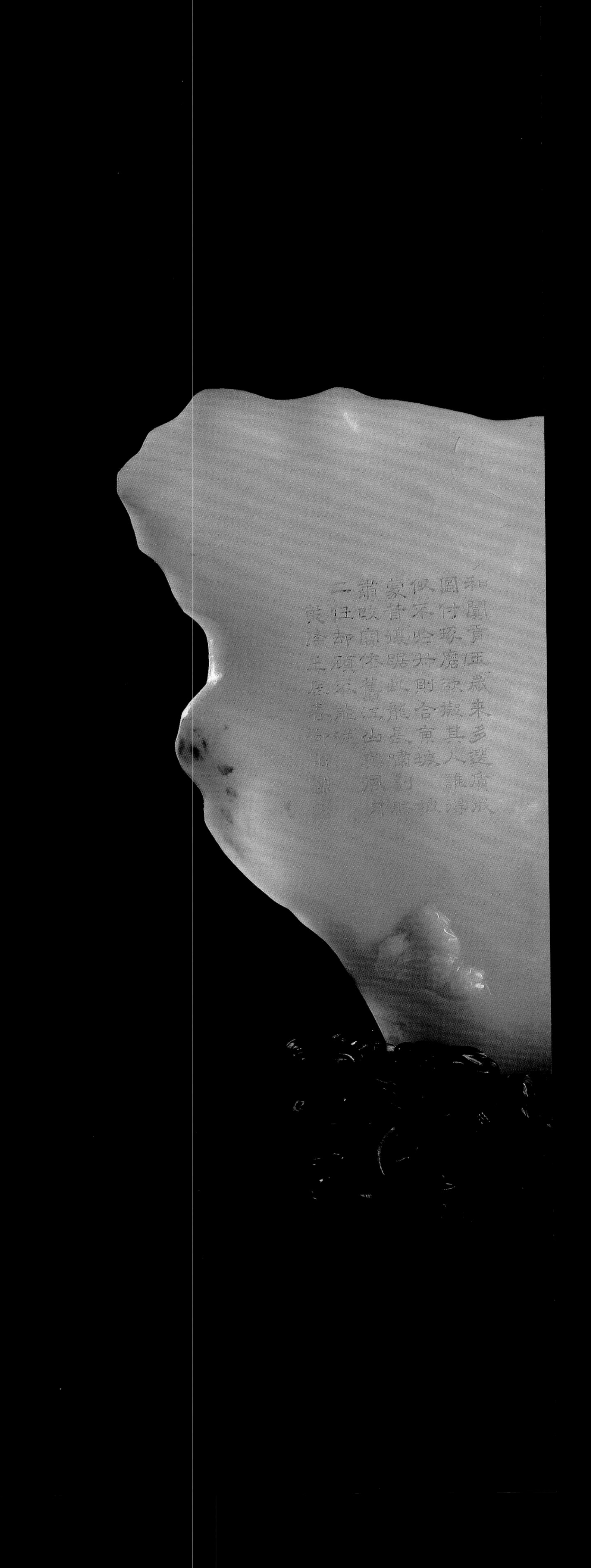
和闐貢玉歲來多
圖付琢磨欲擬其人誰得
乾隆壬辰春御

後赤壁賦

是歲十月之望步自雪堂將歸於臨皋二客從余過黃泥之坂霜露既降木葉盡脫人影在地仰見明月顧而樂之行歌相荅已而歎曰有客無酒有酒無肴月白風清如此良夜何客曰今者薄暮舉網得魚巨口細鱗狀似松江之鱸顧安所得酒乎歸而謀諸婦〻曰我有斗

曾日月之幾何而江山不可復識矣

余乃攝衣而上履巉巖披蒙茸踞虎豹登虬龍攀棲鶻之危巢俯馮夷之幽宮蓋二客不能從焉劃然長嘯草木震動山鳴谷應風起水涌余亦悄然而悲肅然而恐凜乎其不可留也反而登舟放乎中流聽其所止而休焉時夜將半四顧寂寥適有孤鶴橫江東來翅如車輪玄裳縞衣戛然長鳴掠余舟而西也須臾客去余亦就睡夢一道士羽衣蹁躚過臨皋之下揖余而言曰赤壁之遊樂乎問其姓名俛而不答嗚呼噫嘻我知之矣疇昔之夜飛鳴而過我者非子也耶道士顧笑余亦驚悟開戶視之不見其處　蘇軾

甲戌春王上澣臨於三希堂　御筆

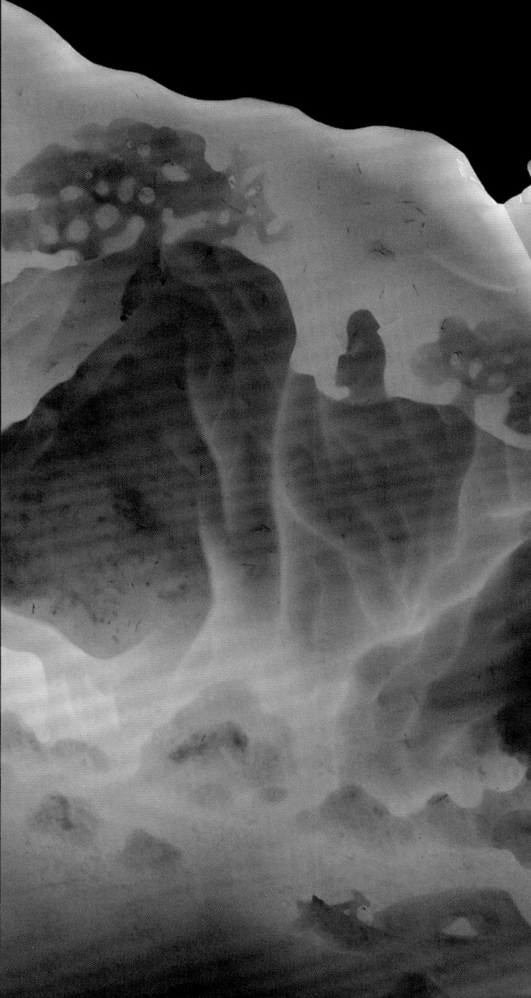

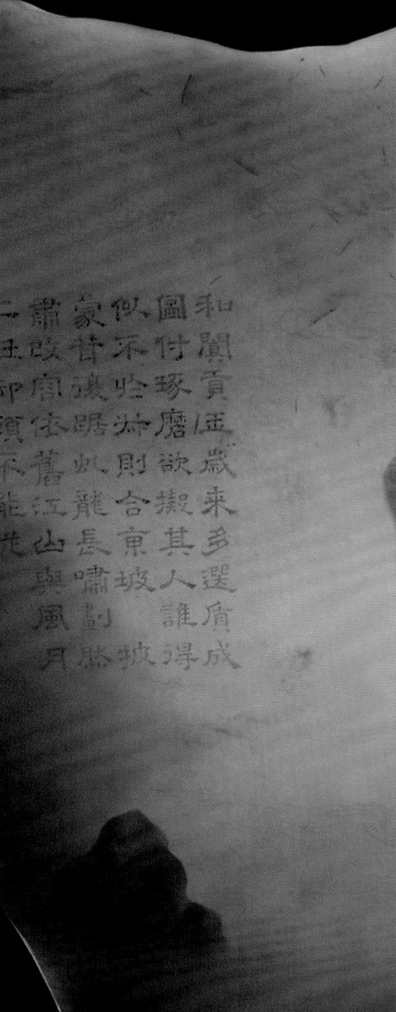

和闐貢玉歲來多選盾成
圖付琢磨欲擬其人誰得
似不吟詩則合東坡披
家昔誤踞如龍長嘯劃胳
肅改宮依舊江山與風月
二玉御題不能先

後赤壁賦

是歲十月之望步自雪堂將歸
從余過黃泥之坂霜露既降木葉
在地仰見明月顧而樂之行歌相答
有客無酒有酒無肴月白風清如此良

清　青白玉　秋山行旅圖　山子

寬12公分　高22公分

器為青白玉質，由整塊籽玉雕製。器作秋天山中景色，用深雕透視技法，層層疊疊，刻出自然界的層次，有林中小徑，茂密樹叢，景分三段，下段流水泛舟，中段山崖小徑通幽，上段山色重疊，林木密集，以染色手法，呈褐紅色，表現秋意濃烈的山色景像，是頗富詩意雅趣的文人書齋擺件。

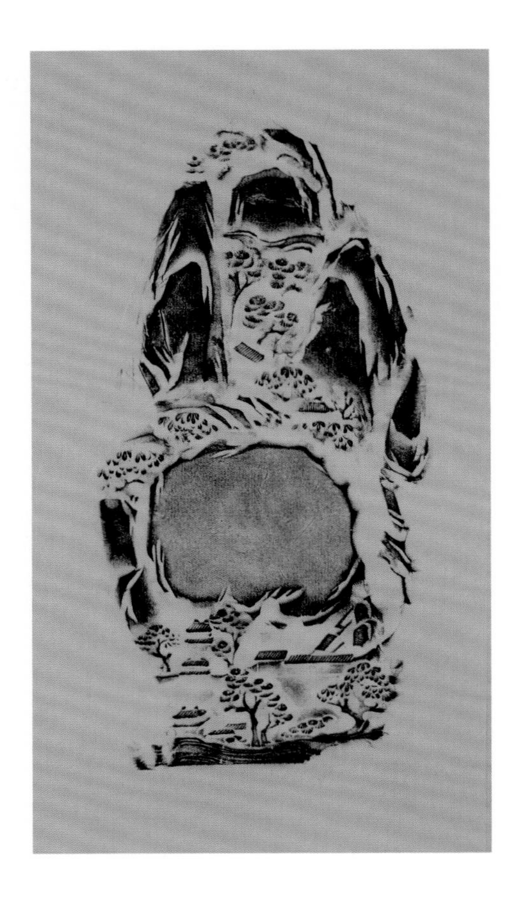

Qing Dynasty
Grayish white jade
Autumn Mountain Scene jade boulder

W/12cm, H/22cm

Grayish white jade — carved out of one piece of seed jade. The scene is a mountain in autumn, carved into a three-dimensional sculpture, with many different layers such as path through the woods, a lush forest. The scene is divided into three parts. The bottom part is a river with a boat, the middle part is a cliff and a path, and the top part is mountain peaks. The dense forest is colored an orange-red color to give it a profound feeling of autumn. This is a library decoration that is full of a literary feel.

寬14公分　高25.5公分

和闐青白玉質，玉質優美而純淨，局部微有黃色沁斑，整組器料未見明顯瑕絀。玉器為仿東周時期的古青銅器方扁壺形制式樣製作而成，蓋頂為平頂式壺蓋，周邊倒角出戢斜成六角形式，蓋頂平斜面琢刻變形寬板交尾夔龍紋。頸部正面鈐刻描金御題詩：「品貢和闐寶，形模博古圖，連環兩百貫，通體密紋鋪，攻錯詠香雅，直方訓大夫，旅獒讀一再，惆若每愁吾。乾隆乙未春。御題」其下鈐刻二小方章，上為「古香」，下為「瑞玉」。玉方壺於頸部兩側高浮雕鏤雕琢一對稱瑞獅鋪首銜環紋耳飾，器腹則淺浮雕一正面雙身夔龍紋與交尾雙鳳紋，全器紋飾以壓地陽刻紋手法完成，寬板線紋身軀，兩邊突起細緻陽線紋，夔龍鳳紋飾佈置繁複、交疊而大器，全器紋飾細緻、拋光潤澤而平整，器底呈扁長方形高圈足，器底鈐刻「大清乾隆仿古」六字隸書款。

根據玉器題詩中詠贊次數的多寡，用以推敲清高宗乾隆鼓勵玉工摹製的器形依序為：鼎、尊、壺、匜等。何以選擇這些器類？主因當是乾隆接受了宋、明以來文人的復古看法和觀念。此外，也與乾隆個人好大喜功的個性有關。就好像他晚年自稱「十全老人」一般，其選擇仿古銅彝器，亦是他對自我成就與功業極度的陶醉表現，這些上古禮器象徵著聖王的文治武功，如今在其手中，並且完成三代至漢等前朝都所無法獲得的大塊新疆和闐玉料來製作，這是何等驕傲之事！

傳此扁壺原為一八六〇年英法聯軍英國軍官MR. PRETICE自圓明園擄回之物，然後賣給倫敦的知名收藏家YULE爵士夫人，一直到一九三四年才將連同此件的一批玉器賣給當時著名的倫敦SPINK & SON公司，一九四〇年由英國SPINK & SON將這件玉器轉賣給美國的MR. S. M. SPALDING.收藏。

Qing Dynasty, Qianlong Era
Grayish green jade "repayment" flask

W/14cm, H/25.5cm

Grayish green jade — fine and pure-quality jade, without even the slightest flaw. It is semi-translucent and bright. It is modeled after ancient bronze flask-shaped vessels. The top has a roof-style stopper, but it is flat. The sides are hexagonal. The front of the neck is carved with a long inscription from the reign of Qianlong. There are two square seals on the top and bottom. There are two handles on the neck carved into dragon patterns. There is a flat rectangular foot on the bottom, which also has a six-word inscription. This flask was sold by Spink & Son of England, and was collected by Mr. S. M. Spalding of the USA. Later, it became part of the collection of the Wu family.

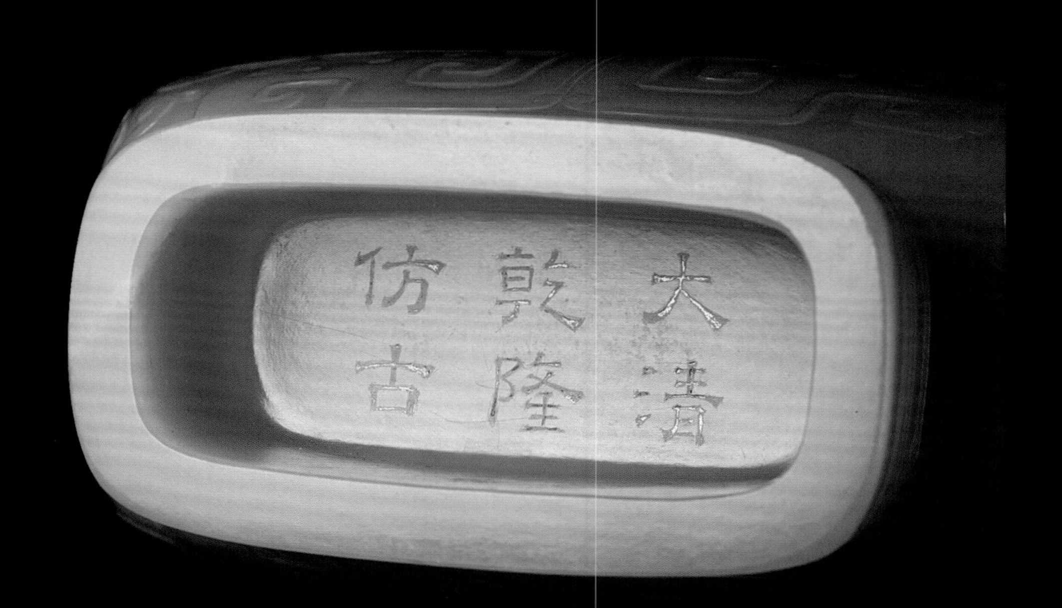

品貢和闐寶
形模博古圖
連環兩百貫
通體密紋鋪
攻錯詠宵雅
直方訓大夫

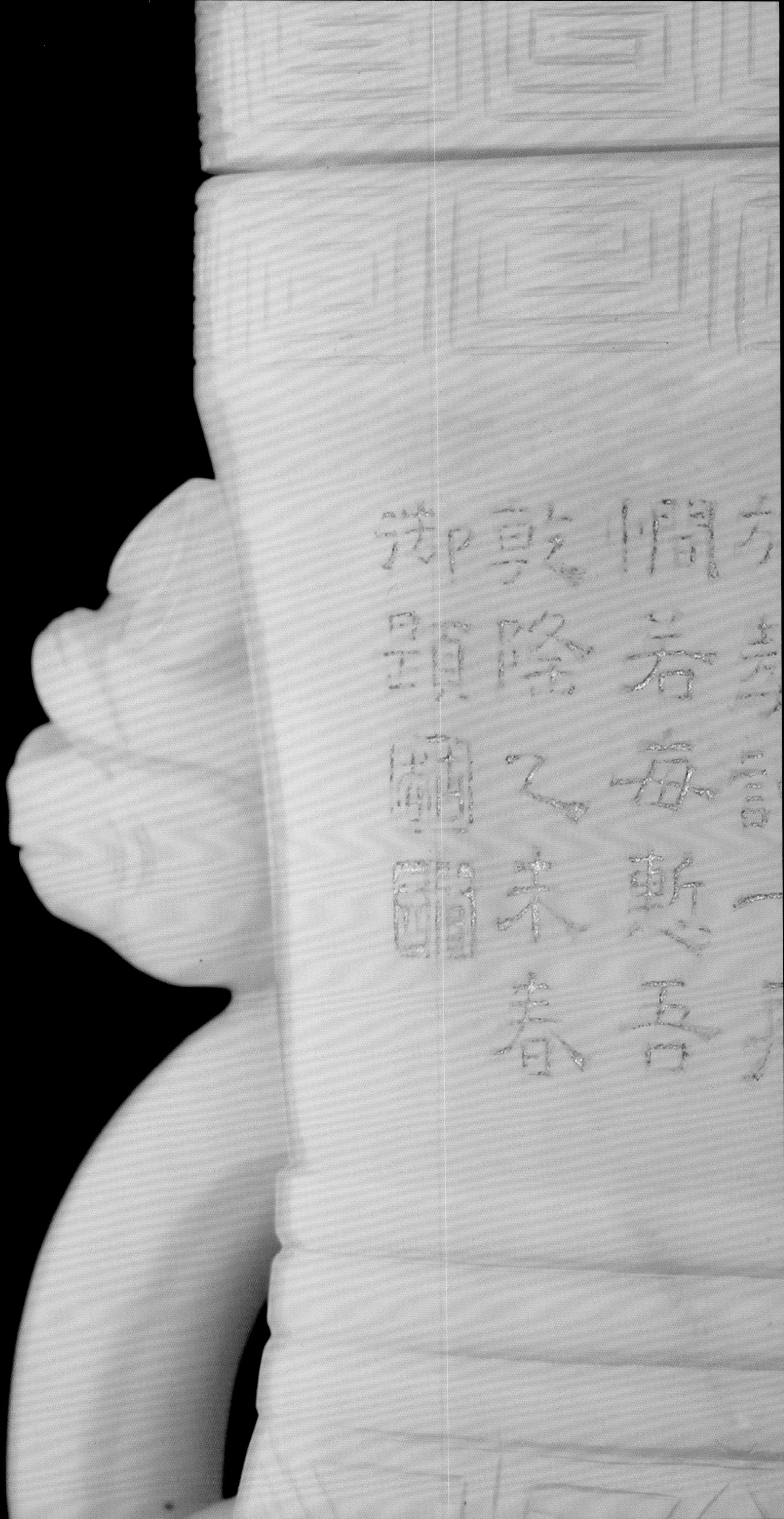
憫若毒螫吾
乾隆乙未春
御題

清　白玉　雙耳蓋瓶

寬8公分　高17.5公分

白玉質，微透明，質佳細潤，整塊羊脂白玉雕製。器有花形圓鈕蓋，口作子母口，小口、聳肩、底內凹平，雙肩附活環耳，器腹以浮雕技法，精刻繪畫式紋飾，刻蓮花、鷺鷥、水草、池塘景色，諧音「一路連科」寓意，意涵連中科舉吉祥慶賀之意，是清代貴族豪門間最佳饋贈禮品。背面刻有「甲子六月，奇光瑾瑜，藏諸櫝韞，瑑飾良工，光華溫潤，乾隆御製」御製詩描金款。

Qing Dynasty
White jade two-handled vase with stopper

W/8cm, H/17.5cm

White jade, slightly translucent, with a fine and lustrous quality, carved from a single piece of suet white jade. This piece has a flower-shaped, rounded stopper handle, and the stopper makes a tight fit with the mouth of the vase. The mouth is small, the shoulders are raised, and the base is slanted inward. There are two ringed handles at the shoulders of the vase. The body of the vase is decorated with painting-style relief carving of lotus blossoms, egrets, water plants, and a pond scene. "Egrets and lotuses" signifies the sending of congratulations for good news in the Imperial Examinations, making this piece one of the finest gifts bestowed among elites of the Qing Dynasty. On the back there is an imperial inscription painted with gold that identifies this piece as having been produced in the Qianlong era.

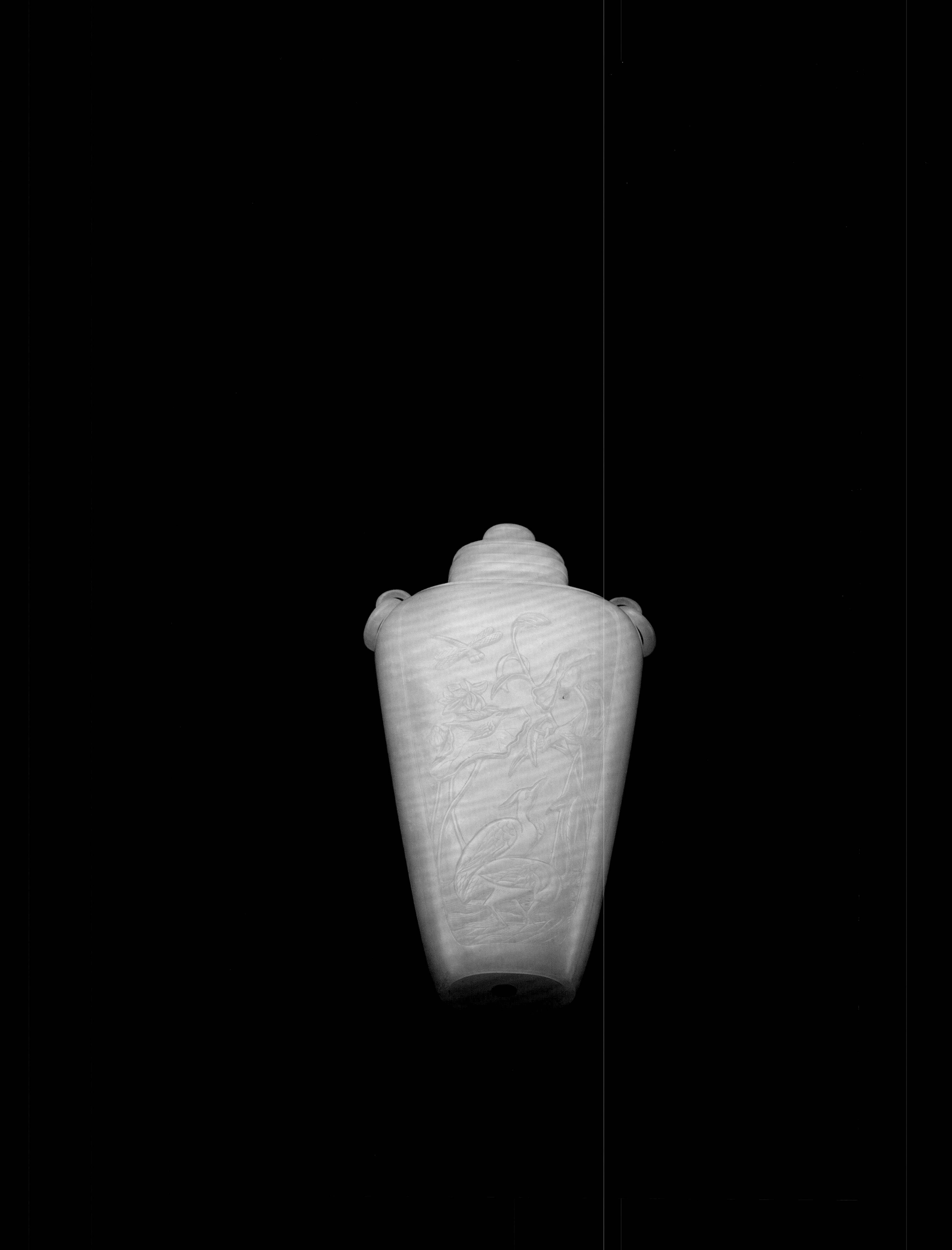

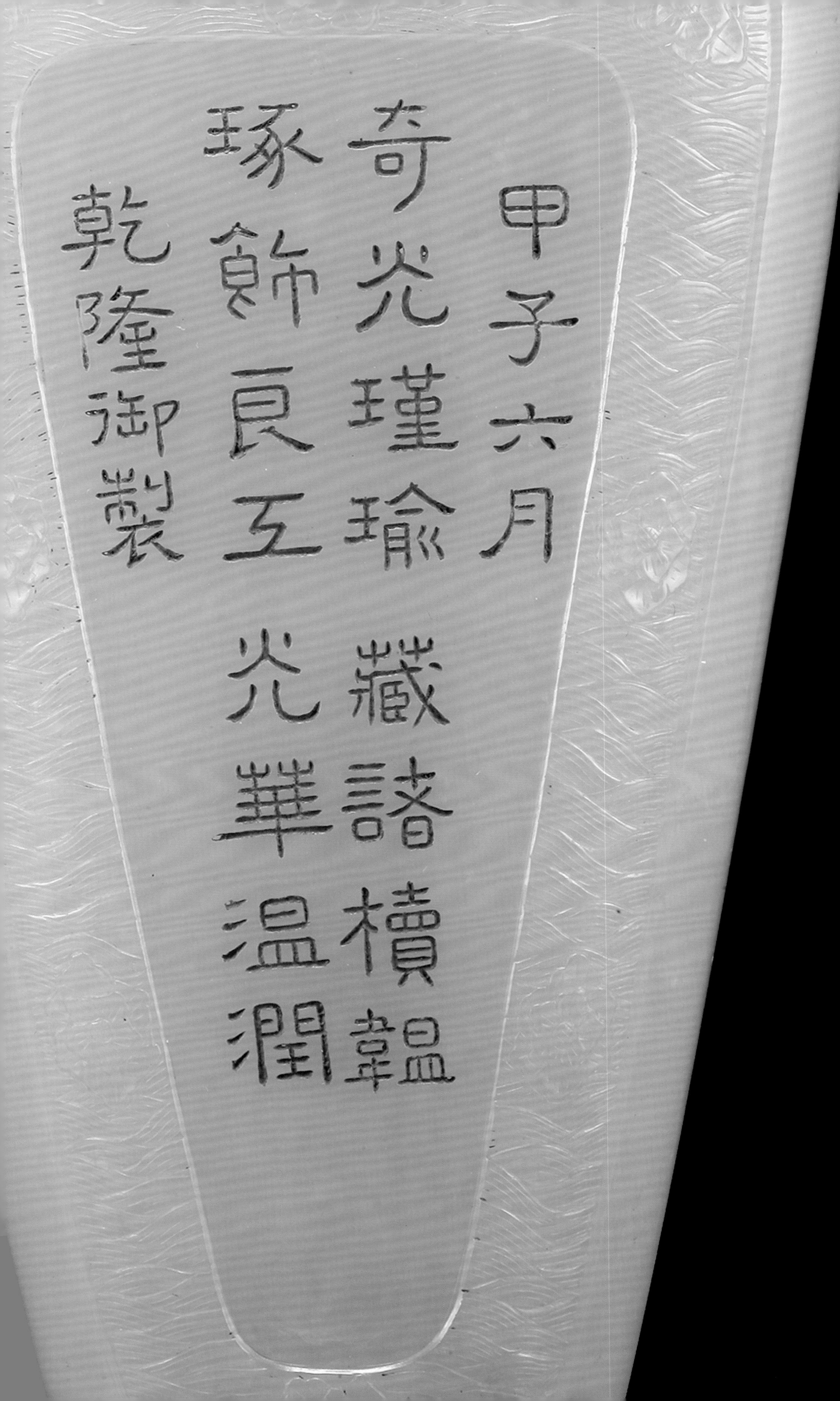

甲子六月

奇光瑾瑜　藏諸櫝韞

琢飾良工　光華温潤

乾隆御製

清　乾隆《古玉軸頭》

長6.7公分　寬6.7公分　高9公分

白玉，質潤，潔白，是上好羊脂白玉，器作圓筒型蓋盒狀，下連方形作，蓋作蓮花瓣形，心為圓形鈕，自頂向下伏視，宛如一盛開蓮花，工藝精絕，具高水準藝術性，筒腹刻乾隆御題詩：「古玉軸頭長二吋，圍一吋…」，最末題「乾隆壬寅秋」，下有刻「乾」圖章，方章「隆」二印款。字體娟秀雅緻，以描金呈現。此盒為收藏扳指所使用。

古玉軸頭

古玉軸頭長二寸圍一寸有去聲分寸五截為二一則琢隸一則就圍圜刻寶叶寶文曰古稀天子用以抑埴書畫可叶隸則佽手覺太

御製詩五集　卷十二

粗中規削半留半取削者玉質乃全呈留者縟華原作土或者用之日以長受汗氣仍玠璘吐既思臂病用不斆入聲刻詠何為意徵憮

Qing Dynasty, Qianlong Era
"White jade rod box"

.l6.7cm, W/6.7cm, H/9cm

Vhite jade—this smooth and milky white jade is a fine specimen of suet vhite jade. The piece is made into a round barrel shape with a lid, while he connected bottom part is square. The lid has a lotus blossom pattern vith a round stem in the center. The top part is shaped like a blooming otus blossom. The craftsmanship is exquisite, with a high level of artistic uality. The body of the barrel shape is inscribed with the imperial poetry f Emperor Qianlong. On the bottom there are inscribed two characters, he name of Qianlong. The script is beautiful and elegant, and traced vith gold. This box was used for storing the rods used for imperial rings.

思辟病用不
斅刻詠何為
意微憮
乾隆壬寅秋
御題 敬勝
古玉軸頭長
二寸圍一寸

古玉軸頭長
二寸圍一寸
有分寸五截
為二一則琢
隸一則就圍
圓刻寶寶文
曰古稀天子
用以抑埴書
畫可隸則倣
手覺太粗中

取背之[illegible][illegible]
乃全呈留者
縟華原作上
或者用之日
以長受汗氣
仍珍璘吐既
思辭病用不
數刻詠何為
意微憮
乾隆壬寅秋
御題

此盒為光緒皇帝為探視其生父醇親王病之玉禮盒。盒面淺浮雕琢刻「☰」乾字號，是乾隆皇帝的專屬符號與標記，乾字卦歷來解釋為「天」，盒面上卦之兩側飾昇龍紋，邊緣再以雙勾雲葉紋為飾，上各雕回首螭龍紋，蓋沿寬凹陷紋，浮刻一對捲雲紋為邊飾。盒身四面，各琢雕有十二章紋各三種，即日、月、星辰，山、龍、華蟲，火、藻、宗彝，粉米、黼、黻等十二種代表古代帝王的尊貴紋飾。這十二章包含了至善至美的帝德，象徵皇帝是大地的主宰，其權力「如天地之大，萬物涵復載之中，如日月之明，八方囿照臨之內。」這十二章紋自周代出現開始，雖歷經兩千多年的朝代更替，因其意義深刻，始終保持著原始的形態，幾乎沒有改變，這也是其他普通裝飾圖案無法比擬的。

下盒器內底刻有「光緒十三年十月二十五日，皇帝來邸視疾，面送醇親王記」下刻二方章，一方為「皇七子」，一方為「醇親王」篆字款。為光緒皇帝為探視其生父醇親王於病榻之時，特命人於宮中藏品中，選有「☰」乾字卦款之玉盒作為禮品，君臣之禮、父子之情、階級身分之殊盡在其中，故之後乃自銘刻款以為記，遂有後記於器底。從此玉盒所傳達的訊息與敘述得知，難以言喻的人倫親情，惟睹此物已表露無遺，這是一種特殊的用心與獨特的心思所在，箇中滋味值得細細推敲與品味。

Qing Dynasty
Altazimuth pair of jade boxes

L/12.4cm, W/12.4cm, H/5.5cm

Hetian white jade. The piece is formed into the top and bottom parts of a box made from the same material. The vessel is made into a perfectly square box with cover which has a hexagram inscribed in the center that is the personal symbol of Emperor Qianlong. There are dragon patterns on both sides of the hexagram as well as a double hooked cloud pattern around the border. On top, a hornless dragon with a turned head is carved, and pairs of curling cloud patterns are carved on the borders of the cover. There are twelve imperial patterns carved on the four sides of the box, which are the sun, moon, stars, mountain, dragon, silkworm, fire, algae, ritual vessel, rice, and the two "fu" patterns. These twelve patterns signify the highest good and beauty of imperial virtue, symbolizing that the emperor is the ruler of the earth and that his authority is endless and enlightening. These twelve patterns were first created in the Zhou Dynasty and lasted throughout the centuries because of their deep significance. They have always kept their original form, with virtually no change, something that cannot be said for other decorative patterns.

The bottom of the box is carved with an imperial inscription, and there are two seal inscriptions. This box was given by Emperor Guangxu when visiting his ailing father, and was in the palace's collection. Presenting a jade box with a hexagram on the top was a sign of propriety between nobles, affection between son and father, and the acknowledgement of high status. A commemoration of this gift was inscribed on the bottom of the box as a record for future generations. The message of this piece is that personal feelings are difficult to put into words, and they can only be expressed through the presentation of exquisite art. This shows a unique thoughtfulness that is worthy of careful reflection.

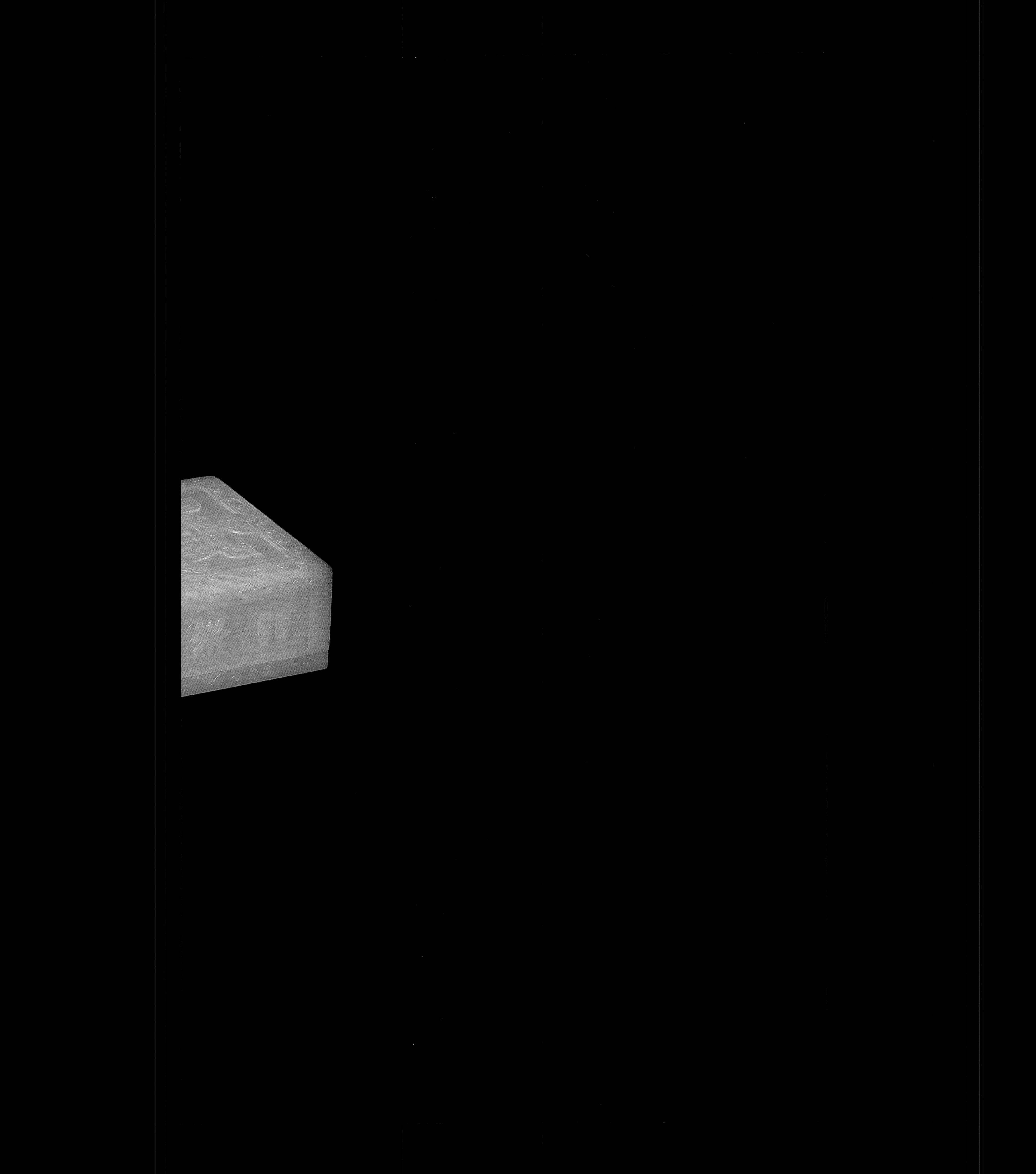

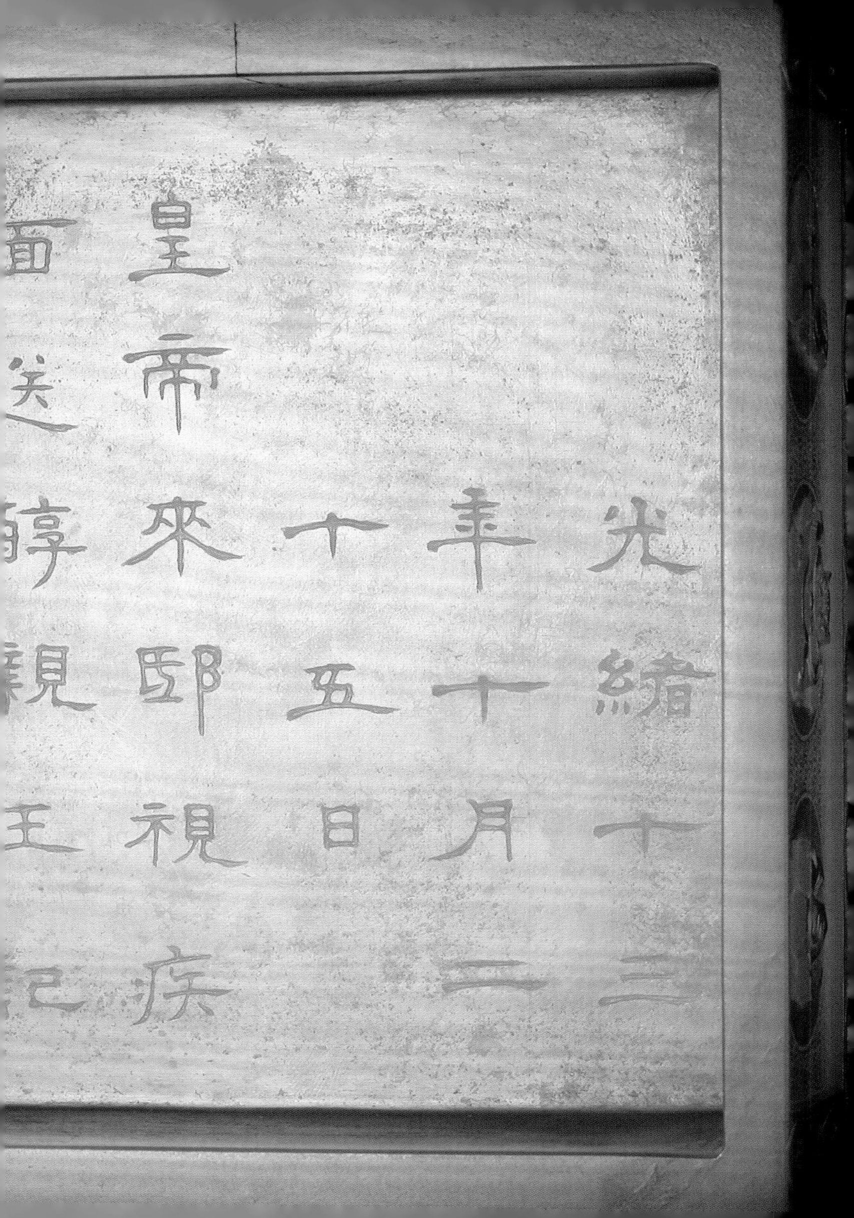

光緒十二
年十月二
十五日
皇帝來邸視疾
面送醇親王記

清 乾隆 御製玉扳指（五件）

1 徑3.3公分 高2.2公分
2 徑3.2公分 高2.5公分
3 徑3.3公分 高2.5公分
4 徑2.7公分 高2公分
5 徑3.2公分 高2.6公分

分白玉及青白玉質，部份入土受沁，部份以烤皮子作色。扳指作圓筒狀，原為古代拉弓使用的「韘」演化而來，後變成裝飾用的佩飾。清代男子流行套於拇指作裝飾品，形制變為圓筒狀。五件扳指中，有在器面刻御題詩，或刻「乾隆年製」等銘款。

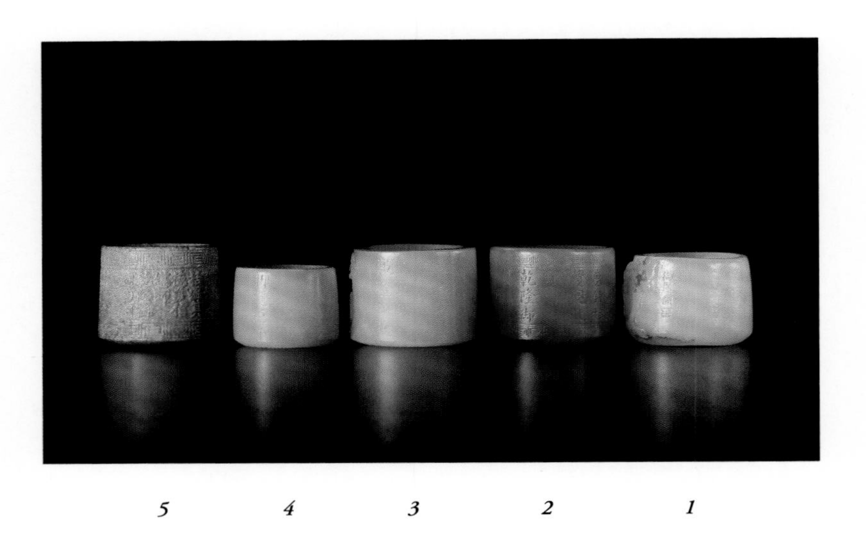

5 4 3 2 1

Qing Dynasty, Qianlong Era Imperial Rings (set of five)

1.Diam./3.3cm, H/2.2cm 2.Diam./3.2cm, H/2.5cm
3.Diam./3.3cm, H/2.5cm 4.Diam./2.7cm, H/2cm
5.Diam./3.2cm, H/2.6cm

Of this set, some are white jade and some are grayish green jade. Some have been discolored as a result of having been buried, and some have been colored by baking of the jade skin. The rings are round barrel shapes. These shapes evolved into decorative accessories from the rings used by archers to assist in stretching the bow. It became popular for Qing Dynasty men to wear these on their thumbs. The mark of the reign of Qianlong is carved on them.

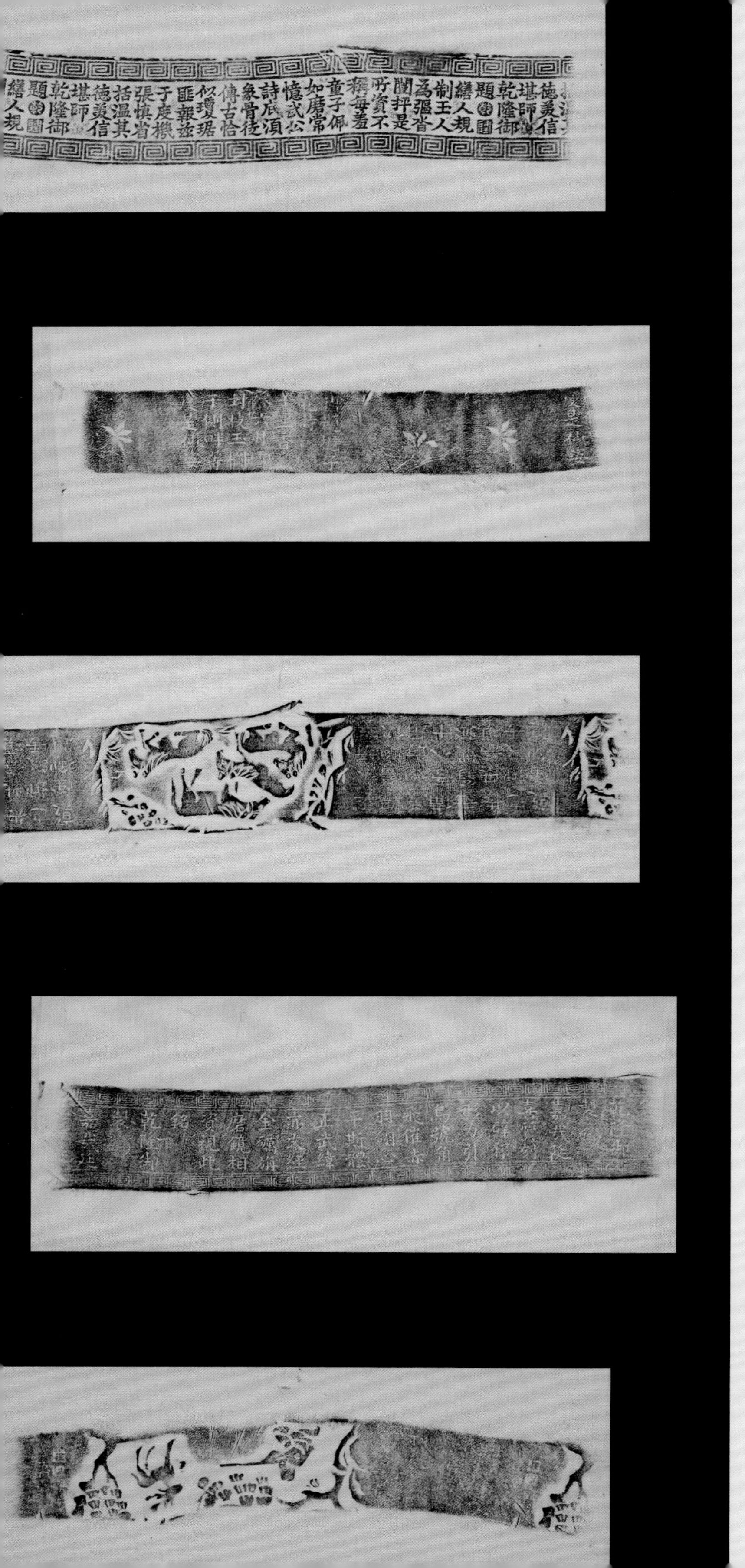

詠玉韘

繕人規制玉人爲彄沓闓抒是所資不稱每
羞童子佩如磨常憶武公詩底須象骨徒傳
古恰似瓊琚匪報茲于度機張愼省括溫其
德美信堪師

梔子

十里香盈谷六月雪封枝玉欄干側畔等度
是仙姿

戲題四駿玉韘

玉人精鑿四名駒欲手如前用備吾八十老
翁罷弧矢此爲頌也抑譏乎

詠玉韘

嘉哉延喜質刻以辟邪形力引烏號角飛催
赤羽翎心平斯體正武緯亦文經金礪旃磨
鏡相資視此銘

題哨鹿玉韘

哨鹿年來久棄之玉工舊稿效前爲挽弓馬
上能無爾持銃林中那有斯顧示衆人仍劼
武迴看昔日祇羸詩至憊力矣中去聲惟巧喻
語子輿猶可思

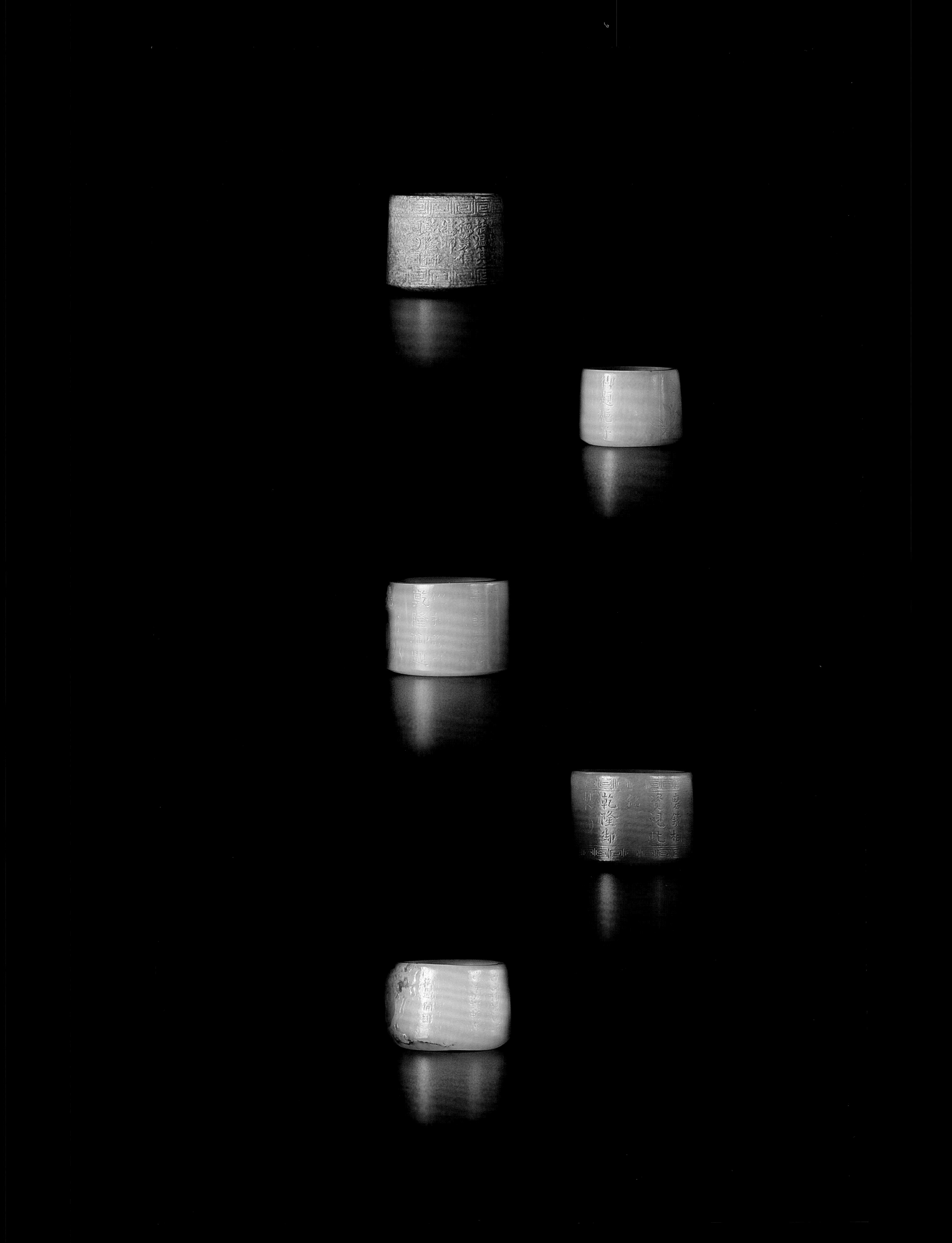

清　青白玉　菊瓣紋扁壺

寬23公分　高29公分

青白玉質，微透明，無瑕光潔。器高直頸小口，作扁圓器腹。下附扁圓型高圈足，在口緣下方附龍形耳，由尾部蜷曲接於頸部，並向器肩延伸龍首，貼附於雙肩部。器面由腹部中央向外緣浮雕菊瓣紋飾，邊緣以回文帶為飾，工細緻，拋光工夫極佳，表面流露勻淨光澤，整件器形仿古青銅器彝器，但紋飾創新，典雅具端莊風情。底足刻有「乾隆年製」四字篆款。

Qing Dynasty
Grayish green with white jade chrysanthemum flask

W/23cm, H/29cm

Grayish green with white jade — slightly translucent, flawless, and burnished. It is tall and straight with a small opening, and a flat, rounded body. It has a high, rounded base, and has dragon handles just below the opening. The tails of the dragons connect at the neck of the flask, and the heads trail down to connect to the body of the flask. The center of the body bears a carved chrysanthemum petal pattern, and there is a pattern around the border. The craftsmanship is exquisite, and the burnish refined. The surface is smooth and shiny, and the entire piece resembles an ancient bronze ritualistic object. The pattern, however, is novel, with an elegant and dignified feeling. The base is inscribed with the four words, "Qian Long Nian Zhi".

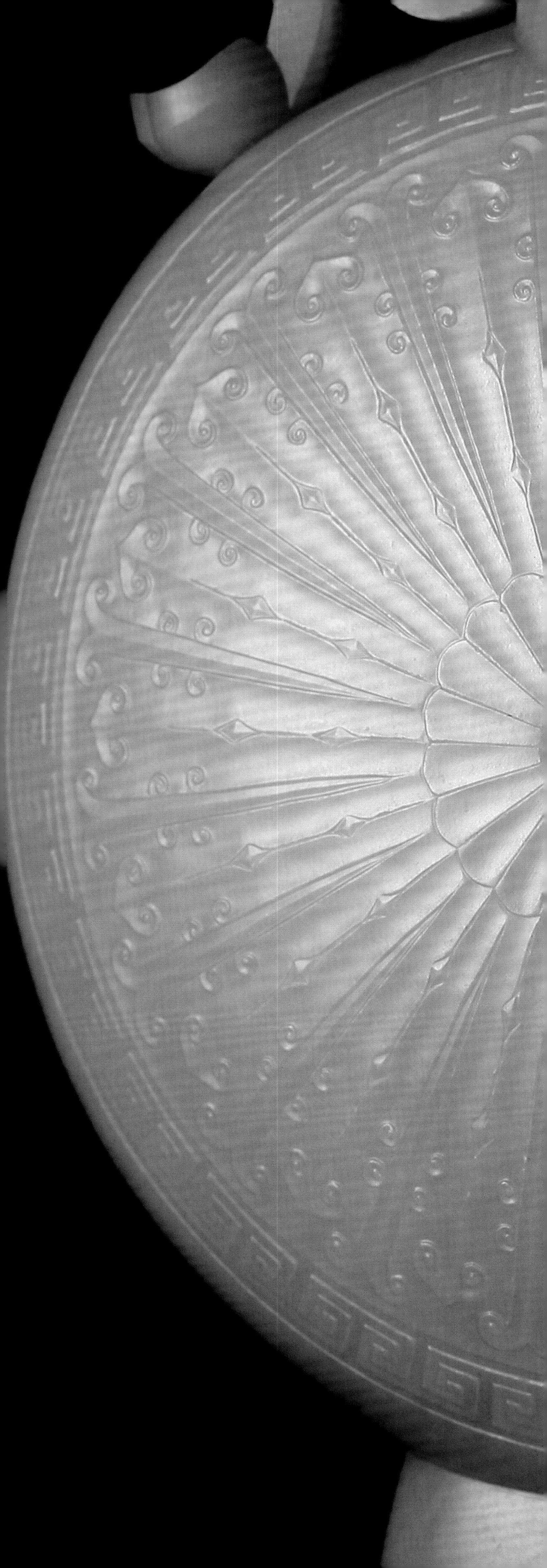

清 白玉 玉碗

徑13.6公分 高6.2公分

白玉質、品質絕佳，羊脂玉質，整塊籽玉所雕挖製成。器圓形，展口、深弧腹壁，底矮圈足，胎瑩白而薄，拋光功夫精絕

央刻方章「乾隆御用」四字篆款，在方章周圍刻「子孫永寶用之」一圈篆字銘文。

Qing Dynasty
White jade bowl

Diam./13.6cm, H/6.2cm

White jade — absolutely pure suet white jade carved from a single piece of seed jade. It is round, with an open mouth and curving walls. The base is short and circular, and the walls are white and thin, showing off an excellent burnishing technique. In the center of the base is a four-character seal-type inscription identifying it as a product of the Qianlong era. There is another inscription around the border.

乾隆御用

清 乾隆 青白玉 玉碗

徑12.8公分 高5.8公分

青白玉質，成對用同一塊水產玉料雕製而成。玉質潔白光潤，是和闐羊脂玉料，呈現美器型優雅，全器光素不加任何紋飾，呈現玉質細潤光澤。器作展口碗形，底有高圈足，中央刻「乾隆年製」四字隸書款，圈足緣邊刻一「乙」字，另一碗亦刻「乙」字，表示成對碗。

Qing Dynasty, Qianlong Era
White jade bowl

Diam./12.8cm, H/5.8cm

White jade — a pair of bowls carved from the same piece of river-gathered jade. The jade is of a shiny and smooth suet white jade quality. These pieces have an elegant style without a single ornamentation, allowing the jade's natural luster to shine. The open bowls have rounded bases inscribed with four characters identifying them as products of the Qianlong era. There are characters carved on the bases identifying them as a matched pair.

清 青白玉 水洗

長8.8公分 寬6.8公分 高6公分

青白玉質，潔淨溫潤，玉質絕佳。係用整塊玉料雕製，器作連座圓鼓形，分上下二段，上面作扁圓鼓形狀，廣口有唇，兩側刻浮雕獸面，象徵器耳，下段乃為器架形式，作八角形。書房水洗的佳品。

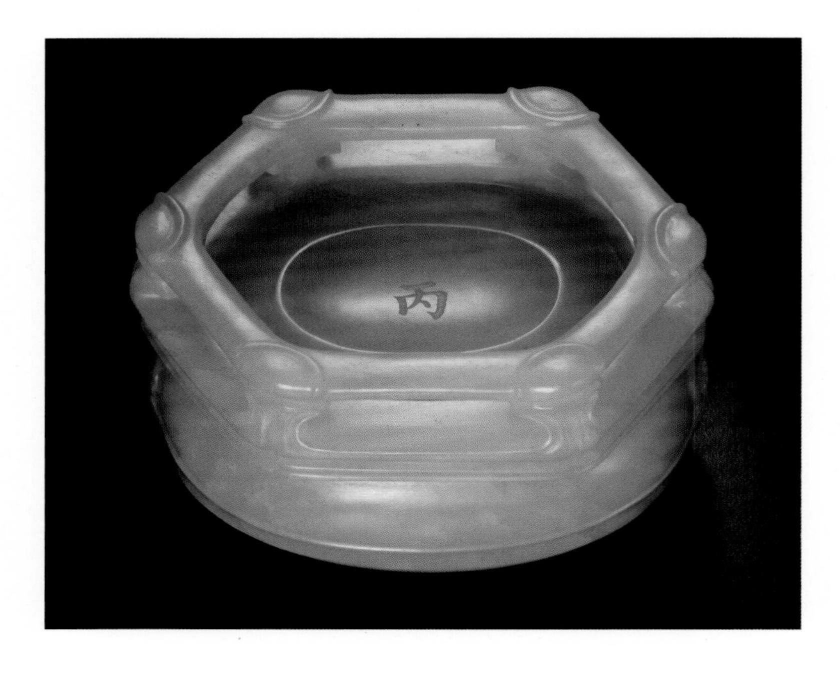

Qing Dynasty
Green with white jade wash basin

L/8.8cm, W/6.8cm, H/6cm

Green with white jade — pure and smooth, the highest quality jade. Carved from a single piece of raw jade, it is made into a round drum shape on a connected base. It is divided into a top and a bottom part. The top part is the round drum shape with a wide, rimmed mouth . The two sides have beast faces in relief, serving as the handles of the vessel. The bottom part is like a frame made into an octagonal shape with an inscription of the character, "Bin". It is a fine example of a court literati studio wash basin.

清 乾隆　黃玉　饕餮耳方杯

長11.2公分　寬8.4公分　高5.8公分

黃玉製成，杯身為方型，表面光素無琢，杯耳飾以饕餮紋，杯底刻有「乾隆年製」篆書款。整器簡明卻又不失精緻，亦突顯了玉質的完美無瑕。

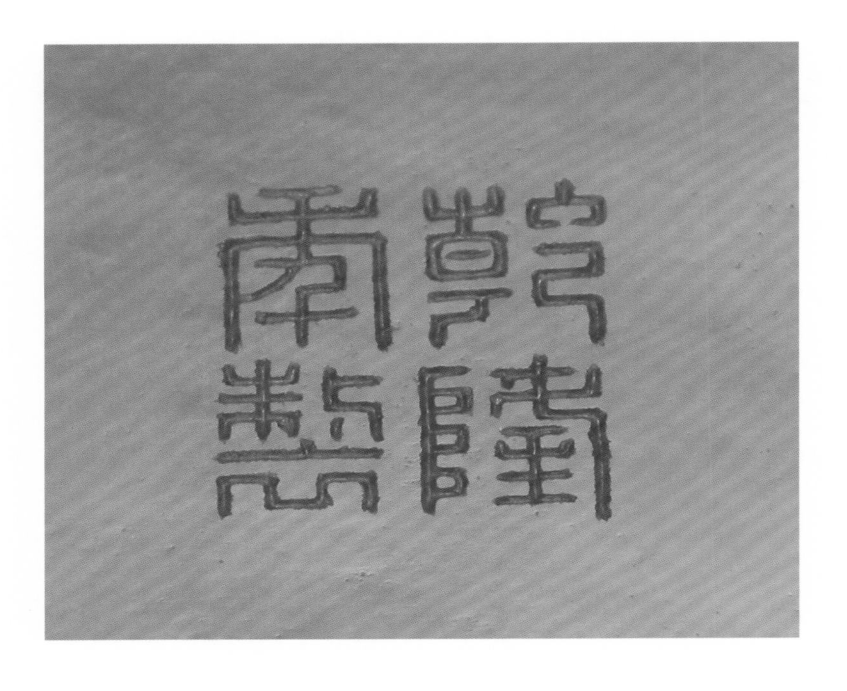

Qing Dynasty, Qianlong Era
Yellow jade ravenous beast handled square cup

L/11.2cm, W/8.4cm, H/5.8cm

Yellow jade — square cup with a shiny and flawless surface. The handle of the cup is a ravenous beast pattern, and there is an inscription on the bottom that identifies it as made in the reign of Qianlong. There is no part of this piece that is not exquisite, showing the flawless quality of the jade material.

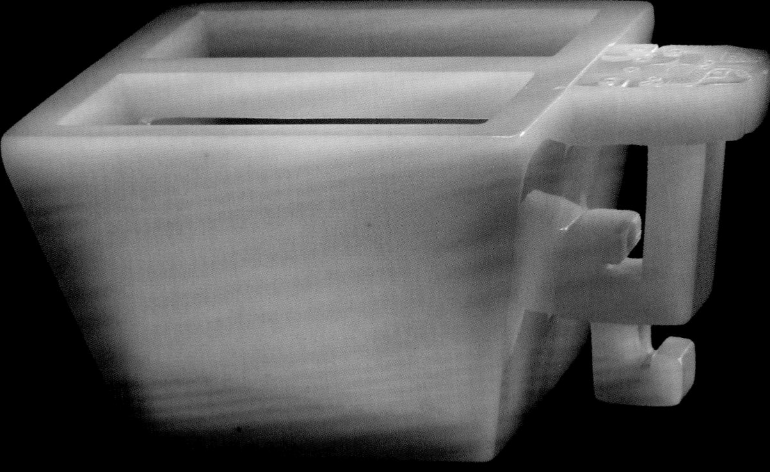

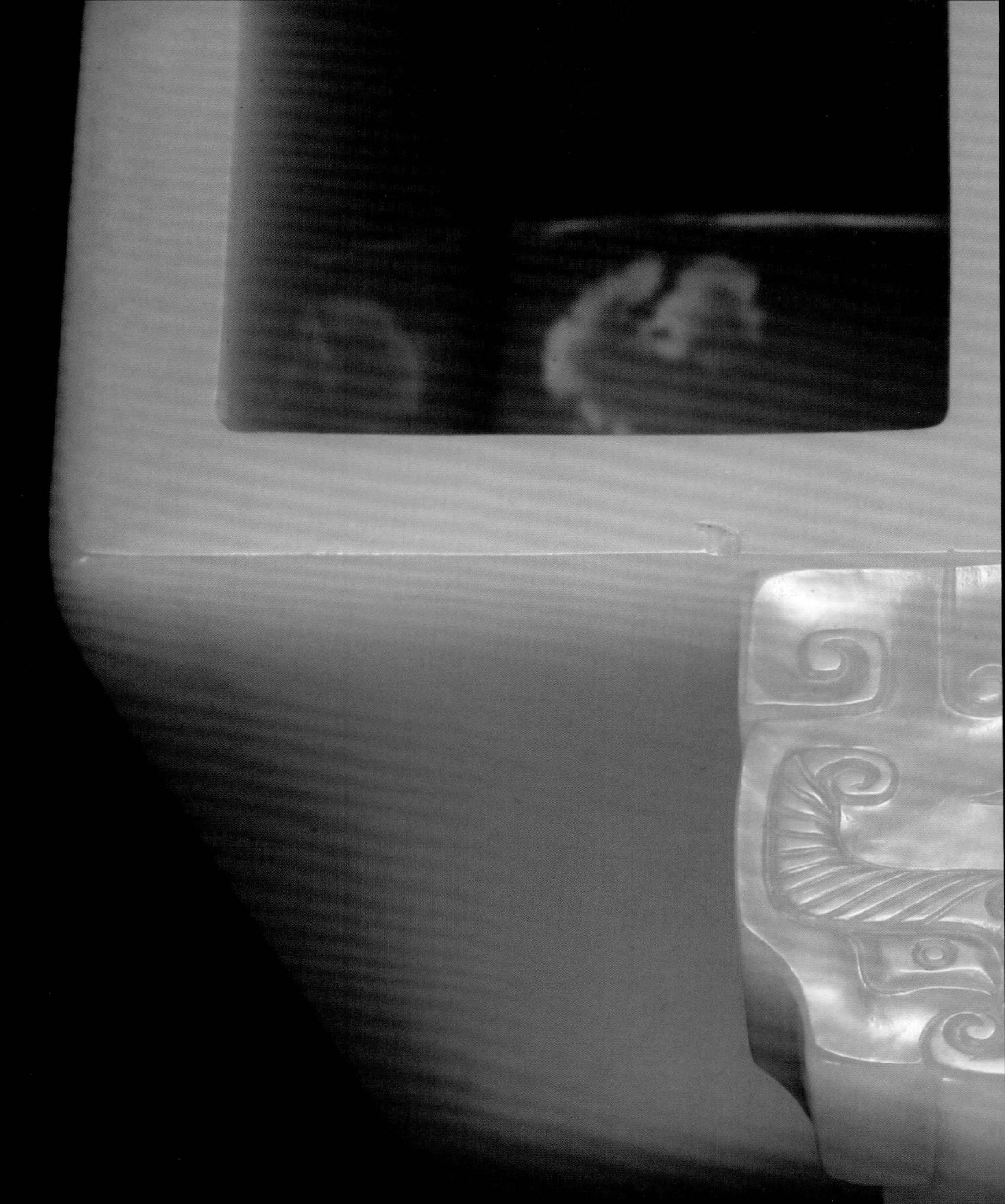

清 乾隆　青白玉　福祿大吉瓶

寬9.8公分　高18.3公分

青白玉質。和闐青白玉製成，器面大部份保持光素，以顯現玉質的溫潤，器附圓形蓋，蓋頂有寶珠形蓋鈕，蓋作子母口，器身上小腹大，形成美好葫蘆形狀，一面浮雕蟠桃枝葉，另一面浮雕「大吉」二字，象徵吉祥寓意。底附橢圓形圈足，此類瓶式，常成對放於轎邊裝飾，亦稱「轎瓶」。

Qing Dynasty, Qianlong Era
Grayish green with white jade gourd vase

W/9.8cm, H/18.3cm

Grayish green with white jade — made from Hetian jade, most of the surface of this vessel maintains its shine, displaying the natural smoothness of the jade. There is an rounded stopper attached, with a jewel-shaped stem on the top and a tight fit. The vessel body is larger at the top and bottom, forming a gorgeous gourd shape. One side is carved with an immortality peach branch and the other side is carved with two characters symbolizing good luck. The bottom has an ellipsoid base. This type of vase usually came in pairs and was placed in palanquin, which gave it the alternative name of "palanquin vase."

大吉

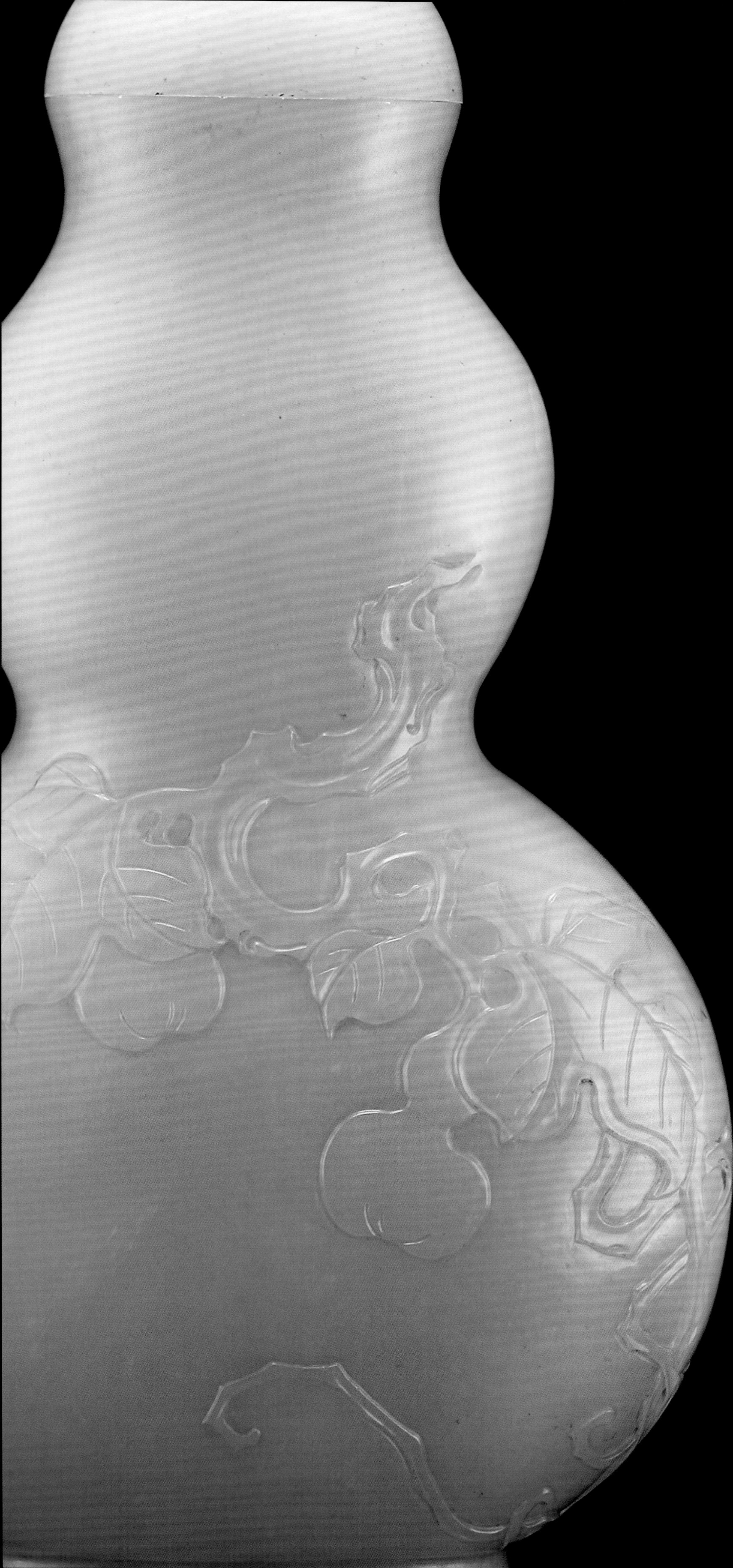

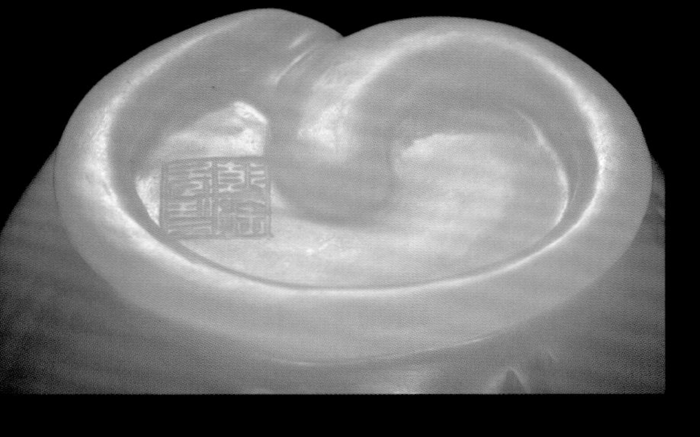

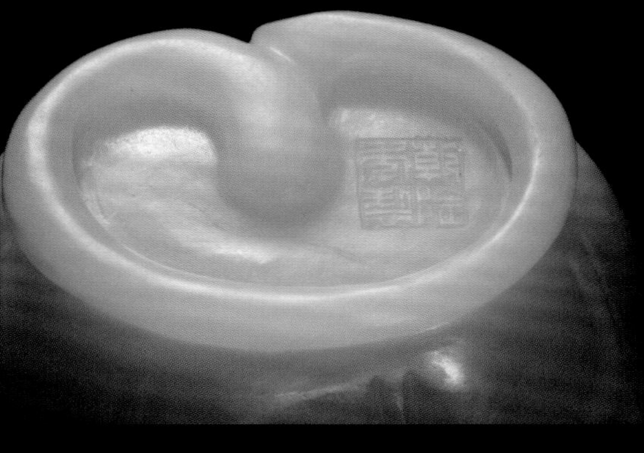

Qing Dynasty, Qianlong Era
White jade orchid cups (pair)

L/6.4cm, W/6.5cm

The bottom of these vessels has an inscription that identifies them as products of the reign of Qianlong. These are made from two pieces of suet white jade of approximately similar size. They were skillfully carved into the jade orchid style. There are curving lines that circle around the sides of the cups. The jade quality is smooth, and the design is uniquely clever and adorable.

器底刻有「乾隆年製」篆書款，器由兩大小相仿羊脂白玉製成，玉蘭花造型，巧琢成杯狀，杯邊翻捲線條靈活，迴環曲折，玉質溫

造型別出心裁，小巧可愛，令人愛不忍釋。

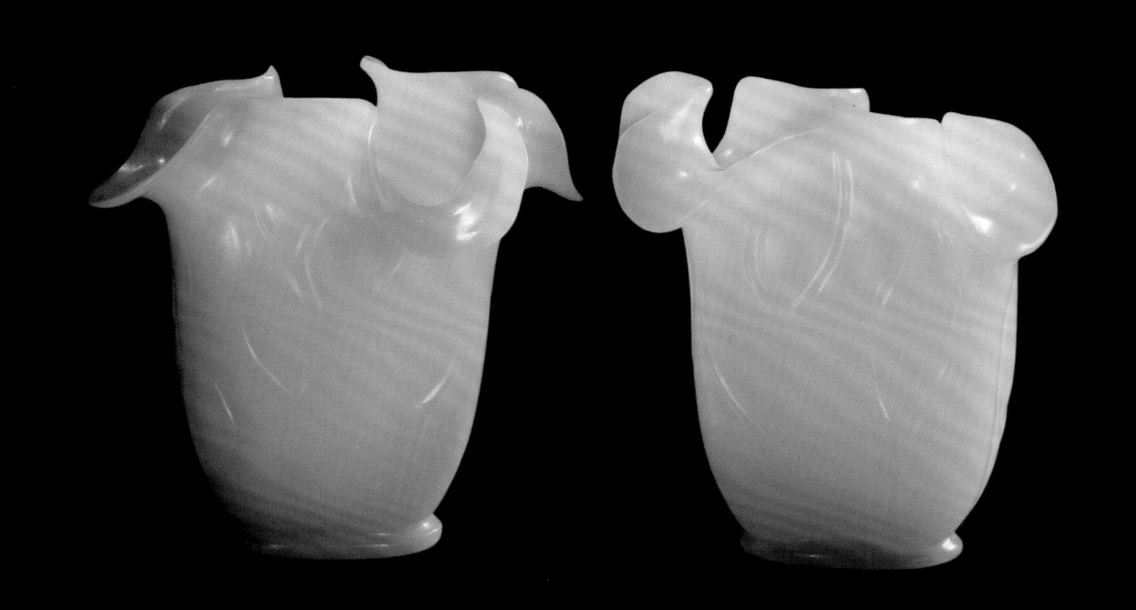

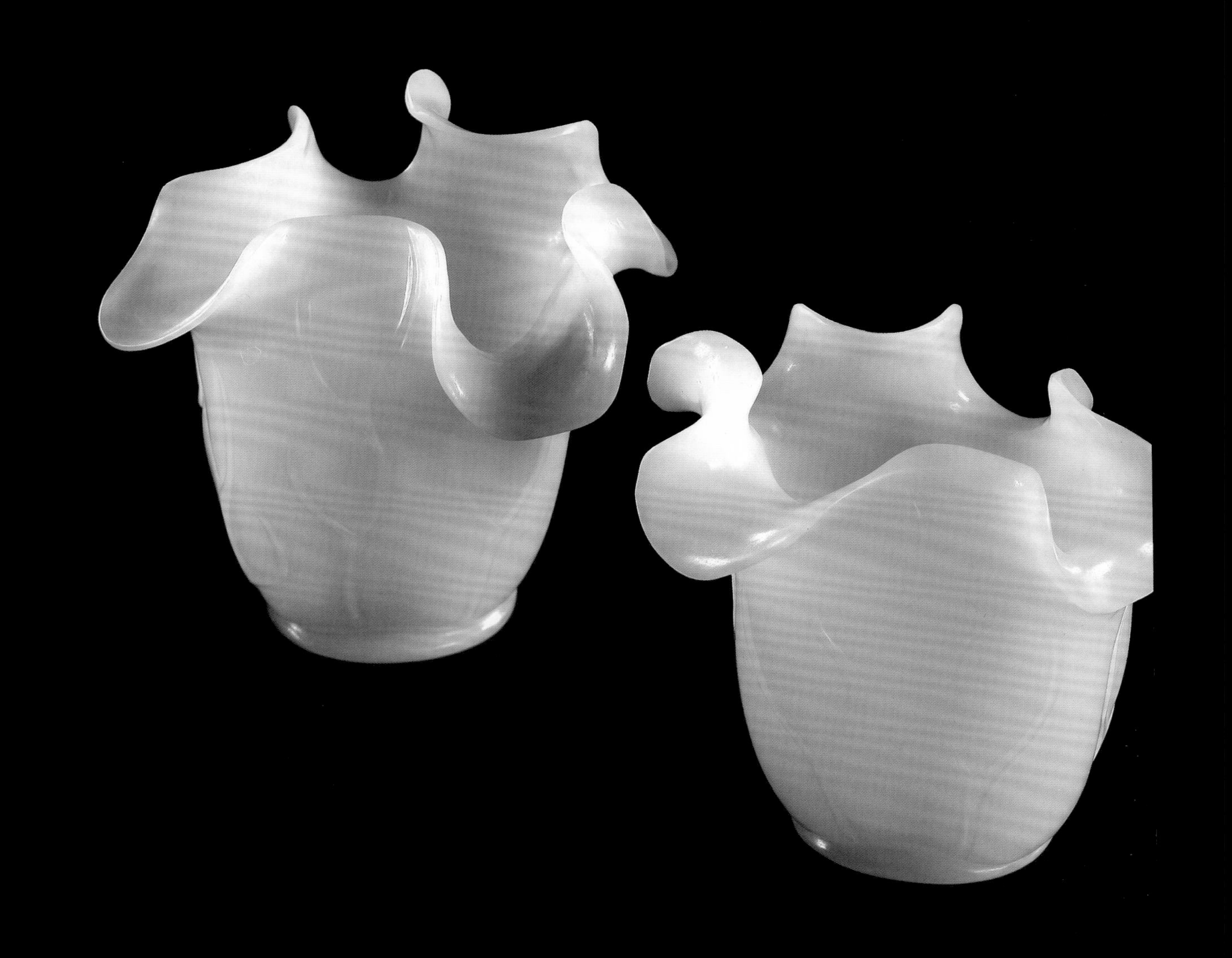

清 乾隆 青白玉 玉牛

長17公分 寬9公分 高5.8公分

青白玉質，和闐籽玉整塊依玉石原形雕成，表面薄留玉皮，使其產生「俏色」效果。牛作伏臥狀，牛首稍回首前望，姿態怡然自得，表情頗似吃畢牧草，俯臥反芻休憩狀。器由籽玉立體雕刻而成，牛首、牛背留著玉皮所留的黃色，極似毛皮自然呈色，乃生肖玉器擺件佳作。腹底陰刻「乾隆年製」四字篆款。

Qing Dynasty, Qianlong Era
Grayish green with white jade ox

L/17cm, W/9cm, H/5.8cm

Grayish green with white jade — carved from a single piece of Hetian seed jade. There is a thin layer of jade skin on the surface that gives it a multi-colored effect. The ox is reclining and its head is looking forward slightly in a relaxed and peaceful position. It looks as though the ox has just eaten its fill of grass and is ready for a rest. The head and the back have a slight yellow color that make them look natural. It is a fine specimen of a jade animal figure. There are four words carved on the bottom, indicating it is from the reign of Qianlong.

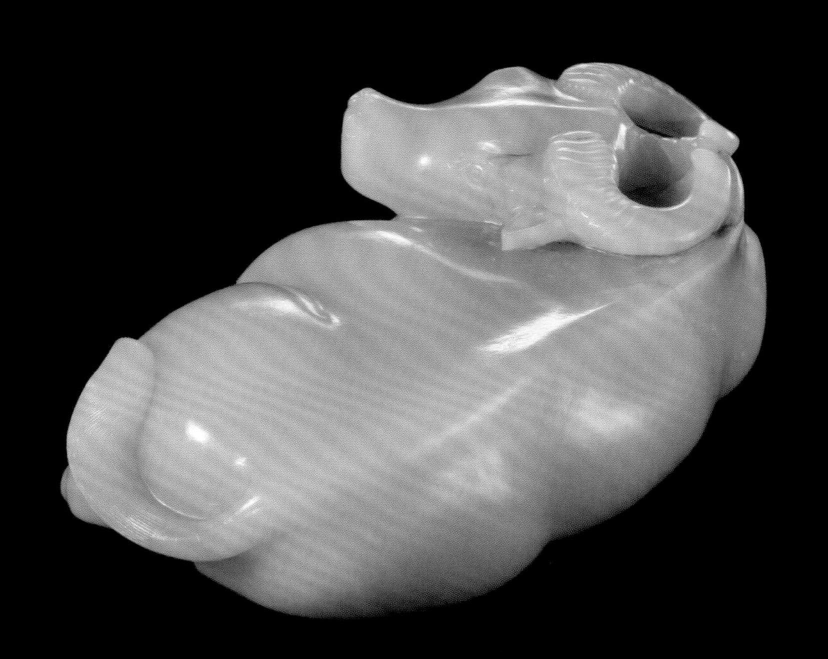

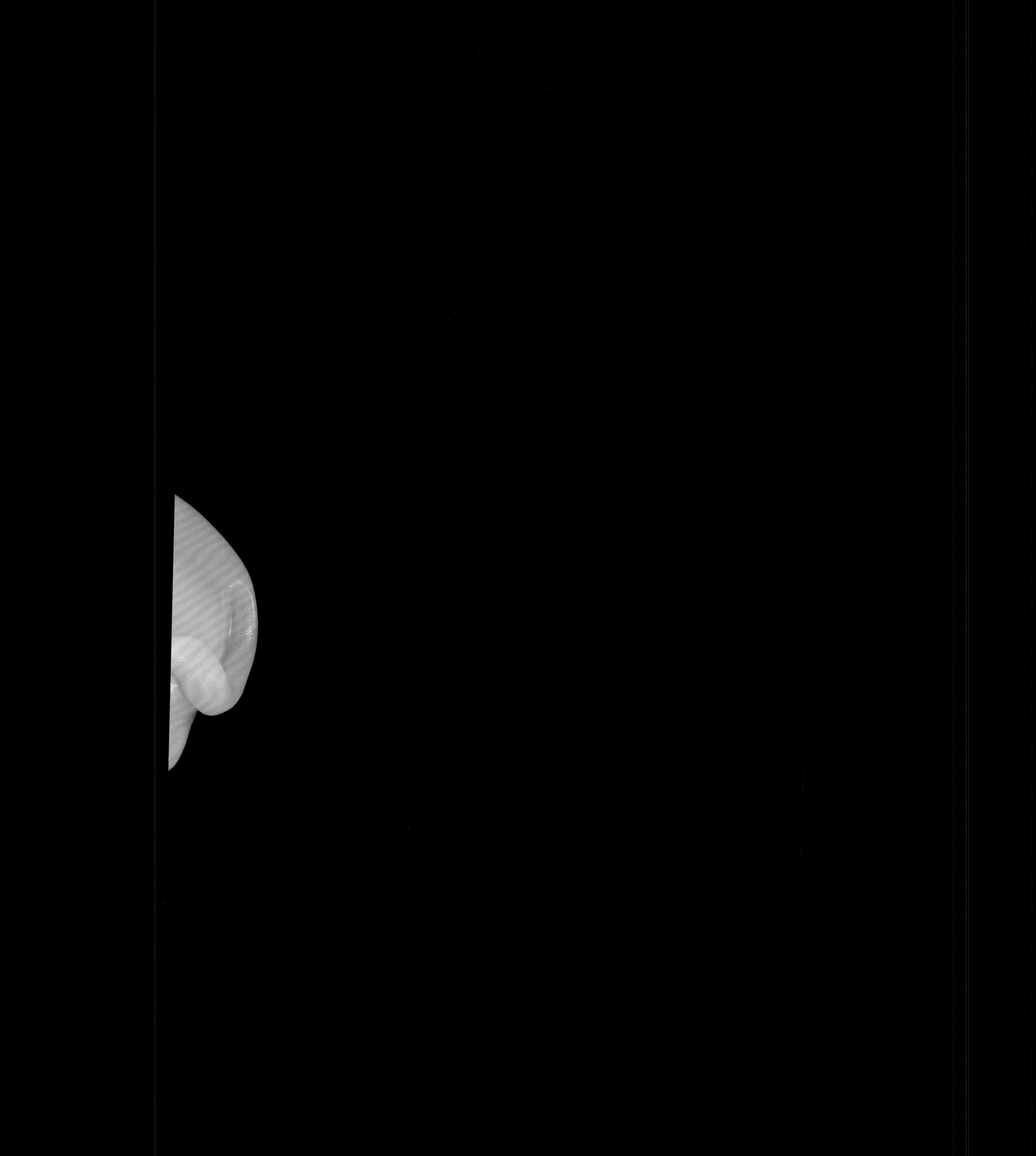

清 嘉慶 碧玉 夔龍紋壺

徑16.5公分 高27.5公分

碧玉質，質呈深綠色，質極純正，間雜黑色斑，乃碧玉自然的質地。仿古青銅器圓壺器式雕製，圓口有唇，圓腹，高圈足中部以一圈綯索紋為飾。頸部飾仰式六出蕉葉紋，器身以弦紋分成三段，均飾夔龍紋飾，幾乎佈滿全部器面，一對銜耳活環飾於頸部兩側，鋪首向外凸起，頗具氣勢。圈足內刻「大清嘉慶仿古」六字篆款。

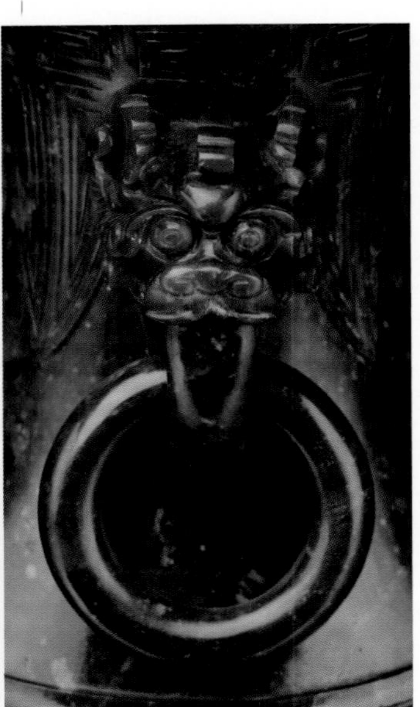

Qing Dynasty, Jiaqing Era
Dark green jade dragon and one-footed dragon pattern pot

Diam./16.5cm, H/27.5cm

Dark green jade — very pure dark green jade with some black spots, the natural quality of dark green jade. It is modeled after ancient bronze round pots. The round opening has a rim, and the body is rounded. There is a high circular base decorated with a ring of a wavy pattern. The neck is decorated with a banana leaf pattern, and the body is divided into three parts by its pattern, with the surface almost completely covered with dragon and one-footed dragon patterns. There are impressive handles protruding on each side. The circular base is inscribed with six characters identifying it as a product of the Jiaqing era.

清　白玉　玉盤

徑22.7公分　高4.7公分

白玉質，為絕佳羊脂白玉雕製，絲毫不見瑕疵，質極純正潔白。器作圓形，展口盤形，低圈足，器面光素，拋光技法圓熟，胎體極薄，幾可透光，足底中央刻「嘉慶年製」四字篆款。

Qing Dynasty
White jade plate

Diam./22.7cm, H/4.7cm

White jade — carved from pure suet white jade without a flaw to be seen. The object is round, with an open plate shape. There is a round base at the bottom. The surface is smooth, with an immaculate burnishing technique. The walls are extremely thin, almost transparent, and the center of the base is inscribed with four characters identifying it as a product of the Jiaqing era.

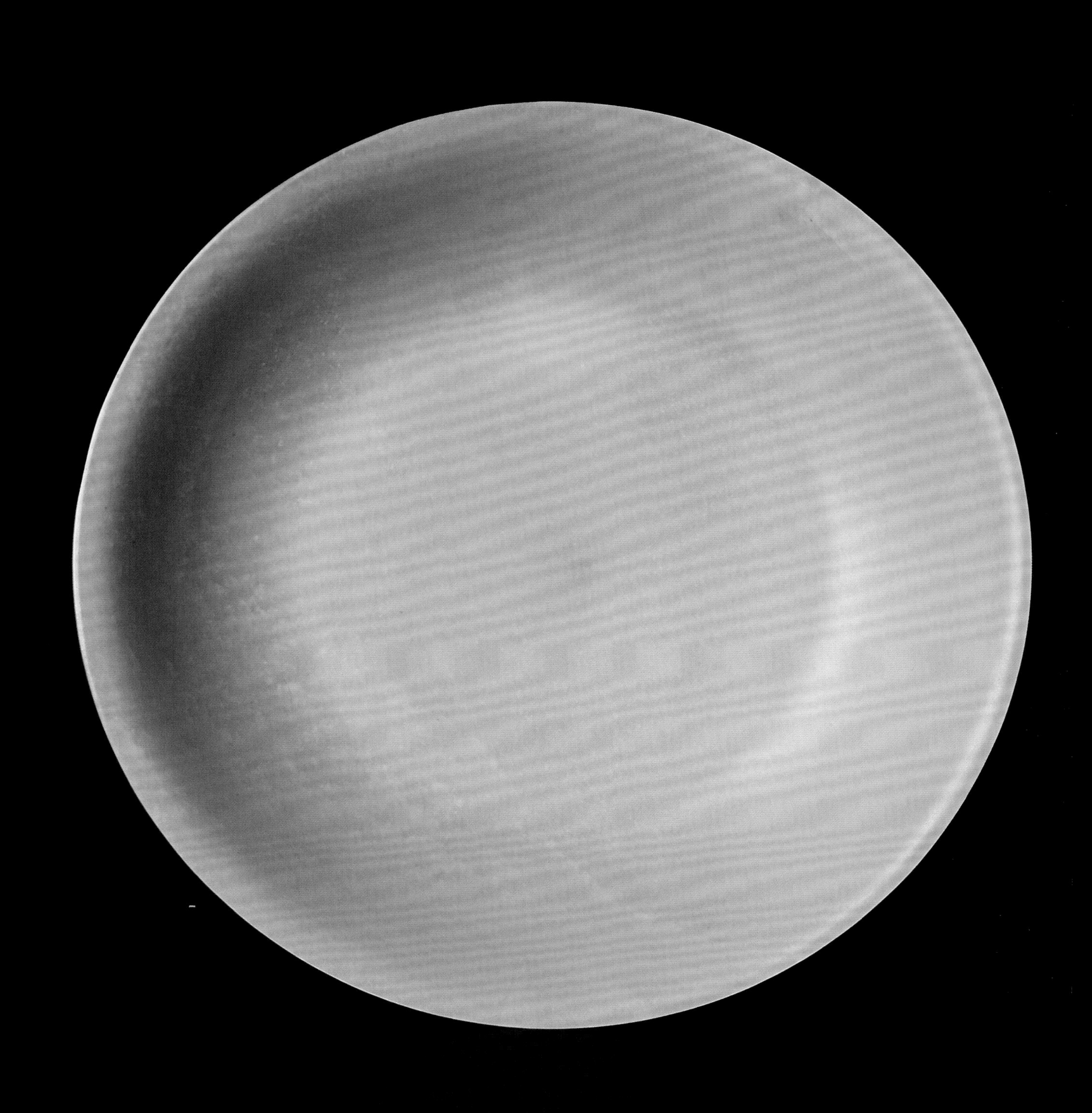

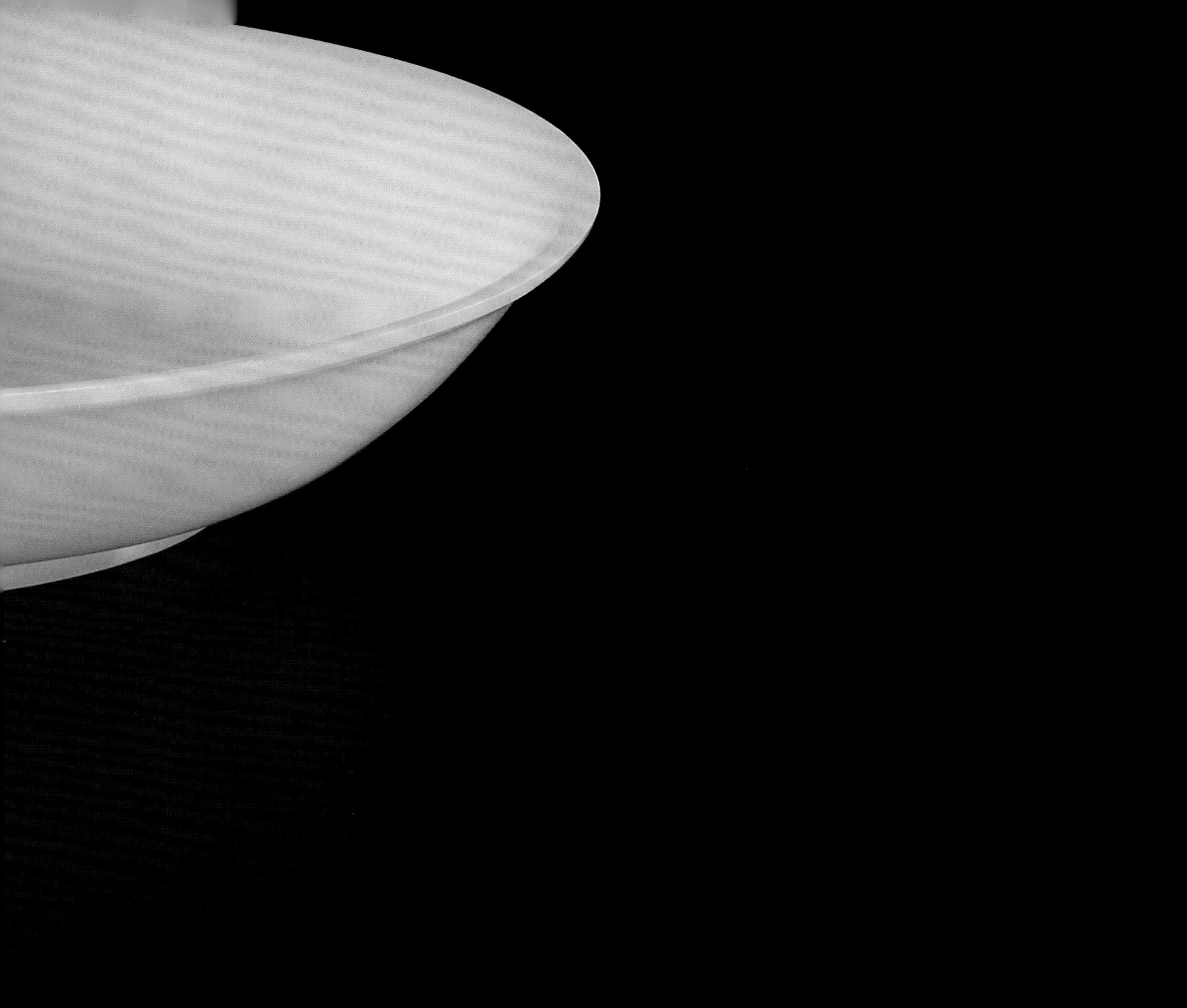

清　白玉　螭耳瓶

徑3.3公分　高10.9公分

此器造型為長直頸口微展、圓腹形成之二階式瓶身，在直頸的兩側加上雙螭虎作耳，全器通體光素無瑕，瑩潤清透，除肩部有雲頭紋裝飾外，無其他紋飾，突顯出螭虎的華麗。底部刻有乾卦紋，乾卦以龍為象，顯示此器可能為御用把玩之物。整體雕工細膩，造型呈現簡潔卻不失高雅。

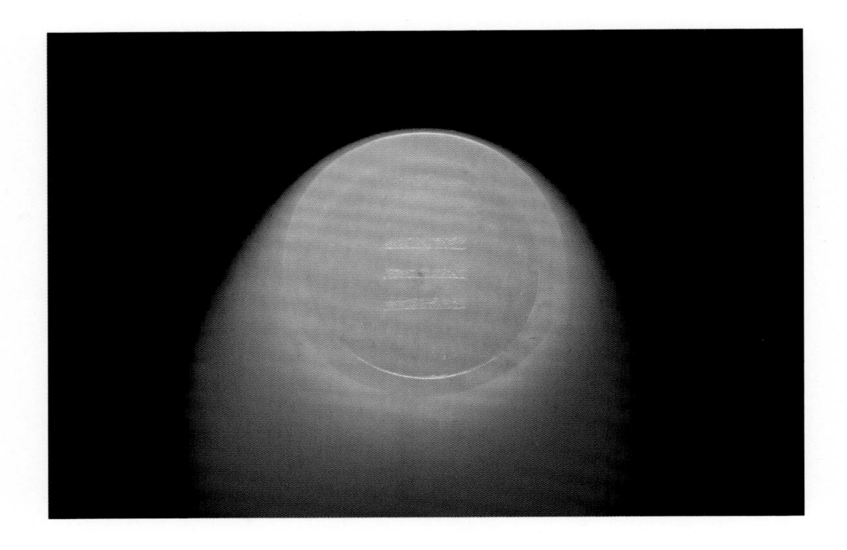

Qing Dynasty
White jade hornless dragon handled vase

Diam./3.3cm, H/10.9cm

This vessel has a long, straight neck with a small mouth, and a round vase body divided into two sections. On the neck section there are two hornless dragon beast shaped handles. The entire vessel is complete, pure, and flawless. It is smooth and elegant. There are no decorative patterns except for the cloud patterns on the shoulder area, which accentuate the beauty of the dragons. There is a hexagram pattern on the bottom, showing that this piece was probably an imperial decoration. The carving work on the entire piece is highly refined, and the style is succinct yet still exquisite.

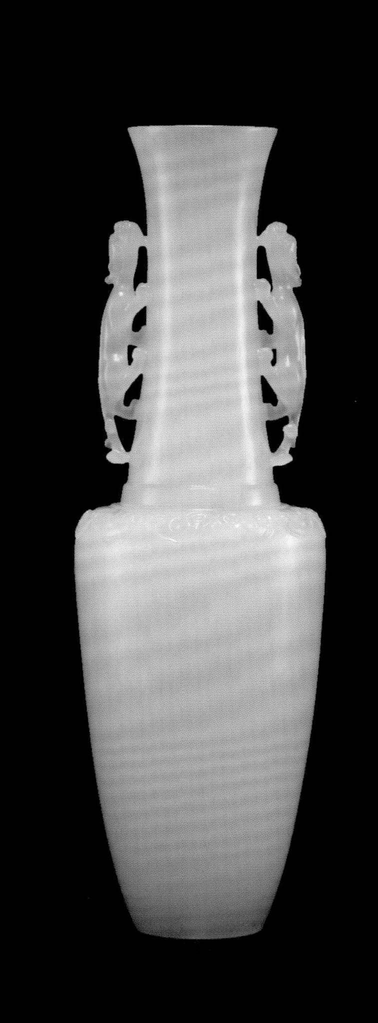

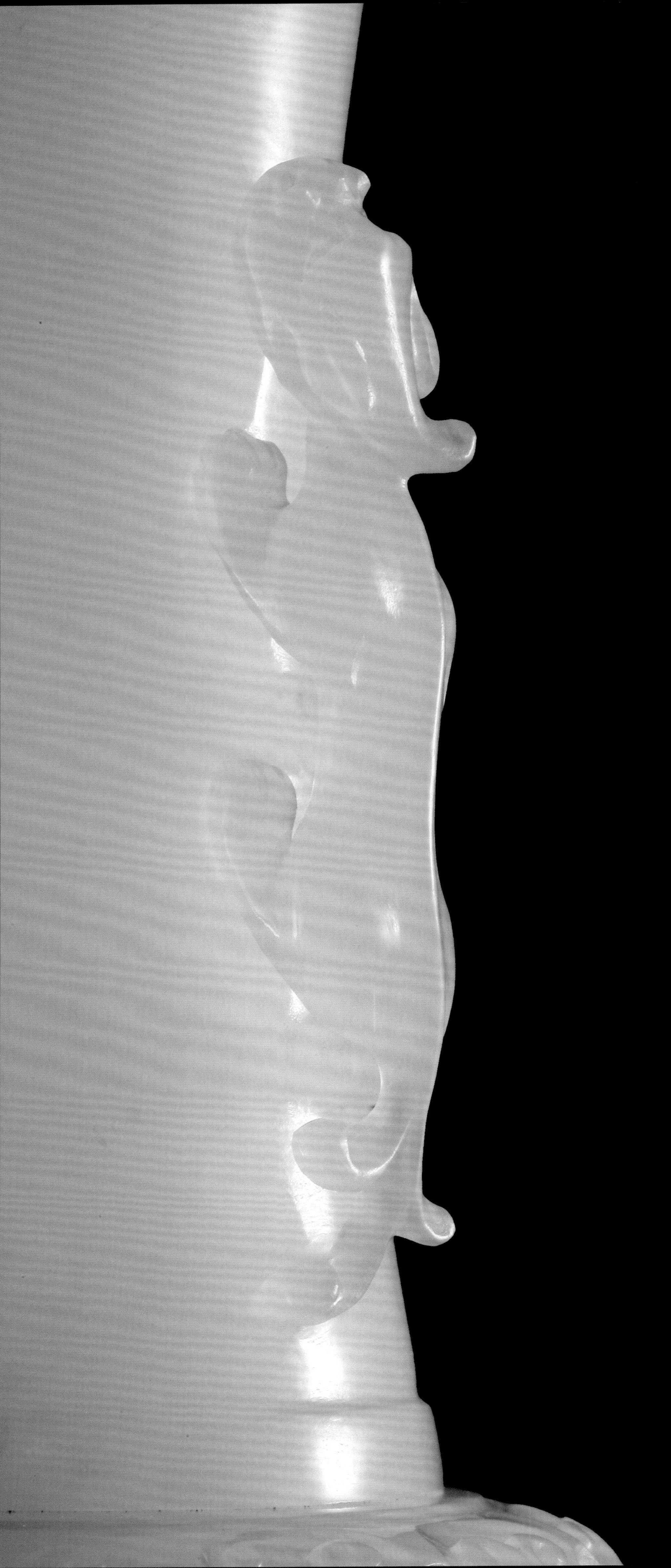

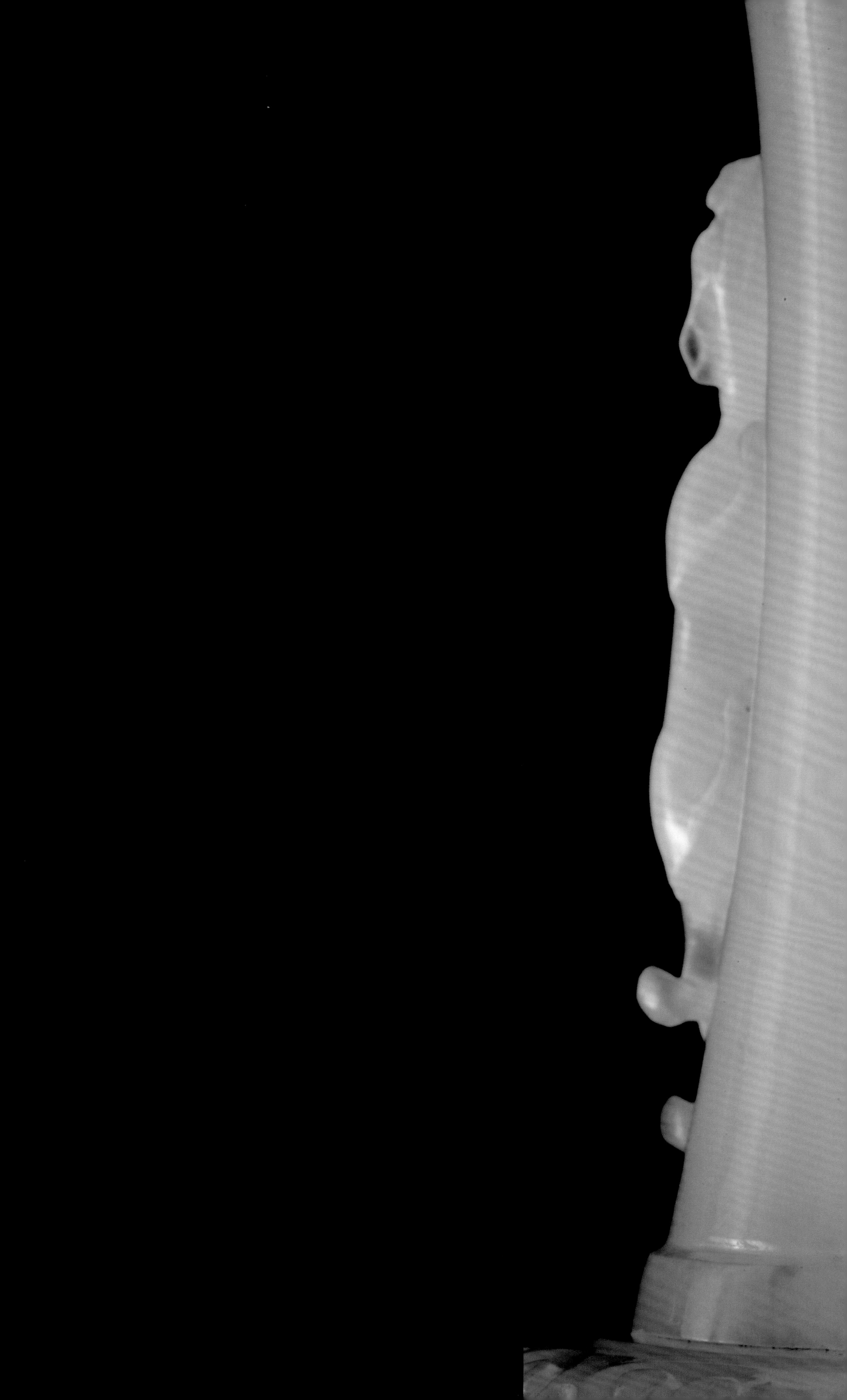

清　青白玉　人物故事扁壺

寬19公分　高29.8公分

青白玉質，整塊和闐青玉雕製，質地絕佳。器扁圓小口，有唇頸部兩側一對龍銜活圓環耳，器身扁圓，下附稍外撇圈足。器腹兩面均雕八位古裝人物紋，但人物的配置兩面並不相同，從人物所持法器，顯然以「八仙慶壽」的主題所雕刻。

Qing Dynasty
Grayish green with white jade human figure story flask

W/19cm, H/29.8cm

Grayish green with white jade — the whole piece is carved from the finest Hetian green with white jade. The opening is small and round, with two dragon-shaped handles on the neck. The body of the piece is flat, with a slightly slanted round foot at the bottom. Carved on both sides of the body are eight human figures in ancient dress, though their positions on the two sides are not identical. By looking at the treasures carried by the figures, it seems that the theme of the carving is, "Eight Immortals Celebrate God of Longevity's Birthday".

清　青白玉　葫蘆型扁壺

寬15公分　高25.5公分

青白玉質微透明，質純淨無瑕。器圓形小口，有唇，器作葫蘆狀頸部，下腹呈扁圓形，附長方形底足，兩側稍外撇，頸肩部附扁葉狀耳。腹部浮雕雙圈紋飾，中心為由花式雲紋所圈圍的太極紋飾，外圈為葉形紋飾，雕工細膩，拋光工夫極佳，器型端麗高雅。

Qing Dynasty
Grayish white jade gourd-shaped flask

W/15cm, H/25.5cm

Grayish white jade — slightly translucent, pure and flawless. The object is rounded, with a small opening and a rim. The neck is gourd-shaped, and the bottom part is flat and rounded with a slightly slanted rectangular base. There are leaf-shaped handles on the two sides. There are decorative patterns carved on the body, and in the center there is a decorative cloud pattern surrounding a tai-chi pattern. The outer circle has a leaf-shaped pattern. The craving is intricate, and the burnishing is of the highest quality, making it an elegant and dignified piece.

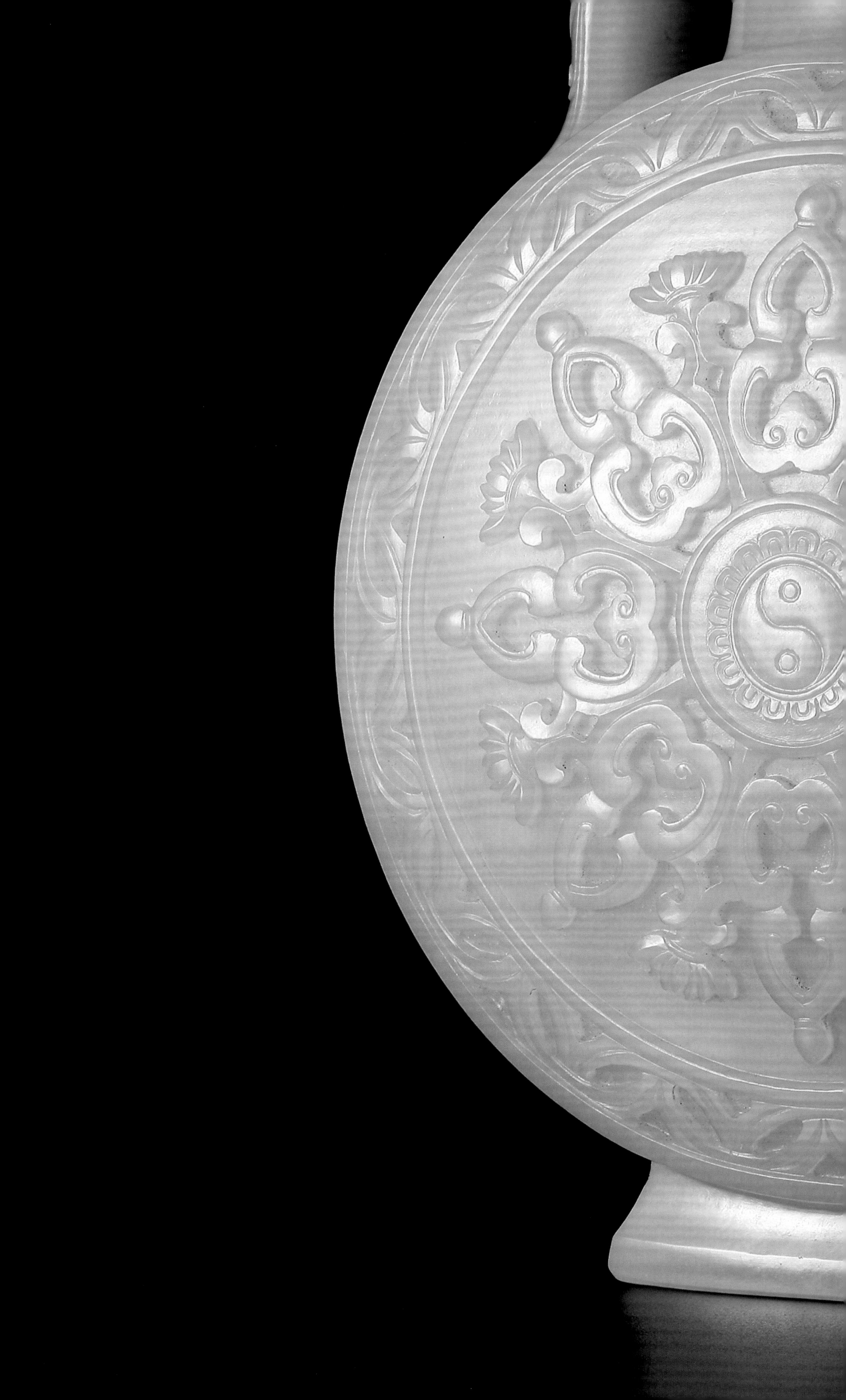

清　白玉　雙鳳羽人蓋瓶

寬10公分　高17公分

和闐白玉質（近羊脂白玉），局部微沁有紅、黃沁色，玉質細潤，富透明光澤。器瓶蓋呈扁圓形，蓋上圓雕有長有一對翅膀的天使形象，顯現出蹲俯的姿態作為瓶蓋鈕飾，自瓶口，沿著長斜頸、折肩、扁腹部兩側外沿，工藝上使用難度較高的鏤空透雕琢刻技法，來表現出花瓶上攀爬有太陽花以及爵床屬植物的藤蔓與葉飾，由上連綴蜿蜒而下，一直延伸至腹部兩側，及至另一側的圈足底部為止，器腹正、反兩面琢刻有變形雙龍鳳紋飾，紋飾繁縟鋪滿器腹，其餘位置玉地打磨平整，拋光精工與細緻，此外瓶身的掏膛工藝特別的薄透而勻稱，因此全器顯現出獨特的輕盈質感。

這是一件非常特殊的玉瓶，除了上述的鏤空透雕技法與掏膛技藝外，表現在藤蔓與枝葉的纖細質感，嫻熟流暢的線條，形成優美裝飾，特別是其間所點綴飾的五個小天使（其中有三位天使羽翼有折損或修飾過），其面容與髮式，仍然呈現中國式的孩童與裝扮，這種獨特的天使形象與太陽花蔓設計，不是中國傳統玉雕上常見的裝飾紋飾與符號，應是在一七一五年受到義大利人Jesuit priest Giuseppe Castiglione（郎世寧）的影響（他同時是一位藝術家與建築師），此玉瓶所呈現出來的特殊風格與裝飾紋飾，應是受其啟發，而此時期其他古典的西方藝術概念，也不斷的傳入中國，也同時影響著其他建築、工藝或藝術作品上。此時期的東西方文化交流與藝術融合現象，正可以藉由此件玉瓶的展示與呈現，完全表露無疑。

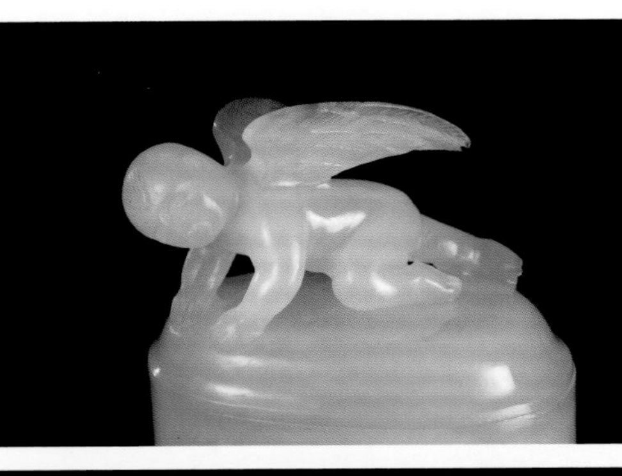

Qing Dynasty
White jade double phoenix sage screen with stopper

W/10cm, H/17cm

Hetian white jade (almost like suet white jade). It has red and yellow soak-induced color in places. The jade is fine and lustrous. The stopper is flat and rounded, with a winged angel sculpture carved on the top in a crouching position. serving as a vase stopper handle. Great skill went into the openwork carving technique of the decorations that flow on both sides from the mouth of the vase, along the slanted neck and flat body of the vase in the form of flowers and ivy climbing up two sides. It starts from the base of the vase on one side, and in the middle on the other. A transforming dragon and phoenix pattern is carved in the middle of the piece's body, filling up the entire space of the body on front and back. The rest of the jade is polished flat with an expert and refined polishing technique. The, "scooping the chamber," technique is also especially delicate, so that the entire piece seems to have a unique, light and delicate feeling.

This is a very distinctive jade vase. Besides the previously mentioned openwork carving and the "scooping the chamber" technique, this piece forms beautiful ornamentation as displayed in the flowing lines and the slender feel of the vines and branches. This is especially true in the case of the five small angels (three of the angels have wings that have been damaged or embellished). Their faces and hair make them seem like Chinese children. This kind of distinctive angel and vine design is not representative of traditional Chinese jade carving decorations. This is probably because of the influence of the Jesuit priest Giuseppe Castiglione (who was an artist and an architect). The special style and decorations of this jade vase were probably inspired by this European. At that time, Western artistic concepts were constantly being introduced to China, influencing works in the fields of architecture, handicrafts, and art. The cultural exchange and artistic fusion between East and West that was occurring at the time is perfectly embodied in this jade vase.

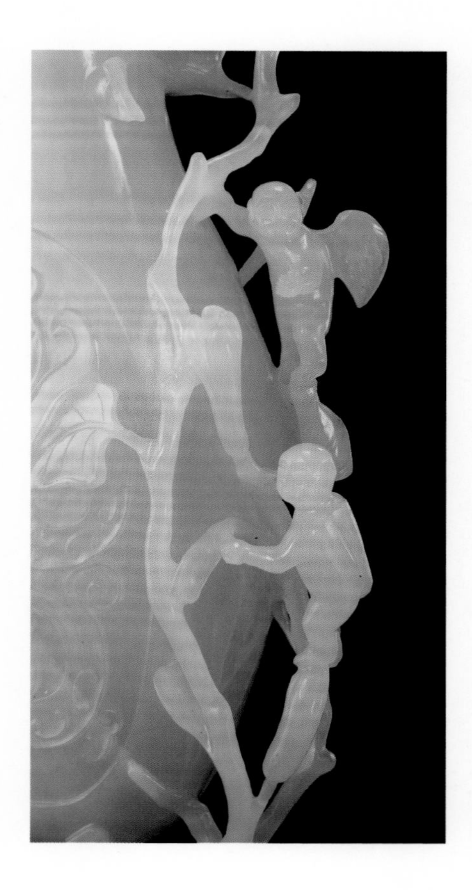

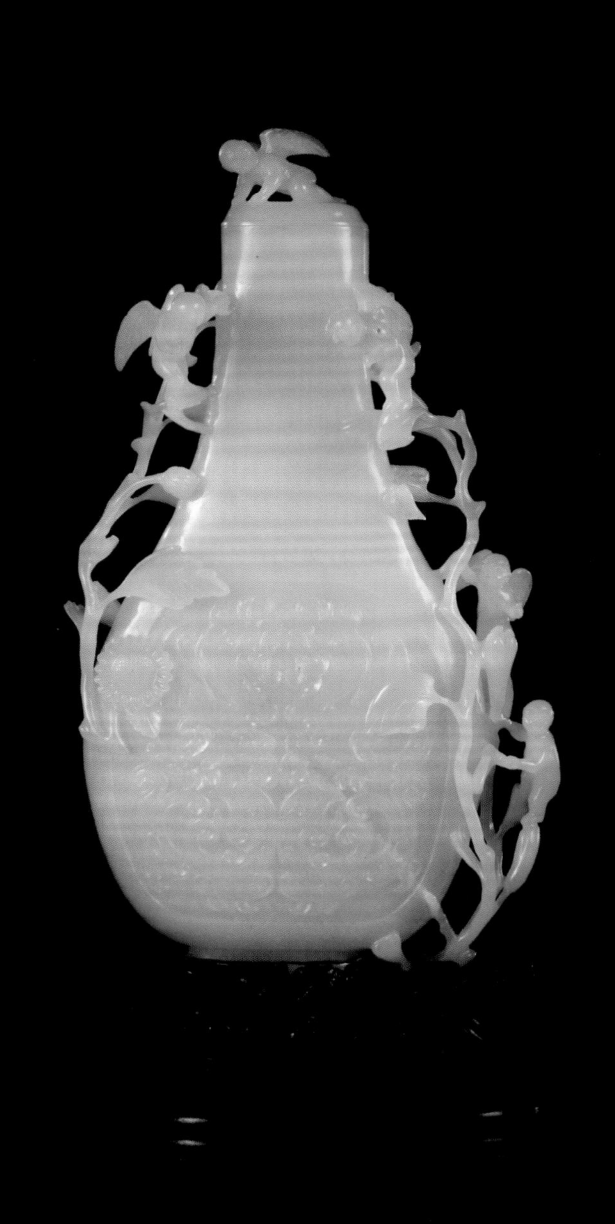

清　白玉　喜上眉梢扁壺

寬13.6公分　高22公分　厚3.7公分

白玉質，由整塊籽玉所雕製，質地呈半透明光澤，白中微閃淡青色，介於白與青白玉之間。器作有蓋扁圓壺形，蓋頂珠寶式圓鈕，為子母口，密合。兩側附銜圓活環耳。腹呈圓鼓形，下附外撇足，腹部器面浮雕梅花、喜雀等圖樣，表「喜上眉梢」寓意，刻工細膩，器式典雅。

Qing Dynasty
White jade "happiness" flask

W/13.6cm, H/22cm, D/3.7cm

White jade — carved from one entire piece of seed jade, it has a semi-translucent luster with some green shining in the white, making the color somewhere between white and green. The jeweled-style rounded stem has a stopper that fits tightly. There are two handles on the sides. The body has a rounded drum shape, and on the bottom is a slanted-out foot. On the body, plum blossoms and birds of happiness are carved in relief, symbolizing happiness. The carving is exquisite and the vessel is elegant.

清　青白玉　饕餮紋扁壺

長13公分　高20公分　厚5公分

青白玉質，質細潤，微透明，品質良好，整塊青玉所雕製。器為蓋壺式樣，蓋頂花形圓鈕，頂平，蓋斜直而下，作子母口，十分密合。肩部高凸透雕葉狀對耳，向外凸起，器身浮雕饕餮紋，仿古青銅器紋飾，底足高圈足，作橢圓形。

Qing Dynasty
Grayish green with white jade ravenous beast pattern flask

W/13cm, H/20cm, D/5cm

Grayish green with white jade—high quality jade that is smooth and slightly translucent, carved from a single piece. It is a pot with a stopper, with flower patterns on the rounded stem. The top is flat, and the stopper is slanted downward, making for a very tight fit. The shoulders have leaf-shaped handles that protrude outward. The body is carved with a ravenous beast pattern and it is modeled after ancient bronze decorations. At the bottom is a tall ovoid foot.

清　青白玉　雙耳瓶

寬12.4公分　高21.5公分

青白玉質，青白玉是和闐籽玉，呈半透明狀，品質極佳。器有蓋，蓋頂附珠寶形圓鈕，蓋光素，呈子母口，短頸，器身作扁長方樣形，方形底足。肩部兩側附花形耳，器腹以浮雕，刻花葉林木圖樣，器形工整優美，設計美觀。

Qing Dynasty
Grayish green with white jade double handled vase

W/12.4cm, H/21.5cm

Grayish green with white jade — carved from one entire piece of Hetian seed jade, it is semi-translucent and of extremely high quality. It has a stopper with a jewel-shaped rounded stem. The stopper is smooth with a tight fit. The neck is short and the body has a flat rectangular shape with a square base. There are two flower-shaped handles on the sides. The body is carved in relief with patterns of flowers, leaves, and trees. The shape is symmetrical and elegant with a beautiful design.

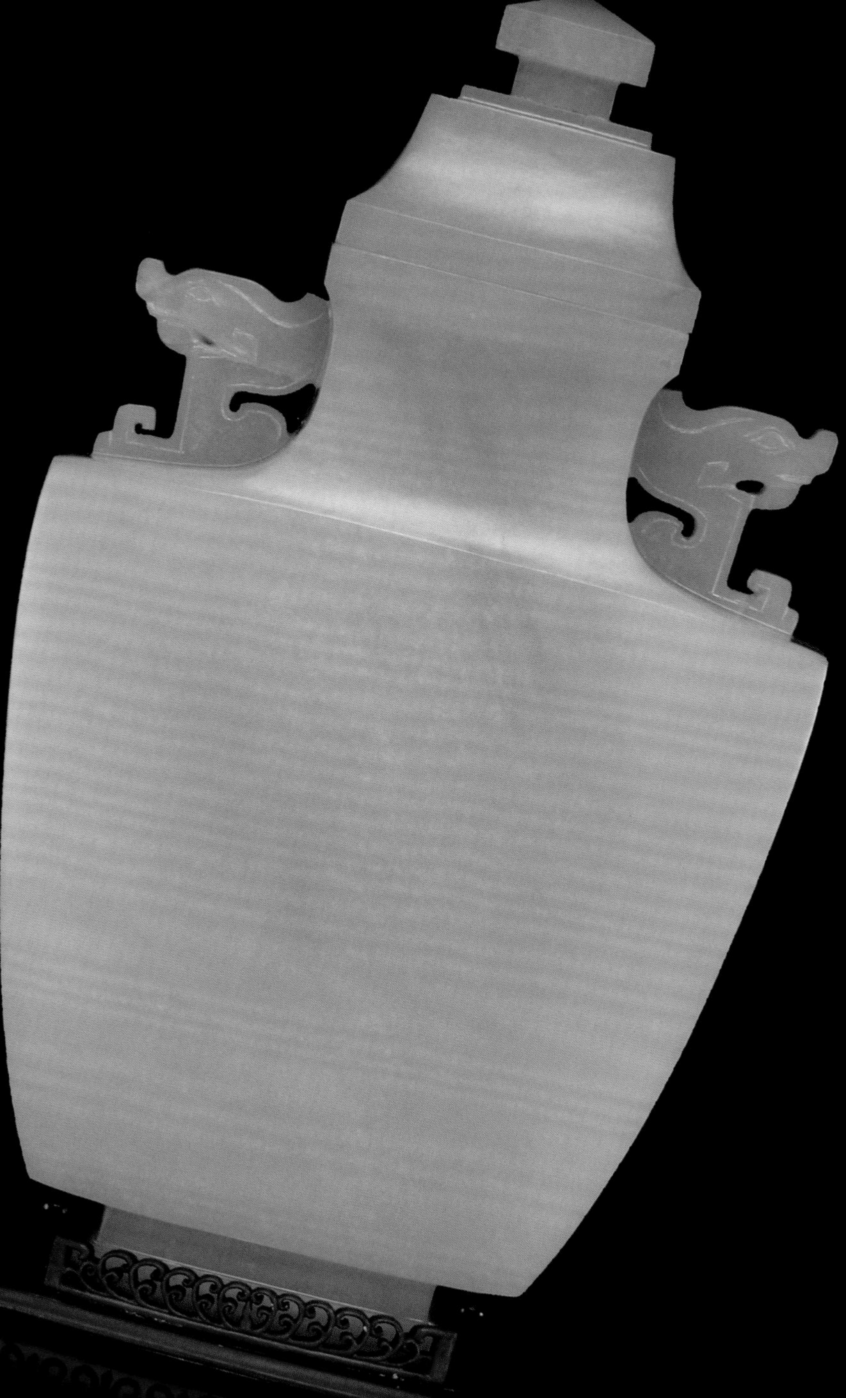

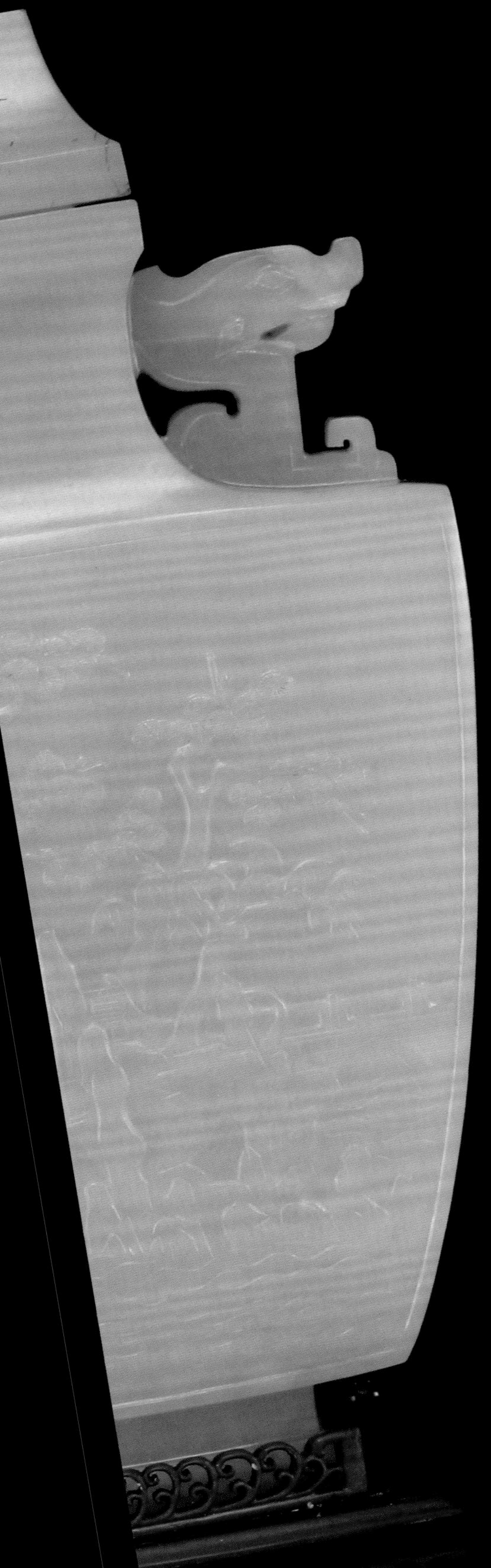

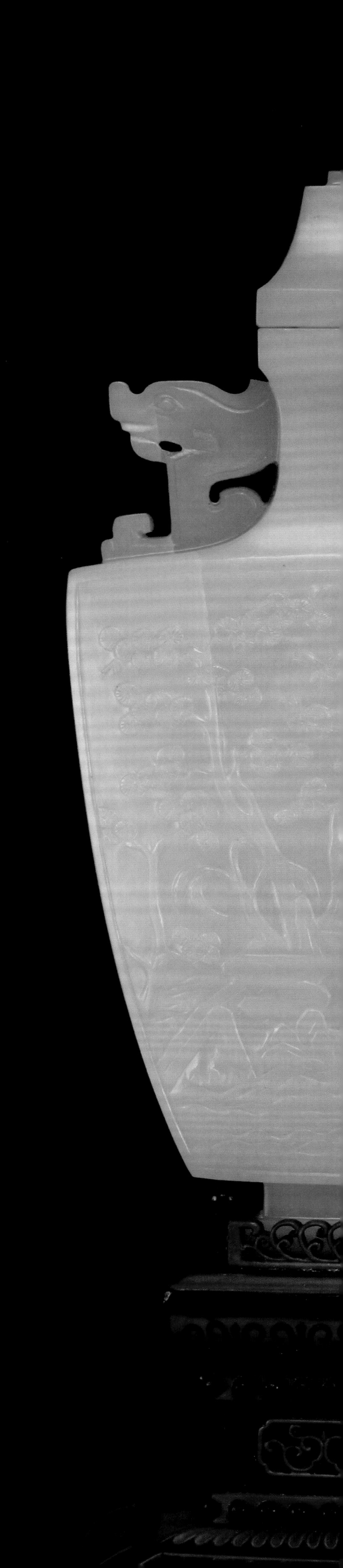

清 青白玉 龍鈕觥形瓶

寬9公分 高14.5公分

青白玉質，白中帶青，閃半透明光澤，整塊水產青白玉雕製，幾無雜質。仿古青銅彝器觥器式所設計的創新造型。器上有蓋，蓋面光素，蓋頂透雕一蟠龍為鈕，器身一側透雕幾何型變形龍作耳。另一側凸雕鳳紋，鳳首向外，身附於器腹，亦可視之為耳。口作斜橢圓形，呈不對稱式樣，底附扁長形圈足，造型設計十分新奇特殊。

Qing Dynasty
Grayish green with white jade dragon handle wine vessel-shaped vase

W/9cm, H/14.5cm

Grayish green with white jade—green and white jade, shiny with a semi-translucent luster, the piece is carved from one piece of homogenous river-gathered jade. It is modeled after ancient bronze ceremonial vessels, but with its own novel design. There is a smooth stopper with a carved dragon stem. The body is carved with geometrical shape-changing dragons as a handle. The other side has a protruding phoenix pattern attached to the body. It can also be seen as a handle. The mouth is slightly irregular, giving it an asymmetrical style, and there is an ellipsoid base at the bottom. The style is extremely clever and unique.

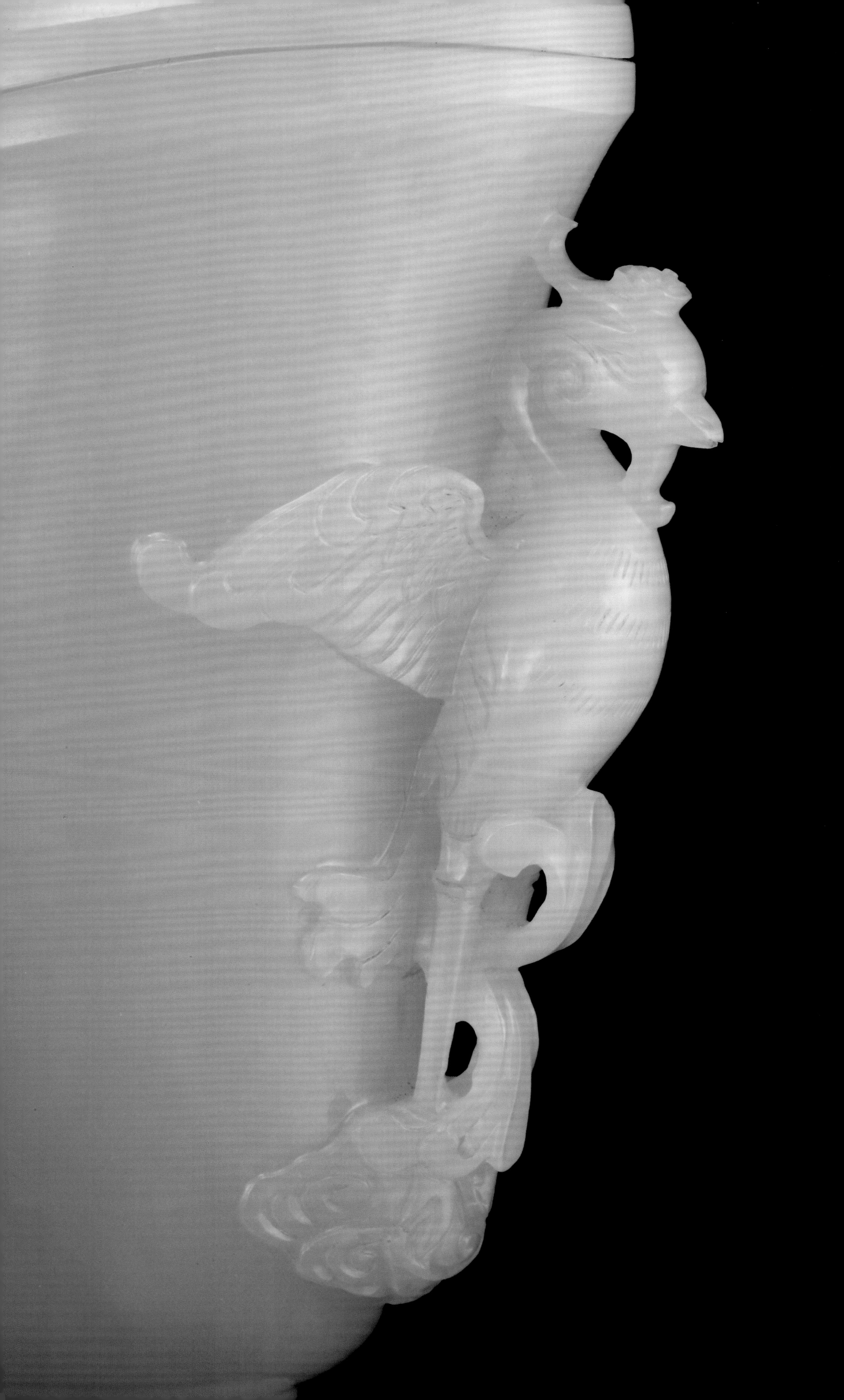

清　白玉　鳳耳瓶

寬10.8公分　高17.2公分

白玉質，閃蛋青色，質地純正。器作橢圓形扁瓶式樣。上有蓋，蓋頂附鏤雕花形鈕，器口作子母口，十分密合。頸短，兩側附鳳首銜活圓環耳，鳳首凸起，鳳身向器腹延伸，以浮雕方式細雕鳳張開羽翅，由兩側向瓶腹中央合攏，似由一對鳳鳥護守，瓶身造型端莊高雅，底足為台座式扁圓形，稍外撇。

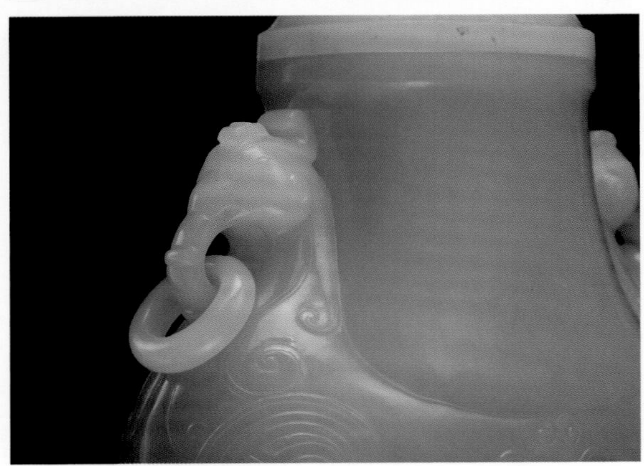

Qing Dynasty
Grayish white jade phoenix handle vase

W/10.8cm, H/17.2cm

Grayish white jade—this jade has a pure quality with a shining eggwhite greenish color. It is an ellipsoid flask style. There is a stopper on top with a carved flower-shaped stem and a very tight fit. The neck is short, and there are phoenix-shaped handles on both sides. The heads of the phoenixes protrude and their bodies extend from the body of the vase. Their wings open up in intricately carved relief and meet in the center of the vase's body as if it were being guarded by the phoenixes. The vase is elegant and dignified, and the base is like a round, slightly slanting platform.

清　青白玉　八角型觚

口徑13.2公分　高27公分

青白玉質，和闐良質青白玉雕製，質地十分純淨，仿古青銅器「觚」形器式，器展口呈八角形狀，頸部附以雙獸頭銜活圓環，器中段圓鼓凸出，亦作八面形，下略縮順八角器身而下，但向底部稍外撇，足內縮呈長扁形。器身保持光素，拋光極佳，器形端正高雅，為廳堂的擺件陳設器。

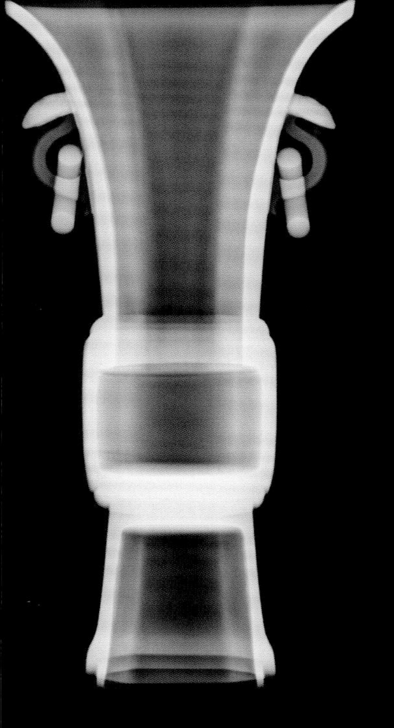

Qing Dynasty
Grayish white jade octagonal gu

Diam./13.2cm, H/27cm

Grayish white jade—carved from extremely pure Hetian white jade, modeled after an ancient bronze wine vessel. The opening has an octagonal shape, and the neck has the heads of two beasts encircling it. There is a protruding section in the middle of the object which also has an octagonal shape. The bottom is slightly smaller, with the same octagonal shape, but the base slants slightly outward, with a rectangular shape at the very bottom. The body of the object is still smooth with refined burnishing, and a dignified and elegant shape, making it a decoration to be displayed in the hall.

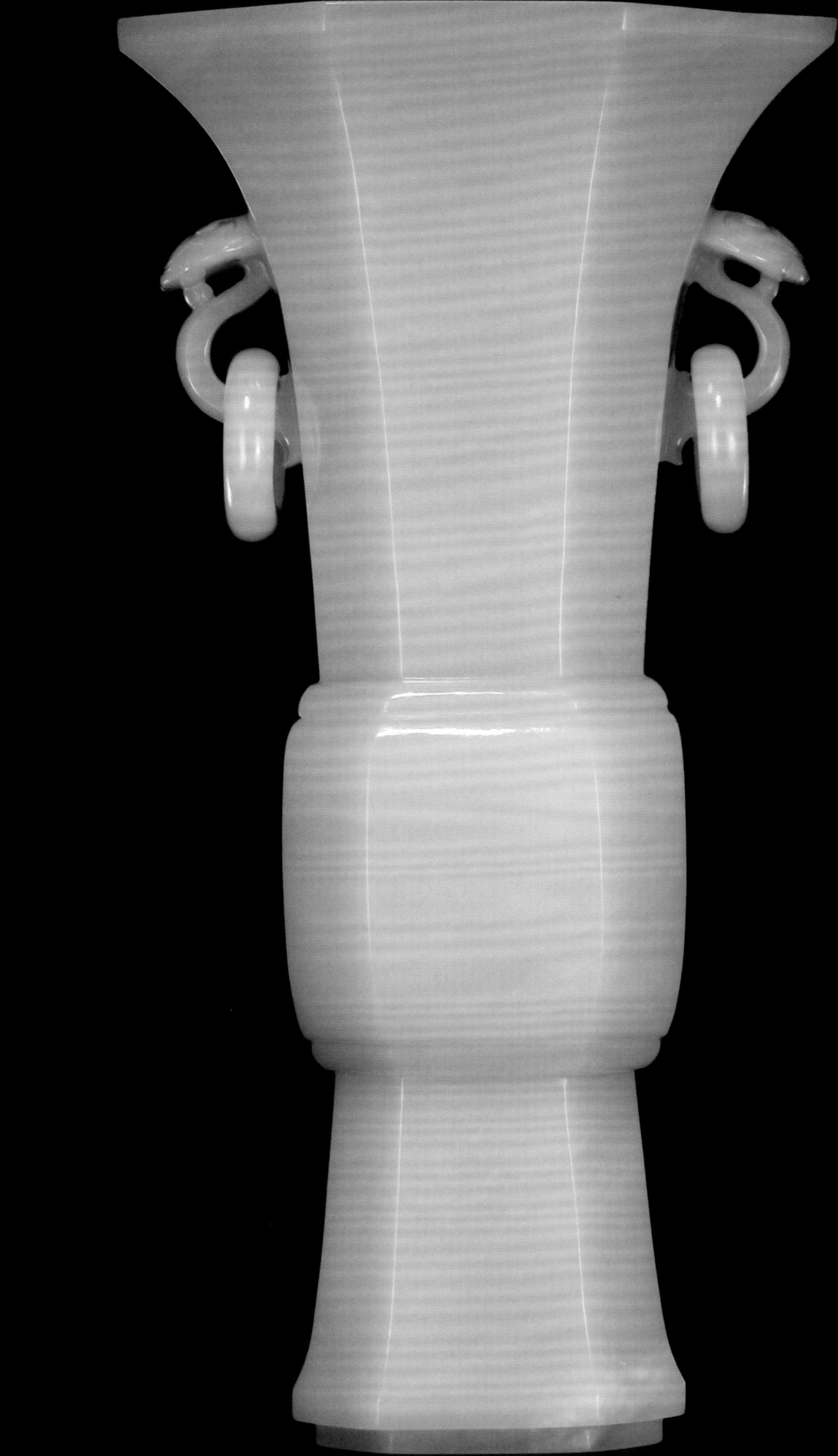

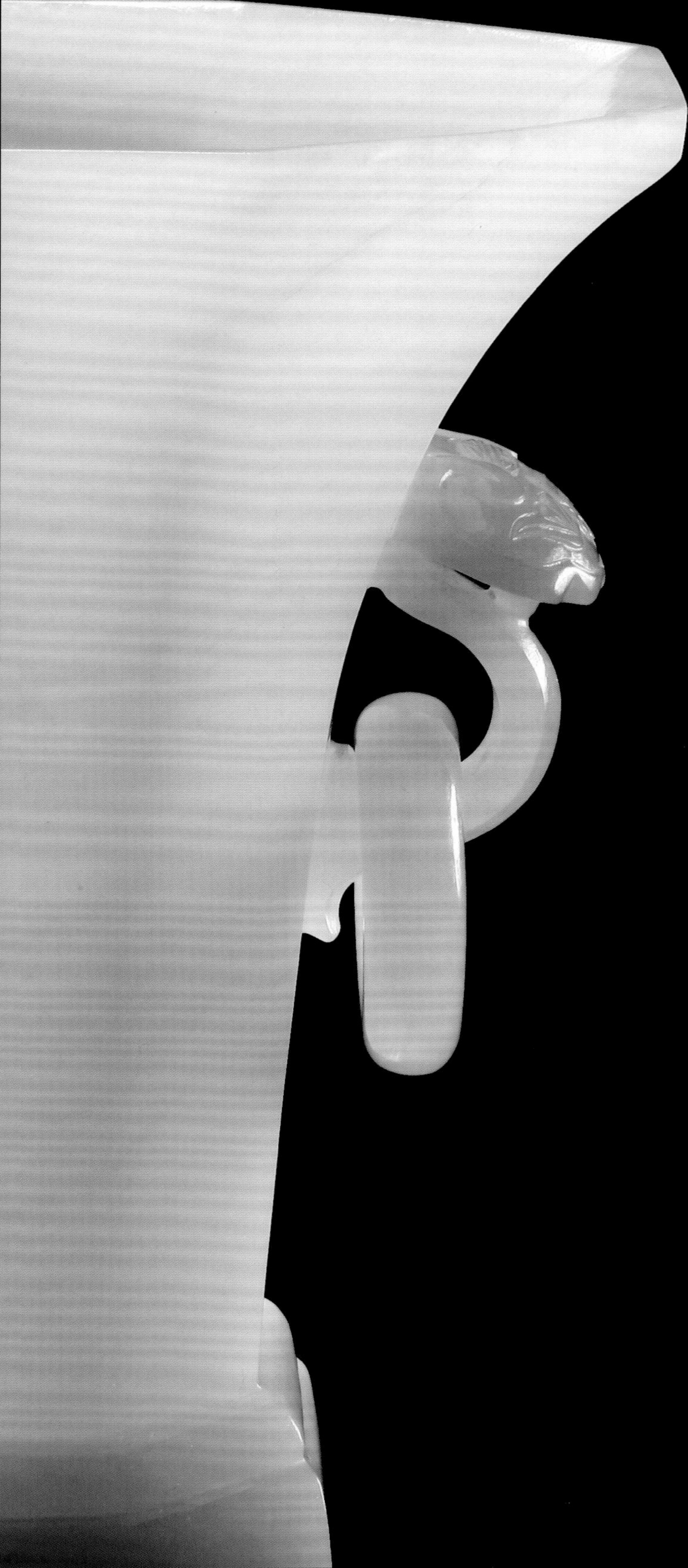

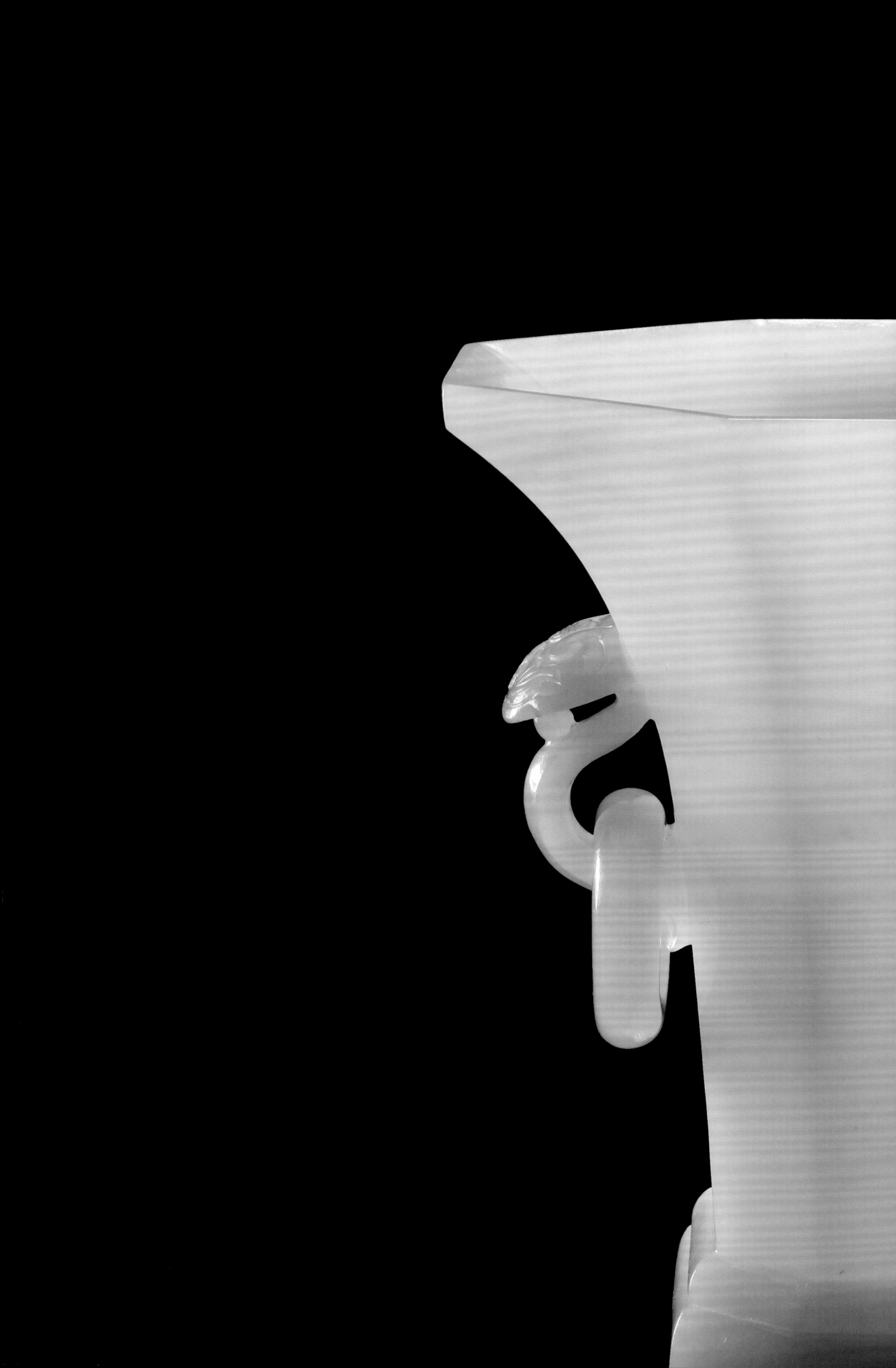

清 碧玉 夔龍紋簋形爐

寬19公分 高11公分

碧玉質，間雜黑斑點，質地純正。器仿古青銅器「簋」的形制雕刻而成。圓形簋有蓋，蓋中央附透雕花型鈕，形狀十分優美，器附銜耳活環，耳上作如意雲頭形，器底高圈足。器面佈滿夔龍及雲紋與古青銅器十分相似。

Qing Dynasty
Dark green jade dragon and one-footed dragon pattern grain vessel-shaped burner

W/19cm, H/11cm

Dark green jade—pure jade with scattered black spots. Its style is modeled after ancient bronze grain vessels. The rounded vessel has a lid with a flowered stem in the center. The shape is extremely beautiful. The vessel has two handles carved with good fortune cloud patterns. On the bottom, there is a high rounded base. The surface of the vessel is carved with dragon and one-footed dragon patterns, and cloud patterns, making it very similar to ancient bronze.

清　青白玉　吉慶福壽洗

寬29.5公分　高10.5公分

青白玉質，色呈蛋青色調，溫潤呈半透明。器圓形，口稍內斂，雙耳以透雕蝙蝠，方勝、磬等吉祥紋飾組成，下附銜活圓環耳，象徵「吉慶福壽」寓意，器下附有四足，腹底中央雕靈芝、蘭草、竹子等吉祥植物紋，器內中央浮雕有蟠桃枝葉，寓意長壽祝賀之意。

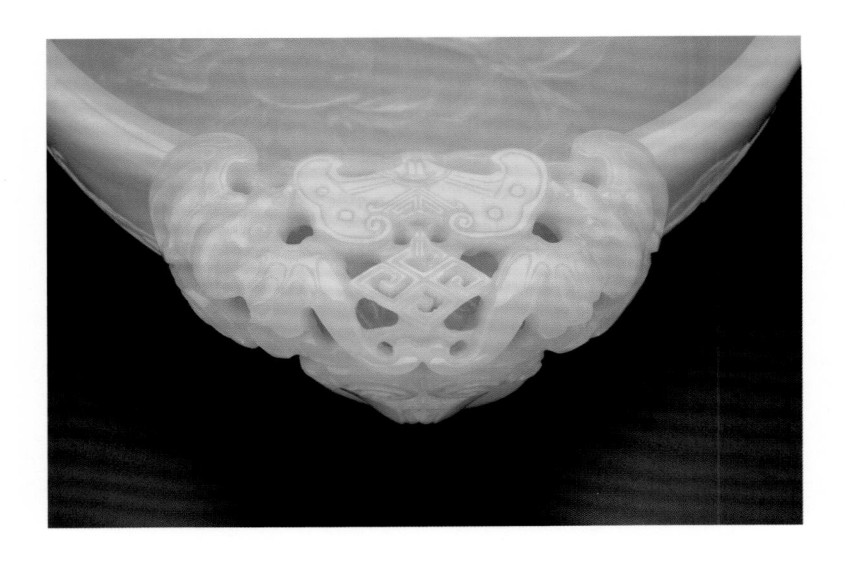

Qing Dynasty
Grayish green with white jade good fortune and longevity wash basin

W/29.5cm, H/10.5cm

Grayish green with white jade—an egg white greenish color, smooth and semi-translucent. It is round with a mouth that curves inward slightly. The handles are carved into bats, forming auspicious patterns. There are ringed handles below this, symbolizing good luck. On the bottom of the object there are four feet, and there are carvings of medicinal herbs and auspicious plants carved on the body. In the center of the interior of the vessel, immortality peach branches are carved in relief, symbolizing longevity.

Qing Dynasty
White jade phoenix handle jar with stopper

W/9cm, H/13cm, ?/7.6cm

Suet white jade—formed from one piece of seed jade, it has some yellow marks with excellent burnishing that shows off the natural luster of the jade. It is formed into the shape of a small jar, with beautiful curves. Because the quality of the jade is extremely fine, the surface is smooth and unadorned in order to keep the jade's natural luster. It has a round stopper carved into the shape of a bird of paradise. Its pose is peaceful and elegant. It is an amazingly beautiful design to substitute a stopper with a bird of paradise.

白玉質，留黃色玉皮，拋光絕佳，顯現自然溫潤光澤，乃籽玉整塊所製成，器作圓肩小腹罐狀，弧度優美，因玉質十分良好，器面光素不雕圖樣，以保存玉面自然光澤，上附圓頂形蓋，蓋中央刻一靜佇立於上的鳳鳥，姿態安祥優美，以鳳鳥取代蓋鈕，設計精絕，令人讚嘆！

清 黃玉 玉碗

徑9.6公分 高5.6公分

黃玉質，呈栗子黃色，上呈局部褐色斑，似為皮色所形成。器作圓形直口碗形，深弧腹壁高圈足外撇，器面光素無紋，拋光極佳，流露玉質自然光澤，黃玉呈色似熟栗的正黃色，雖不加任何紋飾，仍然十分精美。

Qing Dynasty
Yellow jade bowl

Diam./9.6cm, H/5.6cm, D/5cm

Yellow jade—with a chestnut yellow color, with a portion that has brown spots, almost skin color. The object is a round bowl shape, and has a base that slants outward. The surface is smooth and flawless, with excellent burnishing, giving it the natural luster of jade. Though it has no ornamentation, it is extremely beautiful, with its chestnut yellow color.

清　黃玉　龍鳳如意

長37公分

黃玉質，部分留玉皮，作為器面變化的「俏色」，器作如意雲頭狀，雲頭部分凸刻鳳鳥，器柄呈彎曲弧形，器面刻大小龍紋二。清代文人雅士或王公貴族之間，常以「如意」做為彼此餽贈禮品，以表「祝福」、「恭賀」之意，特別是壽辰、婚嫁的賀禮，十分風行。

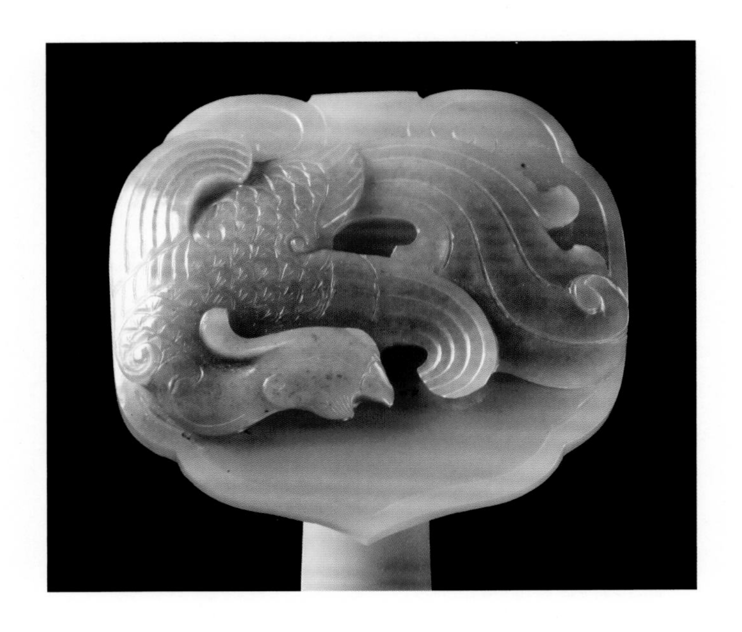

Qing Dynasty
Yellow jade dragon and phoenix good luck ornament

L/37cm

Yellow jade—with jade skin on a portion, the changes on the surface are the natural color of the jade. The piece is a good luck ornament with a cloud shape. The cloud part is carved with a protruding bird of paradise. The handle is curved and ellipsoid, and there are two dragons carved on it, one large and one small. In the Qing Dynasty, lettered gentlemen or royalty often made this ornament as gifts for one another, to wish good luck or offer congratulations, on the occasion of a birthday or a wedding, for example. This custom was very widespread.

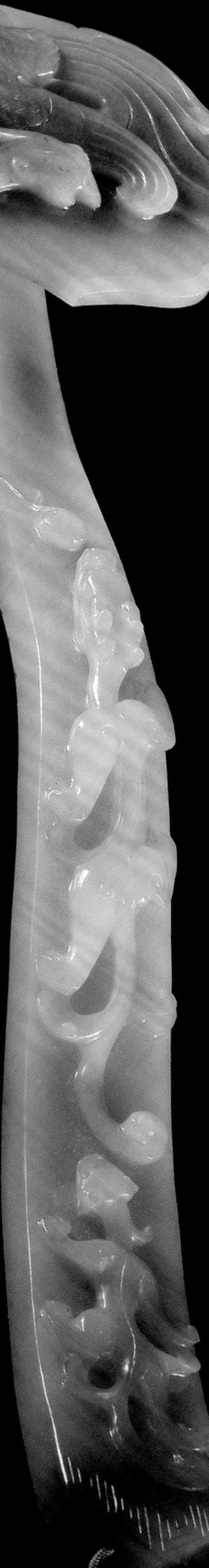

清　青玉　淨瓶觀音

寬10.5公分　高17.5公分

青玉質，青玉稍帶灰，呈灰青色調。像作趺坐狀，右手持淨瓶，左手持念珠，頭上披髮巾自然下垂披於背後，袈裟合度條自然流暢，雕刻技法卓越。法像雙眼向下俯視，嘴角略帶一抹微笑，顯現慈祥神情。頭上髮髻用陰線雕刻，絲絲入扣，雕座為象牙雕刻，雲龍波濤組合成座，相當精美。

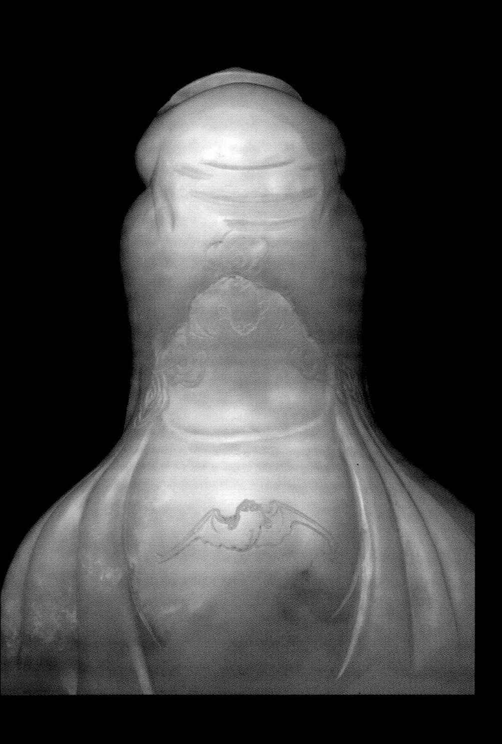

Qing Dynasty
Grayish green jade
Guanyin with Vase of Purity

W/14.5cm, H/21cm

Grayish green jade—this grayish green jade is more gray than green. It is a seated statue that holds the vase of purity in the right hand and chanting beads in the left hand. There is a scarf on the head that falls naturally down the back. The folds of the robe seem to flow naturally, and the carving work is outstanding. The eyes of this Buddhist statue are gazing downward, and the lips are formed into a slight smile in a compassionate expression. The hair bun lines are carved in intaglio with the highest degree of skillfulness. The base is carved from ivory with dragon and wave patterns.

清　翠玉　文殊菩薩像

寬14.5公分　高21公分

乾隆時期開始大量使用緬甸及雲南地區所產翠玉，工匠流行用翠玉的鮮豔「巧色」，雕製玉器。此器乃整塊翠玉雕製而成，文殊菩薩盤腿坐於獅座上，頭上髮髻稍呈現黃色，髮絲刻工細膩，髻正中為花形飾，雕工細如毫毛。身上法衣紗薄合身而自然下垂。法相慈祥優美，雙眼俯視，似觀眾生，手持淨瓶，端坐於獅座之上。翠玉鮮綠，顯現美好翠綠光澤，更顯現法相高貴、慈悲。

Qing Dynasty
Jade Manjusri Bodhisattva

W/10.5cm, H/17.5cm

A large amount of blue jade from Burma and Yunnan started to be used in the time of Qianlong, and the popular carving style was to make objects that made use of the jade's bright color. This piece was carved from a single piece of blue jade into a Manjusri Bodhisattva statue seated in lotus position on a lion throne. The hair on the head is slightly yellow, and the strands of hair are meticulously carved. There is a finely carved flower-shaped decoration in the very center of the hair bun. The Buddhist robes are well-fitting and the folds naturally flow. The beautiful expression is one of compassion, and the eyes look downward as if observing the people of the world. The statue is holding a vase of purity and sits on a lion throne. The blue jade is a shining green that reveals the natural luster of blue jade, making the statue seem all the more lofty and compassionate.

清　黃玉　花形扁盒

長7.5公分　寬5.5公分　高3.5公分

黃玉製作，部份留皮，形成褐黃色。器作花形蓋盒，整塊黃玉一切為二，上作器蓋，下作盒子，上下以子母蓋密合，形成花朵形狀，器蓋做平面有沿花朵形，整體設計一體成形。器面拋光十分講究，不再雕刻圖案，使玉器因為光素，流露玉質自然光澤。盒可作珠寶或粉盒，即古代所稱「玉奩」，是實用與觀賞兼具的佳作。

Qing Dynasty
Yellow jade flower-shaped flat box

L/7.5cm, W/5.5cm, H/3.5cm

Yellow jade—this jade has a brownish yellow color and a portion of it has jade skin. The vessel is shaped from one piece of yellow jade into a two-piece flower-shaped box with a a tight-fitting lid on top. The burnishing on the surface is very thorough, and no other patterns are carved into it. This allows the jade vessel to show its natural luster. The box can be used to hold jewels or cosmetics, and in ancient times it was called a, "jade cosmetics case," with both ornamental and practical functions.

清　黃玉　水盂

徑4.1公分　高1.7公分

黃玉染色，製成俏作玉，使器面更富於變化。器作唇口，圓扁小罐狀，聳肩，扁矮直腹，器面光素，抛光絕佳，器面保持玉質自然光采，染色與原有玉皮溶合自然，具古色古香情趣，乃文人雅士文房擺件，兼實用的玉作擺件。

Qing Dynasty
Grayish yellow jade tea basin

Diam./4.1cm, H/1.7cm

Grayish yellow seed jade with dyed color, making it multi-colored jade and lending the surface more variety. The flat, round jar-shape has a mouth with a rim and wide walls. The body is short and flat, and the surface is smooth and shiny, with excellent burnishing, which reveals the natural brilliance of the jade. The dye color blends naturally with the jade skin color. It has a fantastic ancient feel, and it is a beautiful object that can be used simply as an ornament or for its practical purpose by gentlemen of letters.

清　仿宋白玉珮

長4.7公分　寬3.7公分　深1.5公分

白玉籽玉整件作卵圓形，雕製時僅薄薄去除一層玉皮，部份留存拋光，器一面鏤刻荷花水鷺、山石等水塘圖案，寓意「一路連發」或「一路登科」的吉祥諧音，鏤刻工藝流暢自然，玉器背面玉皮的光澤互相陪襯，如一幅美麗的池塘風光，乃文人隨身佩帶的飾品。玉皮自然呈現點點黃褐色調，如灑金手法，故有「灑金」之稱，此玉珮工藝流行於宋、金時期，從雕工觀之，非早期手法，可能乃清代仿宋作品。

Qing Dynasty
White jade pendant modeled after the Song style

L/4.7cm, W/3.7cm, D/1.5cm

This is white jade carved from a whole piece of seed jade into an ovoid shape. A thin layer of jade skin was removed at the time of carving, and the portion that remained was burnished. A pond scene of lotuses, egrets, and stones is carved into one side, symbolizing good fortune. The carving work is free-flowing. It is matched with the burnished jade skin on the back, making it a lovely pond scene that the literati would wear as a decoration. The jade skin naturally displays yellow and brown spots, which is why it is called "sprinkles of gold". This jade pendant artisanship was popular in the Song and Jin Dynasties. It can be seen from the carving work that it is probably a Qing Dynasty copy of Song styles.

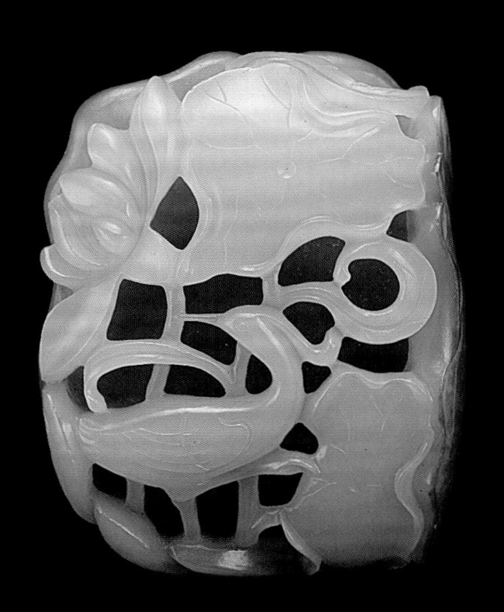

戰國 青玉 龍形珮

長7.3公分

青玉質，器因入土泌成灰褐色，背後局部微露青玉本色。器作S形龍式樣，龍尾向上反勾，龍首向前伏臥。龍張口，下巴作圓弧狀，長鼻向上捲，目為橢圓形梭子眼，耳小作捲雲狀，爪作勾雲狀。器面佈滿圓形卷雲，器身圓弧的中央，穿一圓孔，可以穿組，此佩可單件繫掛，亦可作為組佩組件，是戰國常見裝飾玉。

Warring States Period
Grayish green jade
Dragon-shaped pendant

L/7.3cm

Grayish green jade—this object has turned a grayish brown color because it was buried in the ground. A portion on the back still has its original grayish green color. It is made into an "S"-shaped dragon form, in which the dragon's tail curves upward and the head curves back in a reclining position. The dragon's mouth is open, and its chin has a rounded arc shape, while its nose curls upward. It has an ellipsoid shuttle-eye, its ear is small and curls into a cloud shape, and its claws are made into a hooked cloud shape. The surface is full of rounded curling clouds, and there is a hole right in the center. This pendant could be adorned individually or it could be used as part of a set. It is a commonly found decorative jade piece from the Warring States Period.

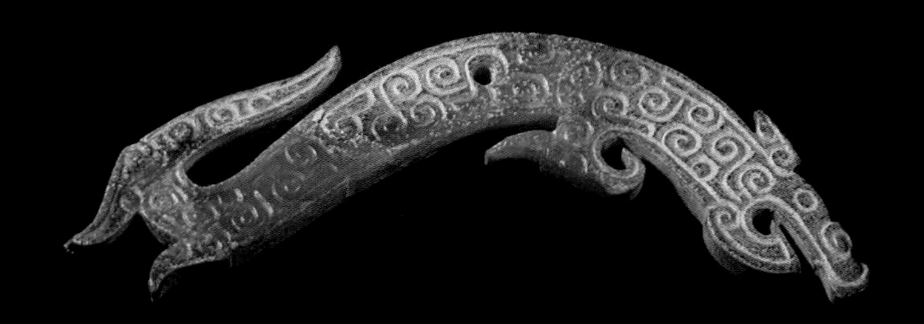

西周　青玉　龍紋勒

寬2.2公分　高3公分　深1.7公分

青玉質，部份受沁變成褐黃色，質地頗佳。器作扁長管狀，上窄下寬，中有圓形穿孔，可穿組，為佩飾或組佩中的組件。器面以複線陰紋，刻出雲龍紋飾，自器上方向下方斜滾而下，線條蜿蜒，自然蟠轉，技法精妙。

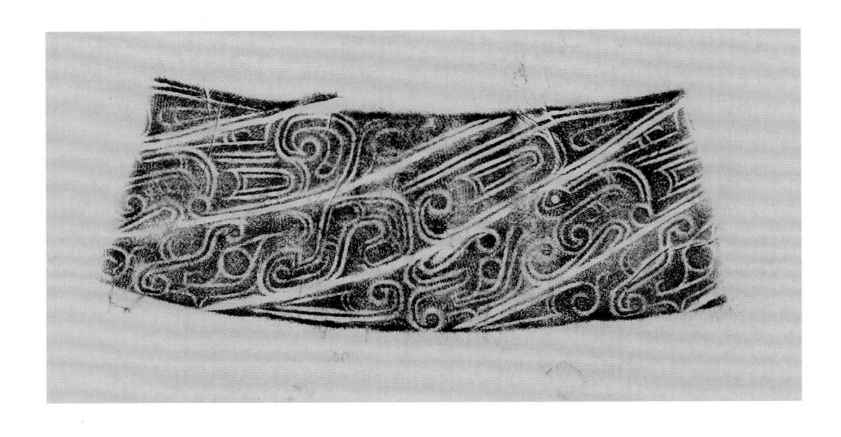

Western Zhou Dynasty
Grayish green jade dragon pattern clip

L/2.2cm, W/3cm, D/1.7cm

Grayish green jade—this jade is of very high quality, and a portion has been changed to a brownish-yellow color. The item is made into a long flat tube shape with a narrow top and wide bottom and a circular hole through the middle. It is a decoration or part of a decoration set. The surface is carved with repeating lines into a cloud and dragon pattern that rolls from the top to the bottom. The curvy lines are extremely fine, displaying consummate carving skill.

明 白玉 髮冠

寬11.6公分 高4.9公分

白玉質，呈半透明，局部可見微黃色沁。器呈花瓣微舒張狀，共四花瓣，向上合於中央花蕊，成為冠頭頂飾。髮冠以玉雕製，最早見於一九七一年江蘇省吳縣所出土的宋墓。此冠似仿宋器所雕製，但比較短小。髮冠由兩側穿一圓孔，用帶有蘑菇形頂飾的長髮簪穿過，簪頭部份稍有曲弧連接頂飾，可用於固髮使用。

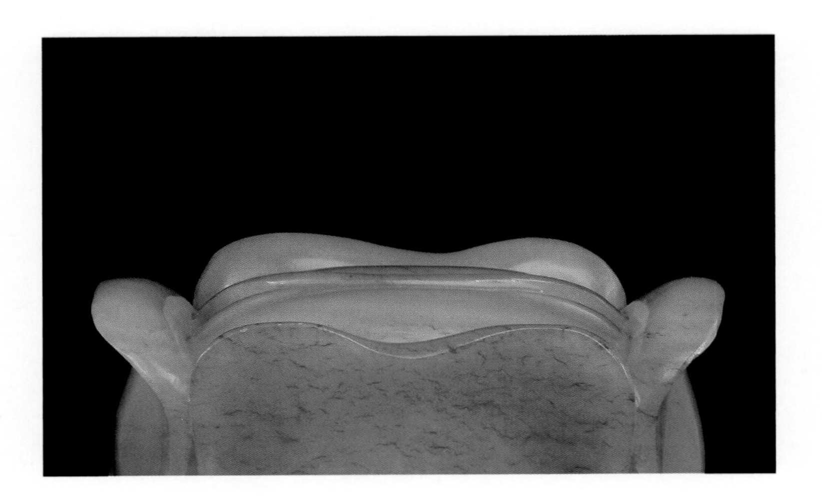

Ming Dynasty
White jade hairpin

W/11.6cm, H/4.9cm

White jade—semi-translucent with yellow color seeping through on a portion. The item is shaped like four flower petals that are slightly open with a pistil in the center. It is an accessory to be worn on the crown of the head. Jade hairpins were first unearthed from Song Dynasty tombs in Wuxian, Jiangsu Province in 1971. This one is a copy of Song Dynasty styles, but it is shorter. There is a round hole through both sides of the hairpin, with a mushroom shaped pin.

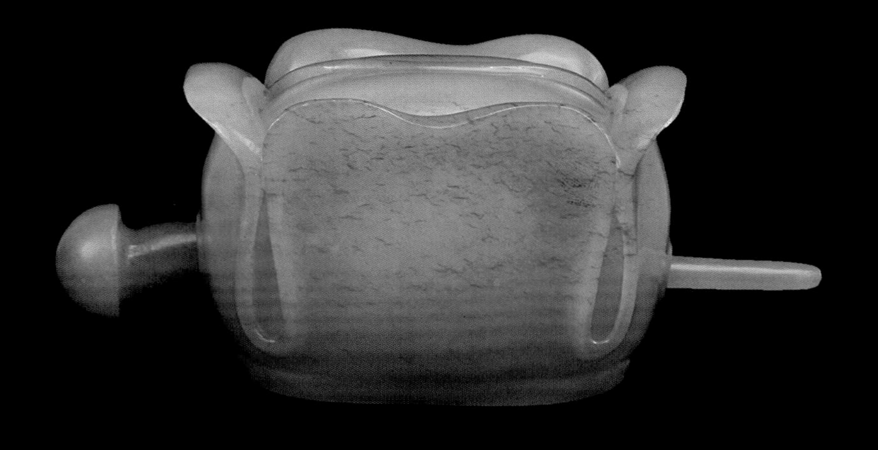

玉犧

長9.8公分　寬2.8公分　高5.2公分

和闐白玉籽料質地，全器呈灑金帶紅皮沁色。犧尊，古時祭祀用之水酒器，器形始見於殷商時期，其酒器常以大型動物作為造型，犧獸則為其中之一，周禮六尊：犧尊、象尊、箸尊、壺尊、太尊、山尊，以待祭祀賓客之禮。此犧形獸，為摹古犧尊形器，器形身軀渾圓，四肢及蹄足粗短，似銅爐鼎之足，周身軀體依勢裝飾華麗花紋，主要紋飾為勾連雲紋、夔形雲紋、雙線紋等，紋飾琢刻較淺而拋光趨於圓潤，是一件仿古器之佳作。

Jade sacrificial beast

L/9.8cm, W/2.8cm, H/5.2cm

Hetian white jade seed material. The entire piece displays sprinkled gold with a red skin soak-induced color. Wine vessels were shaped as animals such as the sacrificial beast as far back as the Yin-Shang times. It was one of the six vessels in the, "Rites of Zhou," used for the rituals involved in showing hospitality to guests who came to worship. This sacrificial beast is modeled after an ancient wine vessel. The body is full and round, and the four legs are thick and short like the feet of a bronze vessel. The body is rich in decorative patterns, mainly the interlocking cloud pattern, the transforming cloud pattern, and the double line pattern. The patterns are carved rather shallow, and the polishing is mostly smooth. The carving technique is unsophisticated, with simple lines, making it a gorgeous piece that is a copy of ancient artwork.

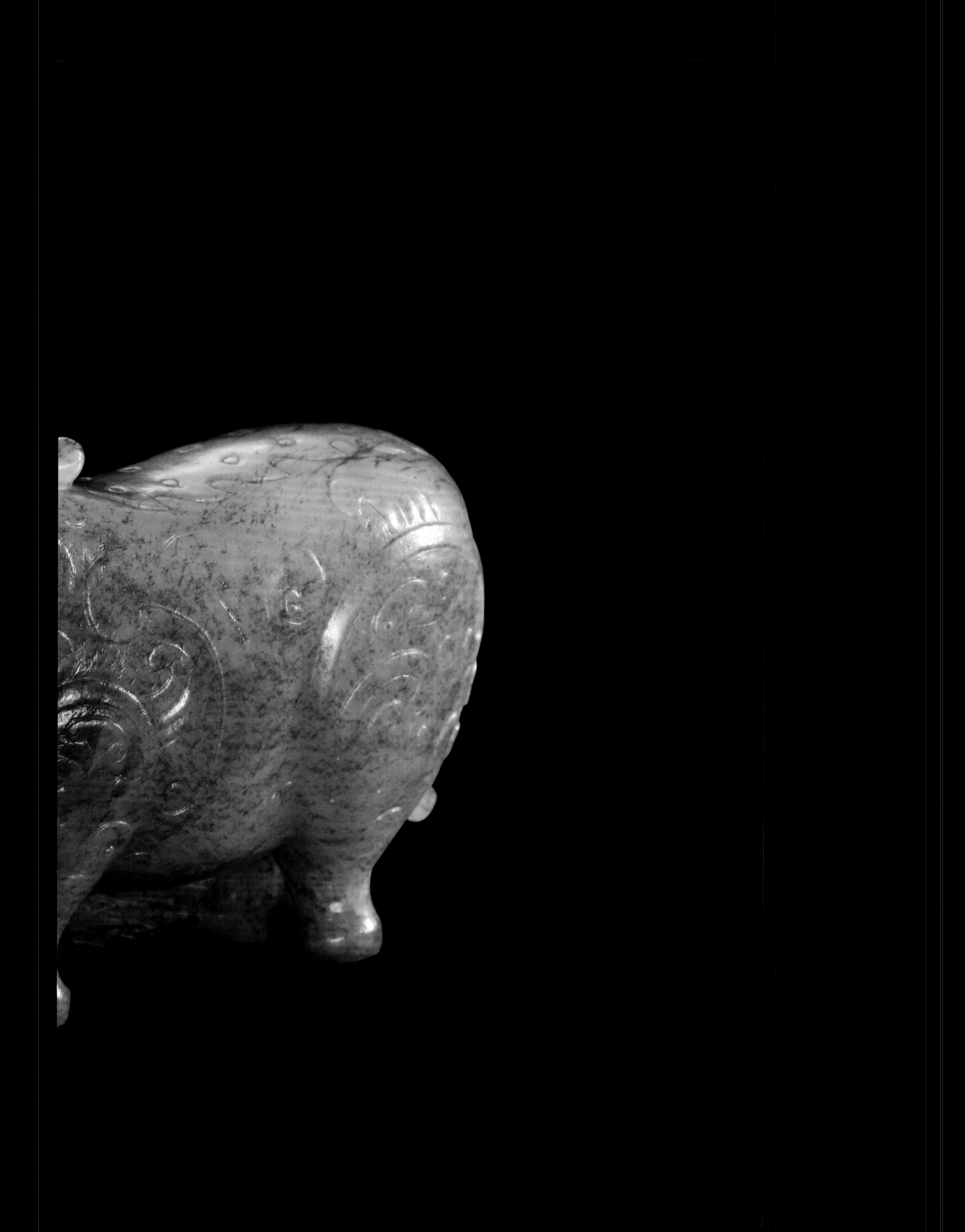

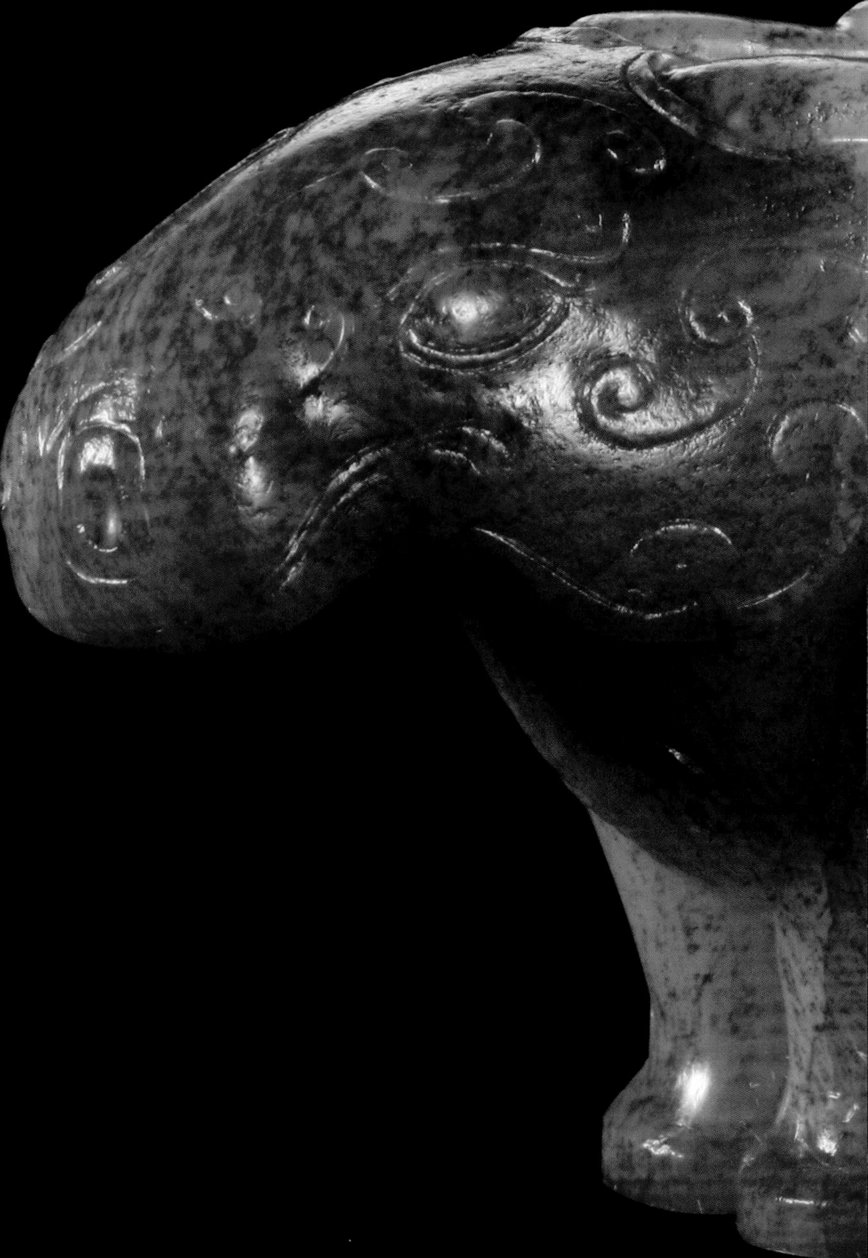

宋玉大觀

宋代玉器研究，歷來都是古代玉器鑑定門類之中的難題，畢竟玉器的傳承與發展，絕不是用「改朝換代」所可比擬的。現在博物館所典藏，以及更多民間傳世的風格相似的老舊玉器，今日仍然難以完全準確地斷定它就是唐代、宋代還是元代的時作玉器，有時甚至將明代早期的精工玉器，都被認定或歸類為具有宋代風格的玉器，而加以珍藏。

同理，保守一點的學者專家，甚至會將某一類形制、紋飾與質變沁色不甚明確的唐宋玉器，直接下修斷定為明代或清代仿古玉器。筆者認為，這對於玉器真品來說是沒有太多實質上影響，或價值上的減損的。我們依然暫且將此類玉器，按照傳統鑒玉方法將其主觀地稱為「宋玉風格」；而比較重要的是，一定要將此類宋玉與明朝中晚期以後製作的仿古玉器，較明確的區分開來，畢竟宋代時作玉器，時至今日依然是十分珍貴與數量稀少，而逐漸鮮明的時代風格與精神特徵，也將會是鑑定宋玉的主要依據所在。

談及古玉的鑒賞與研究，尤其宋代以降的研究，在過去常依附於于金石學之下為多，而所謂的科學性的考古發掘，只有在二十世紀末與本世紀初的近二十餘年，才有較成熟的進展與相對的研究規模。又清代以前，對於宋元以下的傳世玉器，便因年代不甚久遠，或不易辨識為由，因而被忽視了，前輩鑒賞家因其遠離禮器，全歸玩物而不多理睬。現代又因發掘出土的標準玉器少，而難以依此方式從大量的傳世古舊玉器中排比區分出來，雖有以上種種的不利因素，但這並不等於可以忽視宋玉。

雖然過去的鑒賞家僅能依據玉質沁色、玉器形制、紋飾等的明確風格，大致將古玉分為周玉、漢玉和宋玉，並且尤其重視周玉和漢玉的研究，這一方面是由於漢代以前古人高度的工藝技術與精神氣力，確實到達了令世人驚奇的程度所致。

但玉器在每一個朝代，一經琢冶成器即受珍視與珍藏，自隋、唐以後，更由於外來文化因素的影響，玉器在其他工藝的競爭與不利發展的因素之下，不斷的削弱，所以古玉至此早已是非常有價值的文物了。宋代玉器的鑑定與蒐藏，更為近來古玉器門類中特別珍稀之物。

大家知道，我國中世紀（約當是唐宋元明時期）的文明極為輝煌燦爛，比如宋畫和宋瓷（官窯為主）以高度的思想性、藝術性和鮮明的民族性，舉世公認為我國及東方美術的代表，人類美術史上的瑰寶。表現在玉雕藝術品的風格上，自然也有這樣的傾向與變化，就連乾隆皇帝也曾認識到「刻玉為圖斯鼻祖」的讚譽，足見宋代玉器的特殊與精神魅力所在。玉器等工藝美術品亦是以繪畫為基礎，而且服務對象的等級與官階更高，因此必然也有著同樣的時代風格、品評與位階，也應該有相對應的價值與定位，只是時至今日，仍未受當代人士所了解與正視而已。

總歸來說，對傳統古玉真偽的辨別，除了看玉質選材用料之外，主要還是要回歸到玉器藝術的本質，如琢刻工藝、成形工具、工法工序、形制紋飾、盤摩潤色等藝術呈現，以及自然的風化、老化條件與質變程度來加以客觀判斷。

但問題是如何在成千上萬的傳世古舊玉器中，將宋代玉器鑒別出來？目前可依循其形制、紋飾與題材上幾個時代特徵，由幾何變形的圖案轉為注重寫實、強調寫生的神似形象；內容由神怪、異獸為主的題材，轉變為以山水、花鳥、走獸的物我和諧，與自然寫實的風尚等方面去推敲。由於宋代玉器已經逐漸褪去體制與禮制的包袱，走進尋常百姓家，亦是由上層社會所主導與承襲的功業榮華思想，轉向為融入世俗生活的新思維，追求清雅、安逸、自然、優美、復古的人文本質與精神格調。所以，宋代玉器注重表現物件的內心世界，能準確進行細部刻劃，細膩精練、真實自然，故以「形神兼備，品文論質」概括為這一時期玉器的特點，應是比較正確與適切的詮釋。

國立歷史博物館研究人員
郭祐麟

already become a very valuable artifact. In the appraisal and collection of jade, of al
the ancient jades, Song Dynasty jade art is an especially rare item. Everyone know
hat China's civilization in the Middle Ages (during the Tang, Song, Yuan, and Min
Dynasties) was glorious and brilliant. The high level of philosophical quality, artisti
quality, and distinctive Chinese quality of Song Dynasty paintings and Song Dynast
porcelain (mainly Guan kiln), for example, earn them praise as being emblematic o
Chinese and Oriental art. The peak of humanity's art is naturally seen in the trend
and changes in the style of the art of jade carving. Emperor Qianlong's high praise o
ade carvings is enough to prove the special and spiritual charm of Song Dynasty jade
The foundation of arts such as jade carving is the art of painting, but the status or ran
of its patrons was higher, and it similarly had to express style, taste, and status in
manner appropriate for the era. It also had to enjoy a corresponding value and positio
n comparison with those enjoyed by the other arts. It's just that it still has not bee
properly understood and valued by the world to this day.

n summary, the identification of authentic, traditional ancient jade, aside from th
material used to make it, mainly still comes down to the artistic quality of the jad
artwork, such as the carving technique, tools, procedures, style and ornamentation, an
the feel and luster. Natural weathering and aging conditions and degree of qualitativ
change help in the exercise of objective judgment. The problem, however, is how t
determine which ones of the tens of millions of ancient jade artworks are from th
Song Dynasty. Currently, assessments can be based on a few trademarks of the age
such as form, patterns, and subject. During that time, geometric patterns changed int
an emphasis on realism and lifelike images. The contents changed from supernatura
figures and beasts to landscapes, flowers and birds, and harmony with nature, as th
style tended toward realism. Since Song Dynasty jade had already gradually bee
freed from the requirements of government and ceremony and become closer to th
ommon people, it changed from being oriented toward the upper classes and pursuin
he thinking of inherited honors and wealth into a new thread of thought that mainl
ncluded aspects of the lives of ordinary people. It pursued the nature and style o
the literati, which was represented by elegance, ease, nature, beauty, and a revival o
ancient ways. Song Dynasty jade therefore stressed the expression of the inner world o
the object and accurate expression by means of detailed carving, refined craftsmanship
and natural characteristics. That's why the phrase, "both form and spirit," covers th
special characteristics of jade art from that age. This should be a more correct and

The Magnificence of Song Dynasty Style Jade

In the study of Song Dynasty jade, there still exists the age-old difficulty of identifying categories of ancient jade, since the transmission and development of jade art cannot be simply and cleanly divided into different dynasties at a glance. Currently, it is still difficult to determine completely and accurately whether old jade pieces collected by the museum, and similar pieces passed down within the public sphere, were made during the Tang Dynasty, the Song Dynasty, or the Yuan Dynasty. Sometimes fine jade pieces that were made in the early Ming Dynasty are even determined to be jade pieces with the Song Dynasty style, and are therefore collected as treasures. Using the same principle, some more conservative experts will pronounce Tang and Song jade that is unclear in style, pattern, and soak-induced color to be copies from the Ming Dynasty or the Qing Dynasty. I am of the opinion that this does not have too much of an effect on the essence or detract from the value of authentic jade pieces. For the time being, we still subjectively call this type of jade, "Song Dynasty jade style," in accordance with the traditional jade appraisal method. Also, what is more important, is that clear distinctions must be made between this type of Song Dynasty jade and copies of ancient jade made after the mid to late Ming Dynasty. After all, jade made in the Song Dynasty is now extremely precious and rare, and that era's style and the special marks of its spirit, which are gradually becoming clearer, will be the major basis on which to evaluate Song Dynasty jade.

The evaluation and study of ancient jade, was usually regarded as an aspect of epigraphy in the past, especially after the Song Dynasty. Scientific archeological excavations have only achieved a rather more mature state of development and corresponding research scale in the past 20 years, at the end of the 20th century and the beginning of the 21st. Also, Qing Dynasty scholarship ignored the history of jade after the Song and Yuan Dynasties, either because the age was not all that great or because it was not easy to identify. Appraisers of previous generations paid less attention to ceremonial objects because they preferred to appreciate literati study curios. In modern times, because less jade of a certain standard has been unearthed, it has been difficult to make comparisons and distinctions for a large amount of jade treasures using this method. These various difficulties, however, do not mean that we can ignore Song Dynasty jade. Although appraisers of the past were able to generally differentiate ancient jade as Zhou Dynasty jade, Han Dynasty jade, and Song Dynasty jade on the basis of the clear styles of soak-induced color, style, and patterns, they placed special importance on the study of Zhou Dynasty jade and Han Dynasty jade. This is because the high level of artisanship and spirituality of the ancient people in the Han Dynasty and earlier consistently reached standards that are amazing to this day.

Carved jade, however, was treasured and collected during each dynasty. After the Sui Dynasty and the Tang Dynasty, because of the influence of cultural elements from abroad, and also because of competition from other arts and other factors that did not benefit its development, jade art declined constantly. By that time, therefore, jade had

駝形獸

長4.3公分　寬3公分　高5.2公分

和闐白玉帶糖色玉質，局部保留玉皮沁色。作品為玉工遷就玉料設計而成的造型，依勢自然曲俯形成一團臥狀瑞獸，獸作低側首曲頸俯臥狀，瑞獸特別注重筋骨與肌肉的寫實與張力表現，長尾則夾藏於四肢腹部間。此獸首造型似駝，身軀似獸，俗稱「駝龍」，此種姿態自唐代始有（可能是唐代與西方的經貿與文化交流有關），過渡到宋代，則展現得更為圓潤與成熟。此件駝形獸，軀體壯碩，筋肉矯健，狀若蓄勢待發的神情，又從骨架四肢及鬍鬚、尾鬚等部位的生動刻畫與自然的曲線得知，比之前朝的凶猛獸性與神格化形象表現，漸漸轉變為把玩及視覺情趣，更為貼近世俗化的觀賞角度。由於入土與傳世年代皆已久遠，全器風化紋、生坑質變、老化紋及特徵，凹陷沁入肌理現象明顯，表面遍沁黃褐色斑紋，加上沁色分布、風化位置與磨損層次自然，是一件玉質與沁色、造型與工藝皆潤美的辟邪獸雕精品。

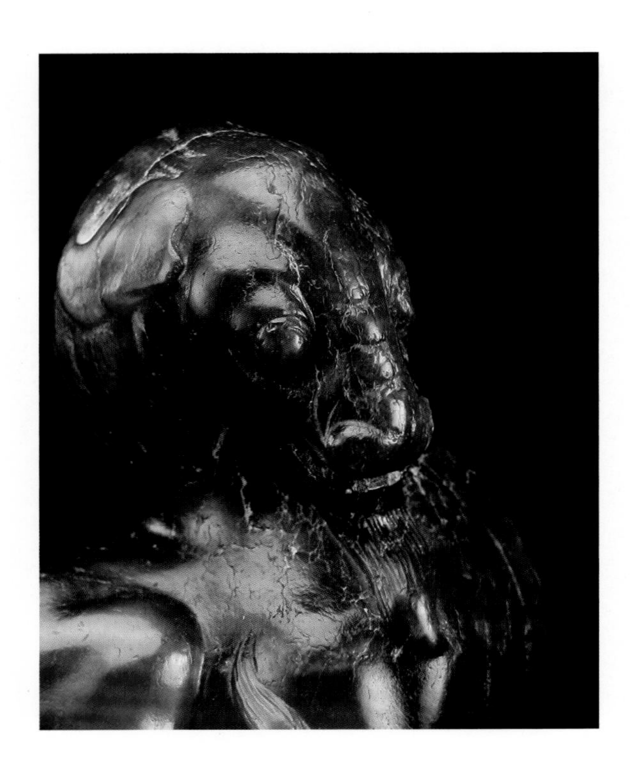

Camel-shaped beast

L/4.3cm, W/3cm, H/5.2cm

Hetian white jade with a molasses-colored quality, and preserved jade skin in places. This piece was carved into a shape based on the jade material, using its natural curves to form an auspicious beast. The beast lowers its head to one side, and has a curved, bowed neck. The auspicious creature has an accentuated physique with muscles carved realistically and powerfully. The long tail is hidden under the resting legs. The head of this beast looks like a camel, and its body looks like a beast. It is called a "camel dragon". This type of style originated in the Tang Dynasty (possibly in connection with trade and the opening to the West in the Tang Dynasty), and became smoother and more mature in the Song Dynasty. This camel-shaped beast has a powerful body and firm musculature, with an air of being poised for action. It can be seen from the lifelike carving and natural curves of the limbs, whiskers, and tail that the style was gradually changing from the fierce creatures and supernatural images of earlier dynasties to one that stressed aesthetic pleasure and visual interest, moving toward an artistic approach closer to folk styles which valued appreciation of the artwork. Because it was made so long ago, this piece has seen weathering, pitting, aging, and marks that clearly show hollowed-in textures on its surface. The surface is a uniform yellowish-brown color with spots. It also has natural layers of soak-induced color distribution, weathered places, and wear. It is an exquisite evil-averting beast piece from the Middle Ages with the perfect combination of jade texture and soak-induced color, and of shape and workmanship.

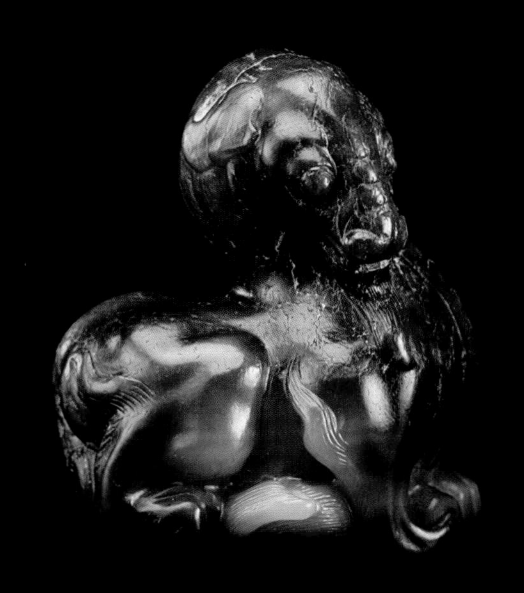

白玉 辟邪器

右：長5.7公分 寬3.2公分 高4.5公分 左：長4.7公分 寬2.5公分 高3公分

和闐白玉質，局部深、烈沁黃褐色釘金斑紋。器作昂首、挺胸、闊步狀辟邪獸，此類辟邪獸風格與姿態，上起自兩漢，大盛於六朝魏晉時期，宋元以降，乃至明清時期圓雕動物皆受其風格影響。辟邪獸軀體端正，獸首作側首曲頸形制，身形又恰與獸首及蜷曲叉式尾，大膽的呈S形骨架與視覺設計。此時期的辟邪獸特別注重精神與身軀骨架的力度表現，裝飾紋飾方面則表現在頭部的獸角、肩部的羽翅、長細蜷曲叉尾、誇張有力的獸爪上。其五官開合，眼、耳、鼻、大嘴與獸首自然協調，形成一種敬瑟的神態，昂首挺胸闊步，十足霸氣，是這一時期的文化體現。從琢玉工法及皮殼沁色面向觀察，精確的砣具定位工法與精緻的琢冶工藝，表現在細緻的層次質感與大跨度的高低曲線變化上，是一件難得的辟邪獸雕精品。

和闐白玉籽料質地，晶瑩白皙，器作玉獾，形象胖圓肥碩，肢體線條流暢，表情靈巧乖順，惹人憐愛。清代動物形體合乎自然比例，琢製細膩，所用題材大都具有吉祥寓意。玉獾靜臥側回首狀，雕工精細，尤其是表現玉獾的肥碩的頭部、腹部、臀部豐滿，神態自若，與辟邪二者並列，表情顧盼，相互輝映，生動活潑，形象可愛，頗富意趣。

獾腹銘有「心賞」楷書款二字，疑似清末知名收藏家吳普心舊藏。

White jade evil-averting piece

Right: L/5.7cm, W/3.2cm, H/4.5cm
Left: L/4.7cm, W/2.5cm, H/3cm

Hetian white jade with partial deep and intense soaked yellowish brown and gold spotted pattern. The piece is in the shape of an evil-averting beast, with raised head and chest, in a wide stride. The style of this evil-averting beast first occurred in the Western and Eastern Han Dynasties and was prevalent in the Six Dynasties and Wei and Jin Dynasties. After the Song Dynasty and into the Ming and Qing Dynasties, the style of animal sculptures was influenced by this style. The body of the evil-averting beast is well-proportioned. The head is angled to one side on top of a curved neck. The body is curved just like the head and its curved, forked tail. It has a bold S-shaped physique and visual design. The evil-averting beasts of this period placed special importance on the strong display of an inner spirit and the physique. Ornamentations are seen on the horns on the head, the feathery wings on the shoulders, the long curling forked tail, and the exaggeratedly powerful claws. Its facial features are all open, with its eyes, ears, nostrils, and mouth naturally positioned on the head, making it a solemn figure. The raised head and chest and wide stride give it an extremely powerful air. It is the manifestation of its era's culture. Precise workmanship and exquisite technique are shown in the jade carving work and the crust's soak-induced color, displaying finely detailed layers of texture and exaggerated curves. It is a rare evil-averting beast masterpiece.

Hetian white jade seed material, with a glittering and translucent whiteness. The pieces are jade badgers with rotund heads and flowing body lines. The expressions are clever and obedient, giving them an adorable look. Animal sculptures in the Qing Dynasty followed natural proportions, with finely detailed carving work and subjects that were mostly auspicious figures. The jade badgers recline with their heads tilted to the side. The carving work is intricate, especially the rotund heads and the full bodies and hinds. They have a self composed manner, and these two evil-averting beasts seem to be looking at each other. They are lively, adorable, and extremely fascinating.

There are two words inscribed on the bodies of the badgers that make it likely that these were from the collection of the famous late-Qing Dynasty collector Wu Pu-Xin.

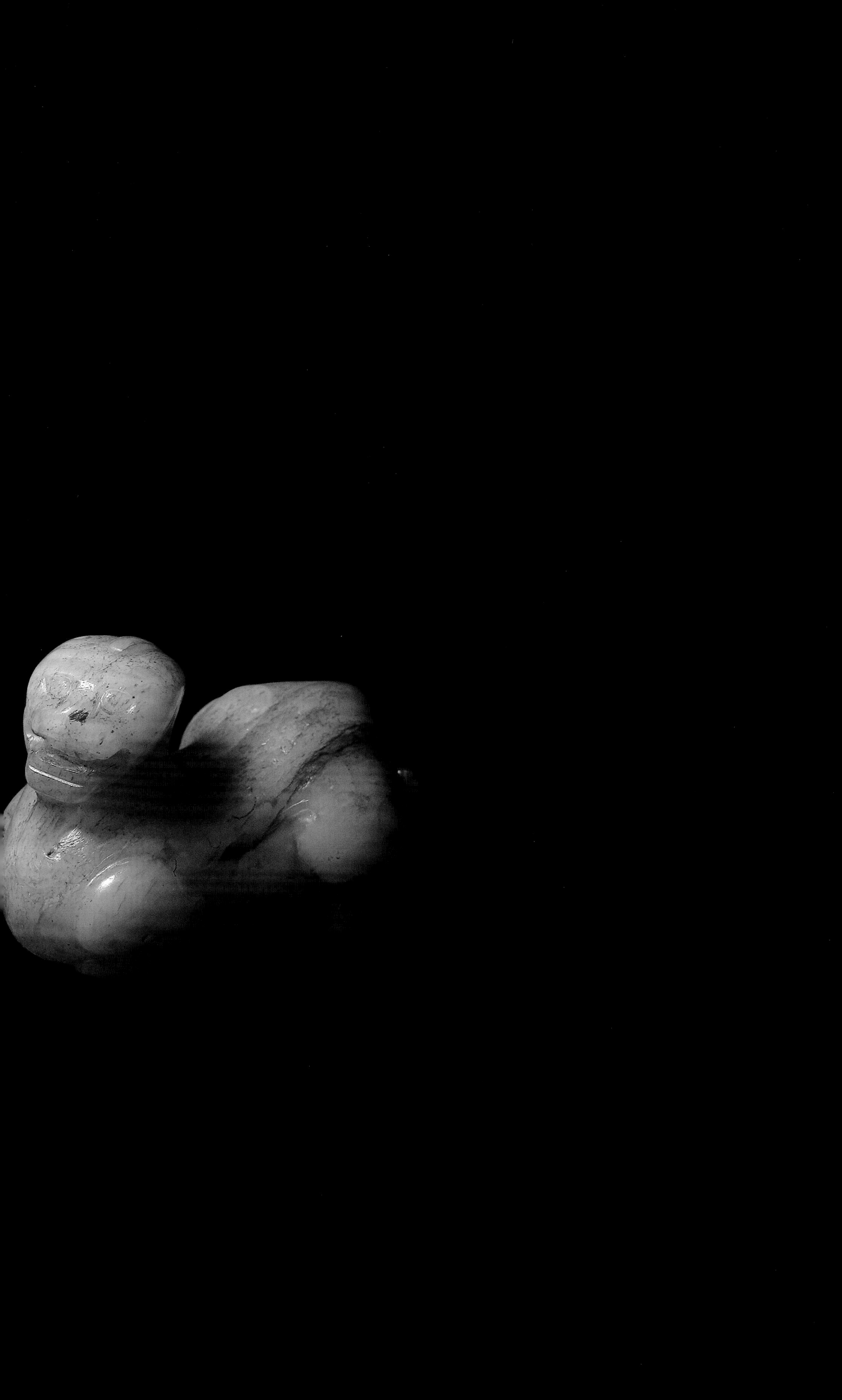

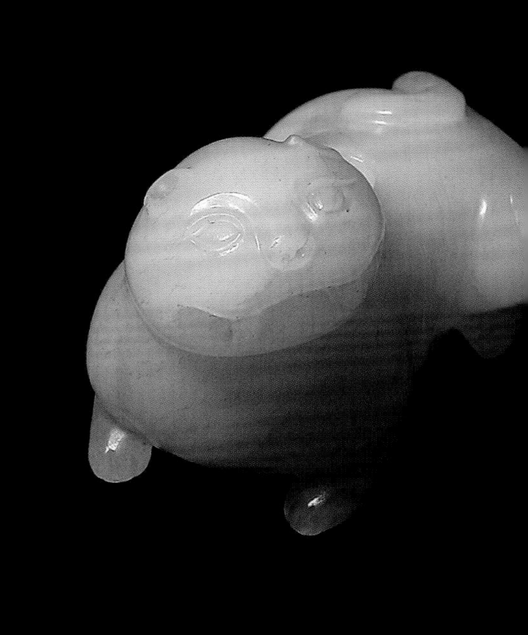

玉獸

長6公分　寬3.2公分　高6.5公分

和闐白玉質，局部帶玉皮沁及黃褐色沁斑。器作回首朝天、闊步辟邪獸狀，此類辟邪獸姿態深受兩漢及六朝時期辟邪獸風格影響。辟邪瑞獸，軀體端正，獸呈回首朝天嘶鳴狀，其身形及蜷曲叉式尾，延續前朝辟邪S形的骨架與視覺設計，亦特別注重動態與精神、骨架與肌肉的肢體力度，裝飾紋飾則表現在頭部的細線陰刻獸角、肩足部的蜷渦紋及短毛，長細蜷曲式叉尾。有其誇張的五官開合，刻劃生動擬人化的眼、耳、鼻、闊嘴、露牙與獸首，自然寫實的身形與神態，回首、闊步、朝天嘶鳴的氣勢表現，是這一時期的復古風格與文化象徵。同樣表現在細緻的層次質感與大跨度的高低曲線變化上，深邃有力的砣具拋磨刀工力度，加上玉匠巧取玉皮沁色，呈現精確的設計與精緻的琢冶工藝，是一件難得的宋代風格辟邪獸雕精品。

Jade beast

L/6cm, W/3.2cm, H/6.5cm

Hetian white jade, with partial jade skin and yellowish-brown spots. The piece is formed into an evil-averting beast with a turned head facing upward and a wide stride. The style of this type of evil-averting beast was influenced by evil-averting beast styles of the Western and Eastern Han Dynasties and the Six Dynasties. This evil-averting auspicious beast has a well-proportioned body, and its head is turned and facing upward, in the middle of a growl. It has a curved body and curved forked tail. The S-shaped physique and visual design extend forward, and the technique especially emphasizes dynamics and inner spirit, as well as the power of the physique and the muscles of the limbs. Ornamentations are seen on the fine lines of the horns carved on the head, the swirling patterns on the shoulders, and the short hair, as well as the long and thin curved forked tail. Its exaggerated facial features are all open, with lifelike eyes, ears, nostrils and mouth carved on the beast's head. The realistic and natural body and aura give power to its turned head, wide stride, and growl. It is a symbol of a return to an ancient style and culture. It also displays, in its finely detailed layers of texture and exaggerated curves, a deeply powerful carving and polishing technique. Its jade carving work leaves a jade skin with soak-induced color, displaying a precise design and exquisite carving workmanship. It is a rare evil-averting beast masterpiece of the Song Dynasty style.

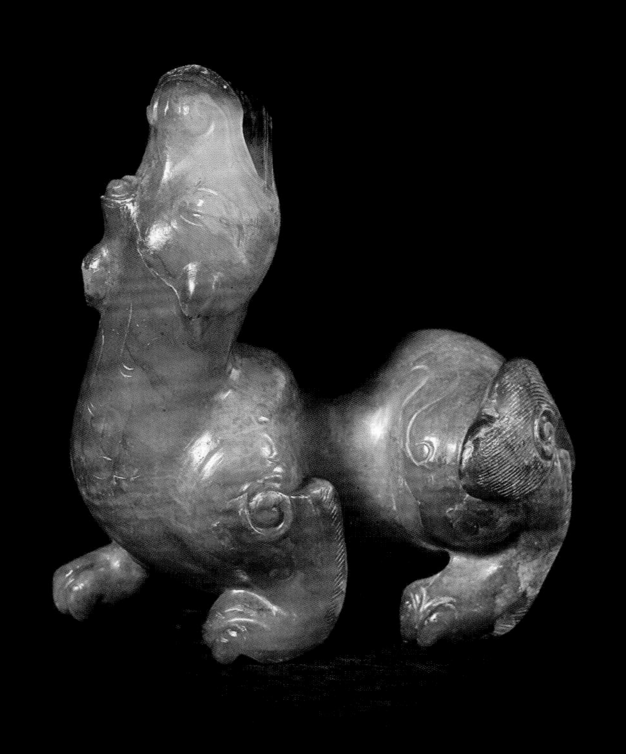

黃玉 角端文鎮

長6.6公分　寬4.2公分　高3.1公分

和闐黃玉質籽料，局部帶黃褐色玉皮沁色。此器身形似牛，頭頂卻只長有一角，故其名曰做「角端」。《後漢書》〈鮮卑傳〉：「角端似牛，以角為弓，稱角端弓…」。據傳能將天下事與福禍吉凶送達君王，是古代君王寶座兩側，不可或缺的裝飾與陪襯神獸。此角端，用料厚實，器作側身回首，表現在文房器用的實用與裝飾把玩上，一手握的滿盈手感，琢工淳樸，線條簡潔明快，神獸體態豐盈，刀工自然而富細膩層次感，完整表現出宋代以來動物形雕玉器文質彬彬的寫實文風與審美觀，絕佳的簡練線條與體積量感，不同於明清時期過分的紋飾與裝飾風格。此外，由於玉質堅實優美，雖已把玩且傳世久遠，仍能完整呈現老練的刀工，加上砣具拋磨細紋交互疊壓錯落的現象，全器呈現包漿與沁色變化豐厚的老化凹陷紋，是一件製作精美的圓雕動物。

Yellow jade one-horned beast paperweight

L/6.6cm, W/4.2cm, H/3.1cm

Hetian yellow jade seed material, with partial yellowish-brown jade skin soak-induced color. This piece is formed into the shape of a "one-horned beast" with the body of an ox and only one long horn coming from the tip of the head. The Han Hou Shu's "Xian Bei Zhuan" says: "The one-horned beast is like an ox, with a horn like a bow, called the one-horn bow..." According to legend, it can report all events in the world and all auspicious and evil signs to the king. It was set on both sides of the thrones of ancient kings, and was an essential ornament and accompanying beast of the gods. This one-horn beast is made of thick and solid material, and the head is turned to one side, displaying its dual use in the literary studio as a utensil and as a curio. It has a substantial feel in the hand, unsophisticated carving work, simple and clear lines, and a plump bestial body. The carving work reveals a natural and finely detailed layered feeling, completely displaying the realistic style and aesthetics of the elegant and refined jade animal sculptures that followed the Song Dynasty. Its absolutely simple lines and solid feeling make it different from the excessively ornamental styles of the Ming and Qing Dynasties. In addition, because of the solidity and beauty of the jade, although this curio is centuries old, it still perfectly displays its accomplished carving work and its fine randomly intersecting and overlapping layers of carving and polishing. The piece shows rich aged hollowed-in patterns with the changes of the shine and the soak-induced color. It is a dedicated animal sculpture.

和闐白玉質地，玉質溫潤而浮透，局部玉瑕絡紋處，深沉黃褐色沁斑。此件仿古立雕動物，依循漢制以來的辟邪形制為題材，其造形似獅而帶羽翼，仍採昂首張口、跨步走遊之狀，叉式卷尾，身軀較漢代時期辟邪動物更為平扁，氣勢不如漢代的豪邁、壯闊與霸氣；亦不如唐宋時期的莊重、文氣與細膩，其紋飾與身形雖強調漢代S形的特殊形象與設計，反而成為明清時期辟邪的鮮明特徵。該玉辟邪瑞獸的製作者，是用一件玉籽「量料取材」而作，自然的一塊玉料，略加施藝，便雕塑成一件既精美又簡樸而不失生動逼真的瑞獸，堪稱「巧奪天工」的傑作。觀賞這件玉雕作品，我們不能不讚嘆古代琢玉工藝與設計大師們的超凡才華。

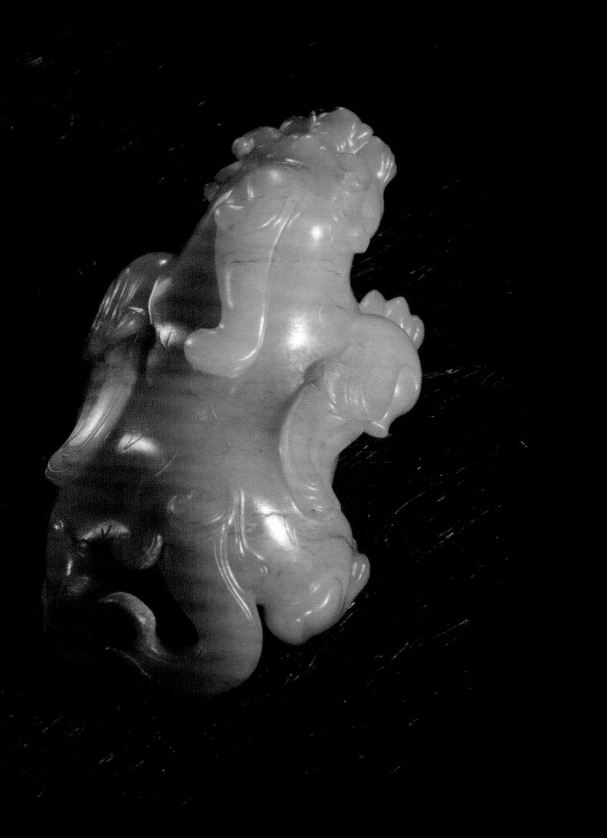

Yellow jade evil-averting beast

/9.6cm, W/2.8cm, H/4.8cm

etian greenish yellow jade. The material has a solid feel to it. This evil-verting beast has angry wide-open eyes and it is shaped like a lion. There s a pair of wings carved on its front paws. It has a curled, forked tail. ts open mouth reveals sharp teeth ready for battle, giving it an extremely ierce look. Its body is rounder than than the bodies of Han Dynasty evil-verting beasts, and its manner is not as bold as Han Dynasty pieces nor s magnificient or dominating as those of the Six Dynasties period. Its xpression of dynamic power conveys another kind of feeling altogether.

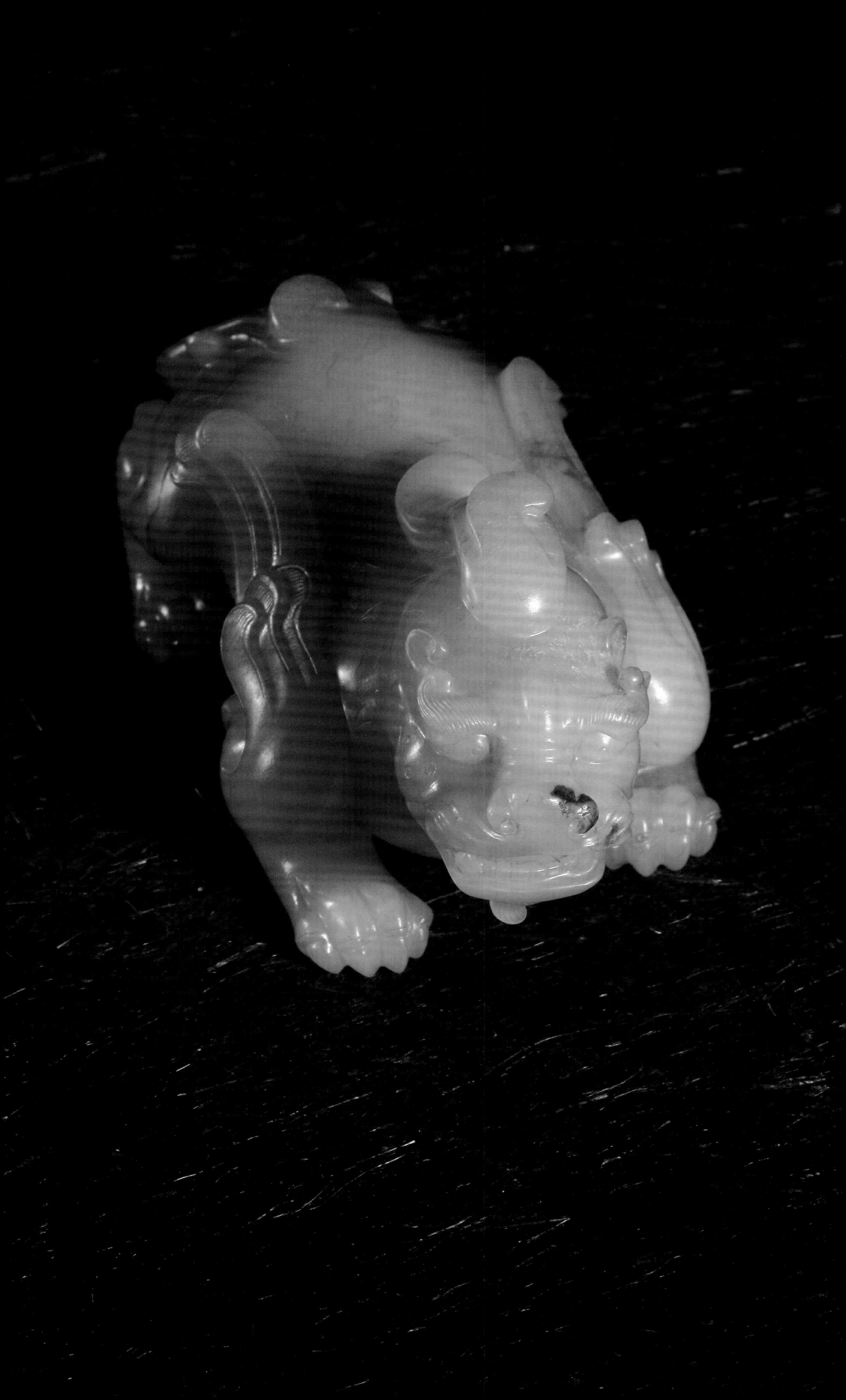

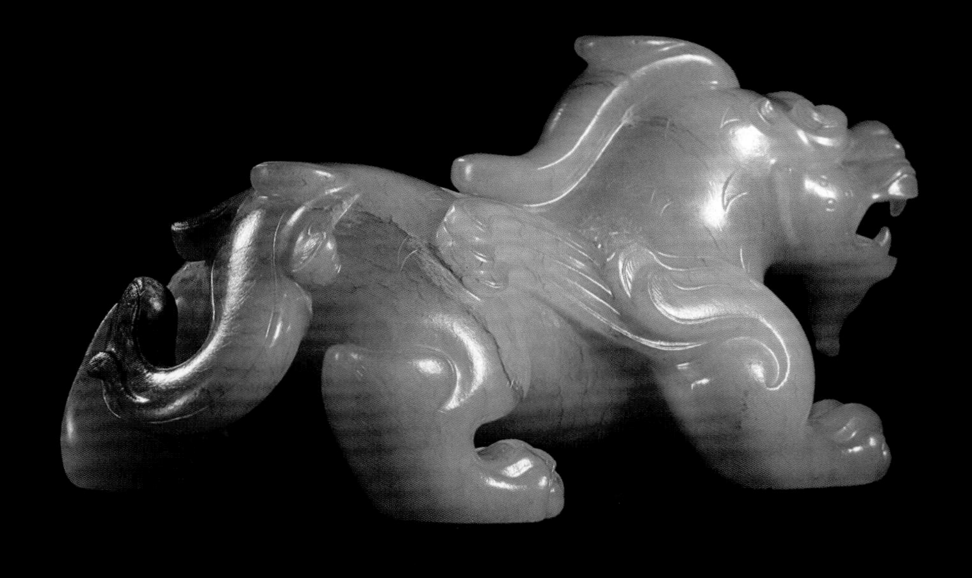

瑞獸硯滴

長9公分　寬5.5公分　高4.2公分

和闐青白玉質地，玉質溫潤而淨透，局部玉瑕綹紋處，沁染黃褐色沁斑。器做昂首辟邪獸形制，這件辟邪前踞後蹲，昂首怒目，斂翼長嘯，張嘴吐舌，利牙外露，雙眼突出，兩耳蜷曲服貼，形似欲撲擊。四肢肥碩粗壯，背上管鑽開口，獸器內腹部掏膛而中空，體中空口處鑲插中空玉筒一枚，器身管壁上琢刻「內府」二字，應是皇室御用之品。

此件仿古立雕動物，依循宋元以來的辟邪形制為其題材，其造型身軀較漢代時期辟邪動物更為平扁，氣勢不如漢代的豪邁、壯闊與霸氣，亦不如唐宋時期的莊重、文氣與細膩；其全身紋飾與身形設計，顯得紋飾繁複與規矩，是明代風格的鮮明特徵。

Auspicious beast water dropper

L/9cm, W/5.5cm, H/4.2cm

Hetian grayish white jade. The jade quality is smooth and pure, with a partial imperfection and dark yellowish-brown spots. This piece shows an evil-averting beast with a raised head. It is squatting on its four legs, and its eyes are full of fury. It has folded wings, and its tongue is hanging out of its open mouth, exposing its sharp teeth. Its two eyes protrude and its ears curl back against its head, making it look like it's ready to pounce. Its four legs are fat and thick, and it has an opening on its back that leads to a hollow body. There is a jade stopper that fits in the opening. The inscription on the side marks it as a utensil used in the imperial palace.

This piece is a copy of an ancient animal sculpture, following the evil-averting beast style of the Song and Yuan Dynasties. Its body shape is flatter than that of evil-averting beasts of the Han Dynasty, and its manner is not as bold or magnificently dominating. It also cannot compare to the solemnity, gracefulness, and meticulousness of those of the Tang and Song Dynasties. The patterns on its body and the design of the body show a complexity and orderliness that is the trademark of the Ming Dynasty style.

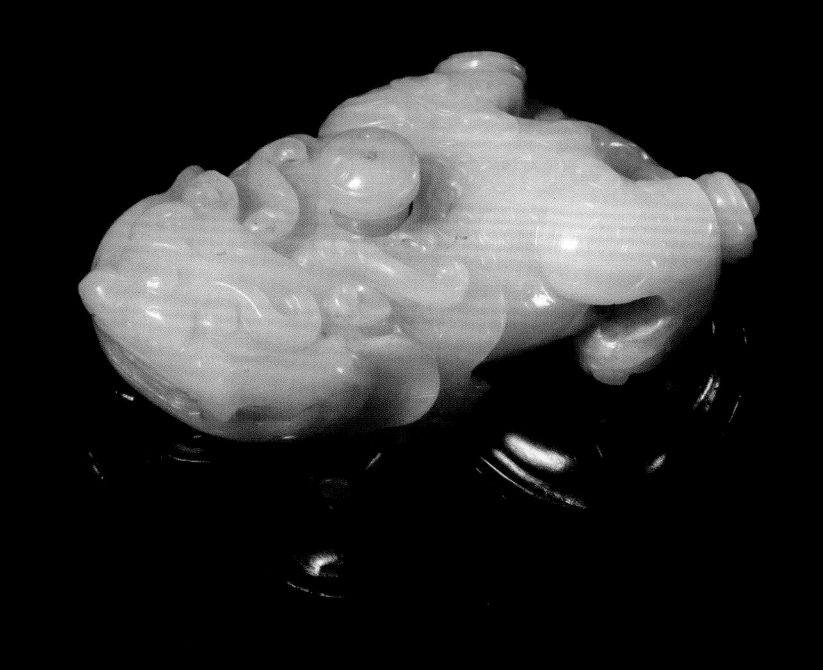

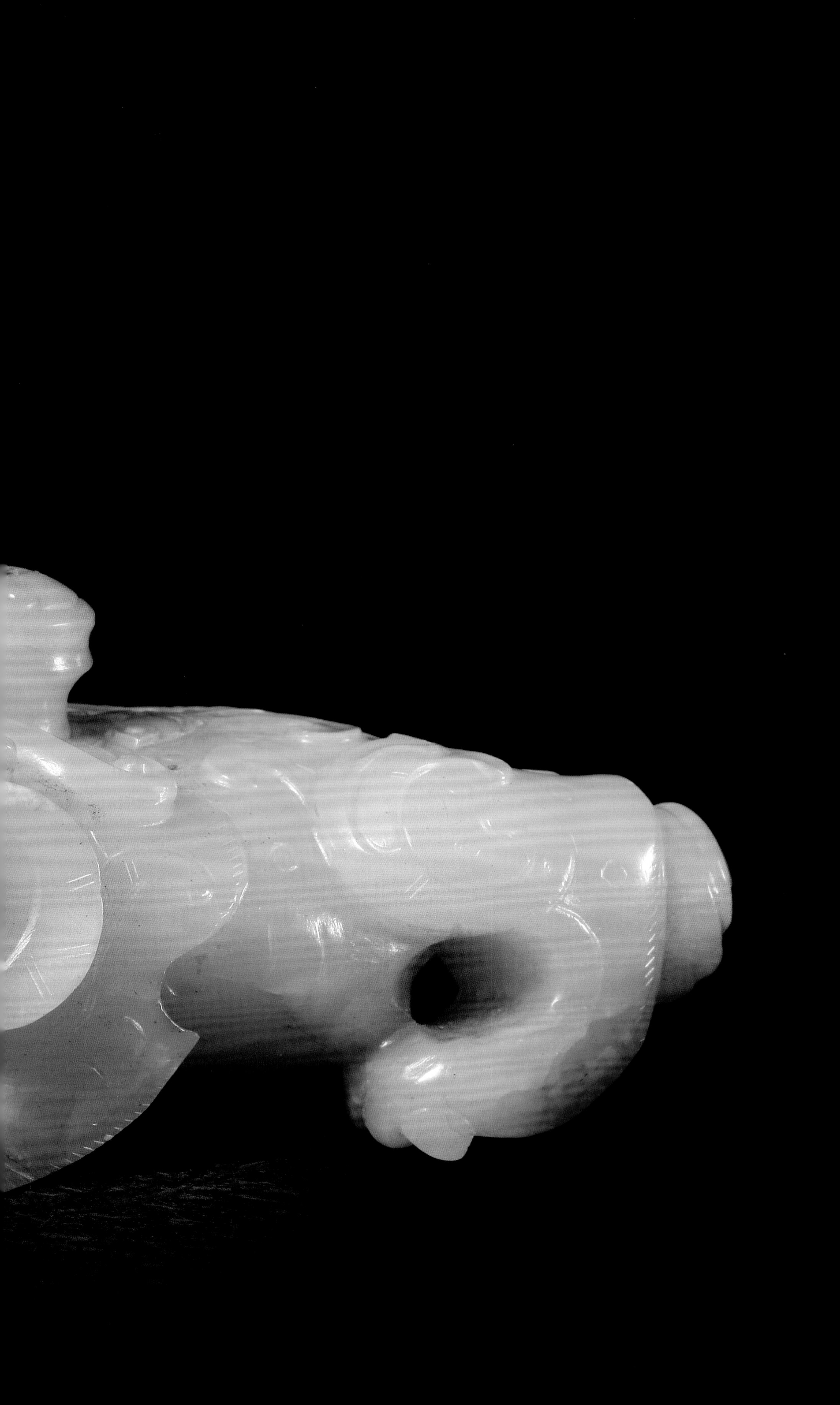

其它

青玉　雙馬擺件

寬8公分　高9公分

青玉質，以整塊籽玉所雕成，清代極重吉祥諧音、寓意，喜用成對成雙的造型設計，馬作成對交首互舔狀，一馬在前，回首後視，一馬在後，首向前伸與其交首互舔，下有圓板狀台座。一馬尾部及另一馬的頭部，留皮色並加染成黃褐色斑塊，姿態親密自然，相當傳神。

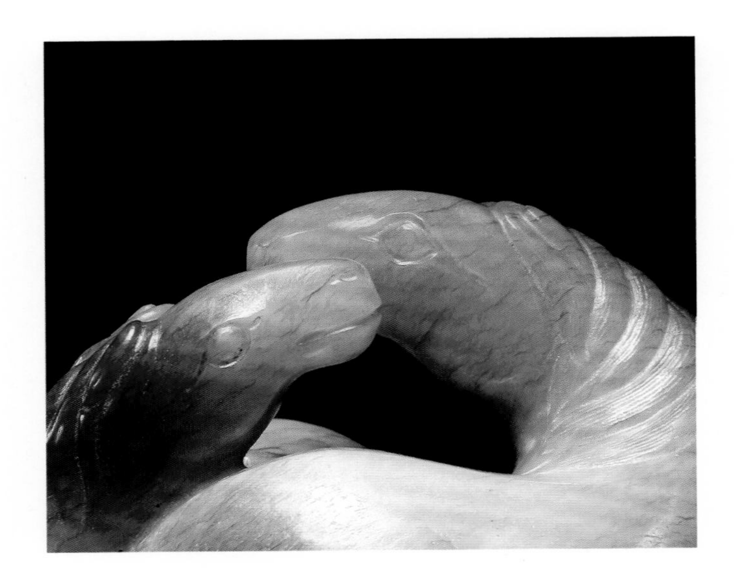

Grayish green jade horse decoration

W/8cm, H/9cm

Grayish green jade—carved from a piece of seed jade. In the Qing Dynasty, the making of pairs of forms that represented good luck homonyms and analogous meanings. This piece is a pair of horses juxtaposed in opposite directions. The horse in the front turns its head back, and the horse in the rear turns its head around and they lick each other's heads. There is a round base at the bottom. There is skin color and dyed yellowish brown spots on the head of one horse and on the tail of the other. The pose is friendly and natural, and full of feeling.

白玉　鹿銜靈芝

長9.5公分　寬6公分　高2.6公分

全器由和闐水產玉石隨形琢碾而成。一鹿臥伏回首，口銜靈芝，身停二隻蝙蝠，陽刻「乾隆御玩」四字，琢碾工藝俐落，不枝不蔓，具見巧思。置之掌中撫，圓潤厚實；置之案前，另有一開之境。「鹿」、「靈芝」、「二隻蝙蝠」在中國象徵「福祿雙全」、「如意吉祥」的意思。

White jade deer with medicinal herbs

L/9.5cm, W/6cm, H/2.6cm

The whole piece is carved from a single piece of Hetian river-gathered jade. A deer reclines and turns its head, and it holds medicinal herbs in its mouth. There are two bats on the body, and there is a four-word inscription identifying it as made during the reign of Qianlong. The carving technique is exquisite. It fits in the palm of a hand, and is smooth and weighty. Deer, medicinal herbs, and bats are all symbols of good fortune in Chinese.

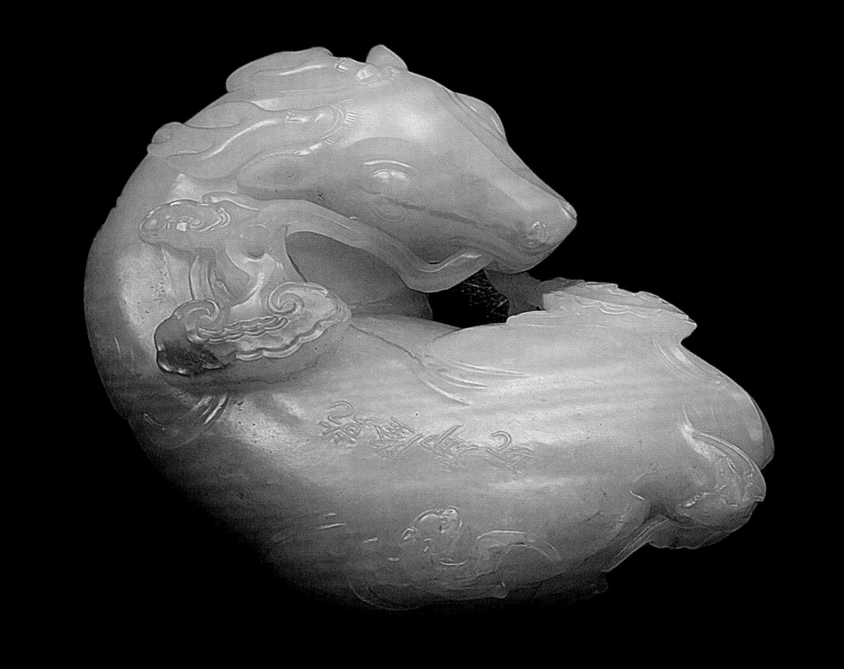

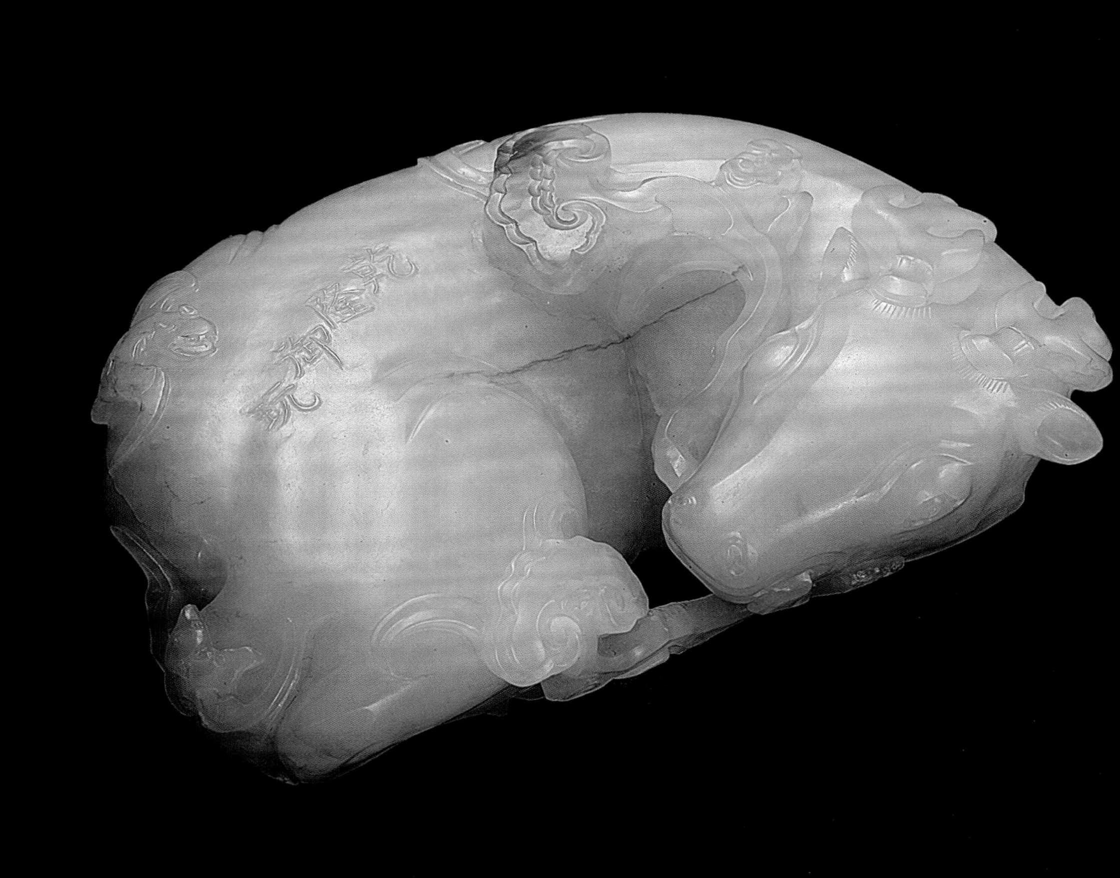
乾隆御玩

青玉　臥馬

長19公分　寬8公分　高10.5公分

青玉質，色呈灰青，較一般青玉色深，部份可見玉綹，但玉工使其呈現似毛皮的巧色。馬採伏臥姿態，前肢一藏於腹下，右前肢微抬，馬首向右轉作回首狀，口部緊閉置放於腹背上，眼微張，尾部極長，自身後向右彎向頸腹部後肢上，自然下垂顯示自在神情，上留玉皮色，並加染呈現更佳「巧色」效果，身上肌理表現自然，可見馬的壯碩。

Grayish green jade reclining horse

L/19cm, W/8cm, H/10.5cm

Grayish green jade—with a darker color than most grayish green jade, and the carving technique skillfully uses the different shades of color. The horse adopts a reclining pose with one leg curled under its body and the right leg raised. The head turns back to the right belly and is resting across its body. The eyes are slightly open, and the tail is very long, curving back across its right rear leg in a relaxed pose. There is jade skin showing, which creates an excellent multi-colored effect, along with a dyed color. The texture of the body is natural, showing the innate dignity of the horse.

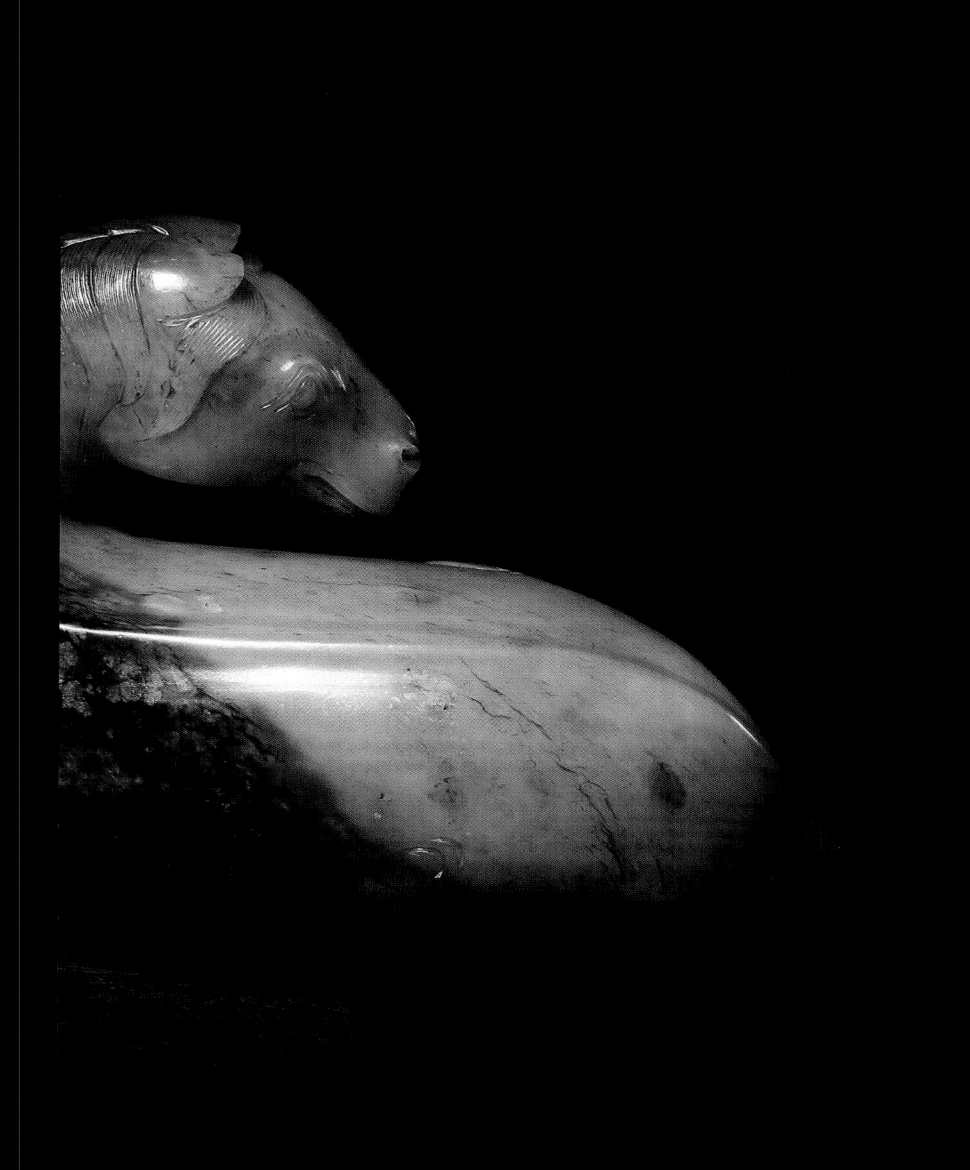

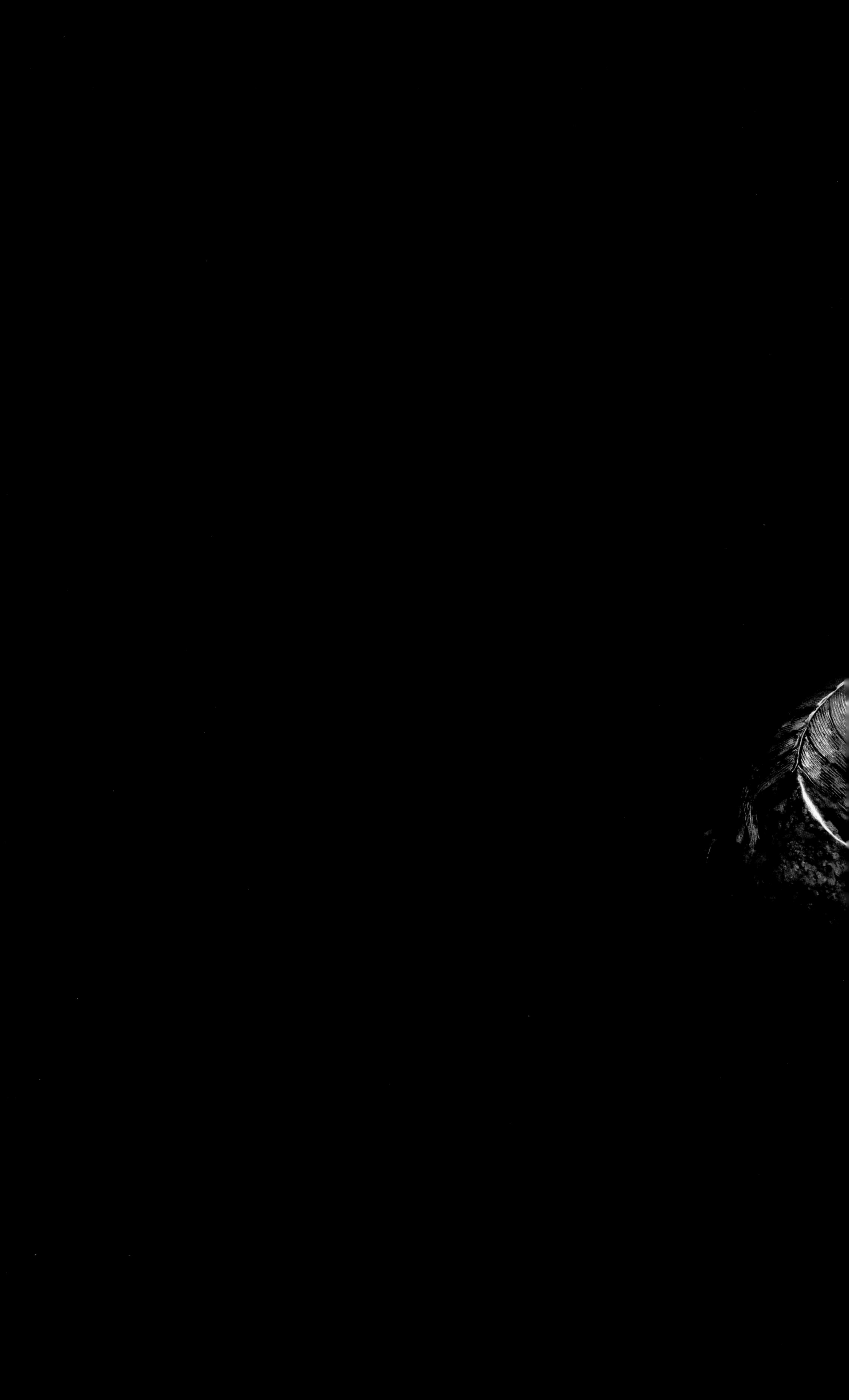

白玉　駱駝

長7.8公分　寬3.4公分　高5公分

白玉質，整塊羊脂白玉籽雕製而成，白色潔淨，可見薄薄的玉皮黃色，似皮毛的自然色澤。以立體圓雕製成駝伏坐的自然姿態，駝首正面前視，四肢彎曲伏坐於地上，雙駝峰凸起於背上，尾部自然下垂，神情怡然自在，肌理自然顯現生命力，技法十分卓越。

White jade camel

L/7.8cm, W/3.4cm, H/5cm

White jade—this is carved from one piece of suet white seed jade. The white color is milky with a thin layer of yellow jade skin, showing off its natural luster. A seated camel shape is carved into a peaceful posture using rounded sculpting techniques. The camel's head looks forward, and its four legs are tucked under its body. There are two humps on its back, and its tail hangs freely, giving it a relaxed look. The extremely outstanding carving technique gives it a shape full of vitality.

黃玉　玉鵝

長5.7公分　高3.5公分

黃玉質，色呈栗黃色，局部呈黃褐色。器採曲頸回首伏臥姿態，雙足隱藏於腹下，雙翅緊貼，顯現優美弧度。利用籽玉圓弧形而設計，乃依料施工，除頭部浮雕出目、口等輪廓，翅膀羽毛以陰線雕刻勾勒形成，其他保留簡潔造型，技法圓熟自然。

Yellow jade goose

L/5.7cm, H/3.5cm

Yellow jade—this piece is mostly chestnut yellow, with some yellowish-brown. The posture is that of a goose with a turned neck in a reclining position, with both feet hidden underneath. The wings are folded close to the body, forming a gentle curve. It uses a curved design carved out of seed jade, following the grain of the material. The piece has a simple style except for the head, the outline of the beak, and the outlines of the wings carved in intaglio. The technique is mature and natural.

白玉　天鵝

長5.7公分　高6公分

白玉質，色青白呈半透明光澤，表面仍留薄薄皮色，現微黃色。鵝雙足伏藏於腹下，首向上延伸，嘴緊閉，雙目前視，尾微上翹，雙翅緊貼身後，翅尾端凸雕，使其更加立體，顯得栩栩如生，技法熟練生動，形姿可愛，可作佩飾，亦可作擺飾品。

White jade swan

L/5.7cm, H/6cm

White jade—this piece has a grayish white color with a semi-translucent luster, with a thin layer of skin color on the surface, displaying a slight yellow color. The swan's feet are folded under its body, and its head is extended upward, with its beak closed. Its eyes look forward and its tail tips slightly upward, with the wings pressed against the body, the wing tips protruding just a little, making it even more lifelike. The carving technique is well-practiced and lively, with an adorable shape enabling it to be used as an accessory or just as a decoration.

圖說作者

璽印

清　白玉　肇祖原皇帝之寶璽印　郭祐麟
清　光緒　白玉　光緒尊親之寶璽印　郭祐麟
清　青玉　宣皇后寶璽印　郭祐麟
清　碧玉　盤螭鈕璽印組（所寶惟賢、嘉慶御筆、所其無逸）　郭祐麟
清　白玉　四方印　楊式昭
清　白玉　圓印（品真、思華）　楊式昭

玉器

戰國　《舊玉穀璧》　林淑心　郭祐麟
清　乾隆　御製《幽蘭玉屏》　乾隆款　林淑心　郭祐麟
清　乾隆《和闐玉鏤東坡後赤壁賦圖》　林淑心　郭祐麟
清　青白玉　秋山行旅圖　山子　林淑心
清　乾隆《玉蟠夔壺》　林淑心　郭祐麟
清　白玉　雙耳蓋瓶　林淑心
清　乾隆《古玉軸頭》　林淑心
清　撫辰經緯　玉盒一對　林淑心　郭祐麟
清　乾隆　御製玉扳指（五件）　林淑心
清　青白玉　菊瓣紋扁壺　林淑心
清　白玉　玉碗　林淑心
清　乾隆　青白玉　玉碗　林淑心
清　青白玉　水洗　林淑心
清　乾隆　黃玉　饕餮耳方杯　洪賓懋
清　乾隆　青白玉　福祿大吉瓶　林淑心
清　乾隆　白玉　玉蘭杯　一對　洪賓懋
清　乾隆　青白玉　玉牛　林淑心
清　嘉慶　碧玉　夔龍紋壺　林淑心
清　白玉　玉盤　林淑心
清　白玉　螭耳瓶　洪賓懋
清　青白玉　人物故事扁壺　林淑心
清　青白玉　葫蘆型扁壺　林淑心
清　白玉　雙鳳羽人蓋瓶　林淑心

清 白玉 喜上眉梢扁壺 林淑心
清 青白玉 饕餮紋扁壺 林淑心
清 青白玉 雙耳瓶 林淑心
清 青白玉 龍鈕觥形瓶 林淑心
清 白玉 鳳耳瓶 林淑心
清 青白玉 八角型觚 林淑心
清 碧玉 夔龍紋簋形爐 林淑心
清 青白玉 吉慶福壽洗 林淑心
清 白玉 鳳鈕蓋罐 林淑心
清 黃玉 玉碗 林淑心
清 黃玉 龍鳳如意 林淑心
清 青玉 淨瓶觀音 林淑心
清 翠玉 文殊菩薩像 林淑心
清 黃玉 花形扁盒 林淑心
清 黃玉 水盂 林淑心
清 仿宋白玉珮 林淑心
戰國 青玉 龍形珮 林淑心
西周 青玉 龍紋勒 林淑心
明 白玉 髮冠 林淑心
玉犧 郭祐麟 洪賓懋

宋玉大觀

駝形獸 郭祐麟
白玉 辟邪器 郭祐麟 洪賓懋
玉獸 郭祐麟 洪賓懋
黃玉 角端文鎮 郭祐麟 洪賓懋
辟邪獸 郭祐麟
瑞獸硯滴 郭祐麟

其它

青玉 雙馬擺件 林淑心
白玉 鹿銜靈芝 洪賓懋
青玉 臥馬 林淑心
白玉 駱駝 林淑心
黃玉 玉鵝 林淑心
白玉 天鵝 林淑心

Qing Dynasty Grayish green with white jade dragon handle wine vessel-shaped vase	Lin Shu-Xin
Qing Dynasty Grayish white jade phoenix handle vase	Lin Shu-Xin
Qing Dynasty Grayish white jade octagonal gu	Lin Shu-Xin
Qing Dynasty Dark green jade dragon and one-footed dragon pattern grain vessel-shaped burner	Lin Shu-Xin
Qing Dynasty Grayish green with white jade good fortune and longevity wash basin	Lin Shu-Xin
Qing Dynasty White jade phoenix handle jar with stopper	Lin Shu-Xin
Qing Dynasty Yellow jade bowl	Lin Shu-Xin
Qing Dynasty Yellow jade dragon and phoenix good luck ornament	Lin Shu-Xin
Qing Dynasty Grayish green jade Guanyin with Vase of Purity	Lin Shu-Xin
Qing Dynasty Jade Manjusri Bodhisattva	Lin Shu-Xin
Qing Dynasty Yellow jade flower-shaped flat box	Lin Shu-Xin
Qing Dynasty Yellow jade tea basin	Lin Shu-Xin
Qing Dynasty White jade pendant modeled after the Song style	Lin Shu-Xin
Warring States Period Dragon-shaped pendant	Lin Shu-Xin
Western Zhou Dynasty Grayish green jade dragon pattern clip	Lin Shu-Xin
Ming Dynasty White jade hairpin	Lin Shu-Xin
Jade sacrificial beast	Kuo Yu-Lin / Adam Hong

Song Dynasty Style Jade

Camel-shaped beast	Kuo Yu-Lin
White jade evil-averting piece	Kuo Yu-Lin /Adam Hong
Jade beast	Kuo Yu-Lin / Adam Hong
Yellow jade one-horned beast paperweight	Kuo Yu-Lin / Adam Hong
Yellow jade evil-averting beast	Kuo Yu-Lin
Auspicious beast water dropper	Kuo Yu-Lin

Others

Grayish green jade horse decoration	Lin Shu-Xin
White jade deer with medicinal herbs	Adam Hong
Grayish green jade reclining horse	Lin Shu-Xin
White jade camel	Lin Shu-Xin
Yellow jade goose	Lin Shu-Xin
White jade swan	Lin Shu-Xin

Commentator

Imperial Seals

Qing Dynasty White jade Zhao Zu Yuan Huang Di Zhi Bao Imperial seal	Kuo Yu-Lin
Qing Dynasty Guangxu Era White jade Guang Xu Zun Qin Zhi Bao Imperial seal	Kuo Yu-Lin
Qing Dynasty Dark green jade Xuan Huang Hou Bao Imperial seal	Kuo Yu-Lin
Qing Dynasty Dark green jade coiled hornless dragon body imperial seal set (Suo Bao Wei Xian, Jia Qing Yu Bi, and Suo Qi Wu Yi)	Kuo Yu-Lin
Qing Dynasty White jade square seal	Yang Shih-Chao
Qing Dynasty Two white jade seals, inscribed with: Si Hua and Pin Zhen	Yang Shih-Chao

Jade

Warring States Ancient jade grain pattern jade disk	Lin Shu-Xin / Kuo Yu-Lin
Qing Dynasty, Qianlong Era "Serene Orchid Jade Screen"	Lin Shu-Xin / Kuo Yu-Lin
Qing Dynasty, Qianlong Era "Hetian Jade Inlay Dongpo's Latter Ode on the Red Cliffs"	Lin Shu-Xin / Kuo Yu-Lin
Qing Dynasty Grayish white jade Autumn Mountain Scene jade boulder	Lin Shu-Xin
Qing Dynasty, Qianlong Era Grayish green jade "repayment" flask	Lin Shu-Xin / Kuo Yu-Lin
Qing Dynasty White jade two-handled vase with stopper	Lin Shu-Xin
Qing Dynasty, Qianlong Era "White jade rod box"	Lin Shu-Xin
Qing Dynasty Altazimuth pair of jade boxes	Lin Shu-Xin / Kuo Yu-Lin
Qing Dynasty, Qianlong Era Imperial rings (set of five)	Lin Shu-Xin
Qing Dynasty Grayish green with white jade chrysanthemum flask	Lin Shu-Xin
Qing Dynasty White jade bowl	Lin Shu-Xin
Qing Dynasty, Qianlong Era White jade bowl	Lin Shu-Xin
Qing Dynasty Green with white jade wash basin	Lin Shu-Xin
Qing Dynasty, Qianlong Era Yellow jade ravenous beast handled square cup	Adam Hong
Qing Dynasty, Qianlong Era Grayish green with white jade gourd vase	Lin Shu-Xin
Qing Dynasty, Qianlong Era White jade orchid cups	Adam Hong
Qing Dynasty, Qianlong Era Grayish green with white jade ox	Lin Shu-Xin
Qing Dynasty, Jiaqing Era Dark green jade dragon and one-footed dragon pattern pot	Lin Shu-Xin
Qing Dynasty White jade plate	Lin Shu-Xin
Qing Dynasty White jade hornless dragon handled vase	Adam Hong
Qing Dynasty Grayish green with white jade human figure story flask	Lin Shu-Xin
Qing Dynasty Grayish white jade gourd-shaped flask	Lin Shu-Xin
Qing Dynasty White jade double phoenix sage screen with stopper	Lin Shu-Xin
Qing Dynasty White jade "happiness" flask	Lin Shu-Xin
Qing Dynasty Grayish green with white jade ravenous beast pattern flask	Lin Shu-Xin
Qing Dynasty Grayish green with white jade double handled vase	Lin Shu-Xin